A STRANGER CAME

It was a bombshell when old Mr. Elsgood
said that a newcomer, Stephen Harmon,
was coming from London to take over the
law firm of Elsgood and Elsey in the sleepy
Midland town of Cheslyn Slade. Nell, Mr.
Elsgood's secretary, was not at all sure that
she was going to like the change – especially when she overheard Stephen Harmon
saying, 'My secretary works for peanuts.
Come to think of it, that's about what she's
worth.'

A STRANGER CAME

by

JANE DONNELLY

MILLS & BOON LIMITED
17–19 FOLEY STREET
LONDON W1A 1DR

First published 1972
This edition 1972

© *Jane Donnelly* 1972

ISBN 0 263 71406 3

Made and Printed in Great Britain by
Cox & Wyman Ltd.,
London, Reading and Fakenham

CHAPTER ONE

THE staff of Elsgood and Elsey, family solicitors, had all known that Mr. Elsgood was considering retirement. At sixty-eight he was entitled to opt out of the rat race. Not that Elsgood and Elsey had ever gone for anything tooth and claw, their line was mainly straightforward probate and conveyancing. When they represented clients in the magistrates' courts the cases were routine and humdrum. Local newspapers usually gave a line or two, because readers are always fascinated by the troubles of their neighbours, but they had never made the national press since the firm was founded.

This was no discredit. They were a respected firm of small town solicitors. Business was conducted with unfailing sympathy and decorum. They won a fair proportion of their cases, they gave value for money.

Mr. Elsey had died several years ago, and Mr. Elsgood had carried on, with the aid of the articled clerk who had recently qualified. Norman Rowe had been working in Mr. Elsey's room anyway. He just took over the bigger desk. It hadn't been necessary to change a thing. Even the name on the letterheads stayed the same.

Occasionally, during recent months, Mr. Elsgood had talked of retirement. Mrs. Elsgood was hankering for a bungalow in Bournemouth. But there seemed a fair chance that he would carry on for a few more years.

His farewell announcement caught the staff unprepared. Friday night he had wished them all good night and a pleasant week-end. He hadn't retired on Friday. His secretary, Ellen Attlesey, had been making appointments for him running into next month.

But when she arrived on Monday morning he was in the office ahead of her. That was a thing she could never remember before. Nell always arrived at nine, went through the mail and generally prepared the way, and Mr. Elsgood came in around ten.

The offices were the upper floor of what had been a Victorian house; there was a glass-panelled door at the top of the stairs with 'Elsmore and Elsey' printed neatly on the panel. The staff trooped through, discussing how they had passed their Saturday and Sunday. Nell took off her coat in the tiny wash room, and went along to Mr. Elsgood's room, and there he was behind the desk.

Her instinctive reaction was, 'What's the matter?'

He smiled benevolently, sitting back and joining the tips of his fingers. 'Nothing is the matter, my dear Miss Attlesey, but I have an announcement to make. Would you ask the others to come in?'

Nell gathered them: Norman Rowe, and Alexander Baker the clerk, from Mr. Elsey's room, next along the corridor; Mrs. Storey and Joan Frisk from the room nearest the top of the stairs, labelled 'Inquiries'; and told them all, 'I don't know why. He says he's announcing something.'

'Do you think the firm's gone bust?' Joan Frisk was twenty and engaged and would have found that exciting. Mrs. Storey and Mr. Baker turned on her. Mr. Baker clicked his tongue impatiently, and Mrs. Storey hissed, 'Don't be so stupid!'

'All here?' said Mr. Elsgood, looking around as though he had a staff of dozens instead of five. 'Well, this is rather a sad moment for me. I have to say good-bye to you all.'

They were sorry. Now it had come it was a wrench, because he was a kind and tolerant employer. 'Oh dear,' sighed Nell. She had worked with the firm since she left secretarial college; she was twenty-one now. She asked mournfully, 'When?' and Mr. Elsgood said,

'The new head of the firm will be taking over on Wednesday.'

The day after tomorrow! They stared at him, speechless. Mr. Elsgood had never made a quick decision in all the years he had sat behind that desk. He could dither almost indefinitely. Several members of his staff were wondering if this was mental relapse, it was so completely out of character.

He realized this, and said apologetically, 'I should like to have given you all more warning, but I had very little advance notice myself. I was approached a few days ago on the matter, and it was settled over the weekend. I must say I had

6

expected a much longer period of negotiations. Of course I shall be around for a week or two in an advisory capacity.'

'I see.' Norman Rowe was hurt. When he was alone with Mr. Elsgood he would register bitter affront. He was not a partner in the firm, he was simply the assistant, but he had worked wholeheartedly for Elsgood and Elsey and this was not the treatment he would have expected.

He had been asked, when the retirement question first came up, if he would be interested in buying the practice and said no. He didn't want a firm of his own. He felt happier if ultimate responsibility rested on another man.

But this, without warning, was shattering. He asked stiffly, 'Do we still consider ourselves employed here?' and Mr. Elsgood couldn't reassure him fast enough,

'Of course, of *course*. That was the very first thing we discussed, the safeguarding of employment for all of you.'

Come off it, thought Nell, with a flash of cynicism; although she believed it had come high on the list and that Mr. Elsgood had done the best he could for them.

He said, 'Mr. Harmon is prepared to give you all a three months' contract, and assures me it is unlikely he will wish to make any staff changes.'

'Harmon,' Alexander Baker repeated the name slowly, as though he was trying it out. He had worked here for thirty years. If the filing cabinets had blown up he could have jotted down most of the data from memory. He had grey hair, and now a tinge of greyness had spread to his skin, emphasizing the deep dragging lines. He looked older, and he felt it.

Mr. Elsgood said, 'Stephen Harmon. He was previously a partner with a London firm.'

'*London?*' echoed Norman Rowe. 'And he's coming *here?*'

There was nothing wrong with Cheslyn Slade. It had been a pleasant and picturesque little Midland town for centuries, surrounded by heather-covered moors and fir tree woods. The coal mines on the hills, that had once been a main industry, had closed one by one during the last ten years, but the farms continued to prosper, and small factories had sprung up, and trade in the shops was brisk. It

7

was a comfortable place to live and work, but it was only a little town, and if Mr. Stephen Harmon was looking for a change from London he had found it in every way.

'Health reasons,' said Mr. Elsgood.

That didn't sound too promising. Mr. Elsgood was elderly, but he had rarely had to take time off; and although the pace was gentle here if Mr. Harmon was in poor health the staff could find themselves with a load of extra work and worry.

'What's the matter with him?' Mrs. Storey sounded suspicious that he might be arriving on a stretcher, and Mr. Elsgood said reproachfully,

'I believe he had a slight coronary, and his doctor advised a less strenuous routine. And now,' he smiled his fatherly smile, 'there is a great deal to be done if everything is going to be ship-shape and Bristol fashion.'

Norman Rowe said sulkily, 'If we'd had a bit more notice we'd have whitewashed the coal.' Mr. Elsgood let that go. He said quietly,

'You're due in court, aren't you, Mr. Rowe, at ten o'clock? The shoplifting case?'

All the staff but Nell left, hurrying and anxious to talk this over among themselves.

When they got into their office Norman Rowe and Alexander Baker would commiserate with each other on this small betrayal. They were both shaken. They had both believed themselves in Mr. Elsgood's confidence.

Mrs. Storey had worked here for some time too, but Joan was simply saving up for marriage. It didn't matter to Joan who sat behind Mr. Elsgood's desk – she typed for Mr. Rowe anyway. Mr. Elsgood was Nell's responsibility.

Nell said with honesty, 'We'll be sorry to lose you.'

'I'll be sorry to be leaving,' said Mr. Elsgood, 'but we can't go on for ever, can we?'

He looked around wistfully. The office had hardly changed over the years of his practice here. The desk was solid mahogany, the pictures on the walls were steel engravings of the Cries of Old London, and the books behind the glass-fronted shelves were leather-bound classics that had never been opened since they were first slotted into place. The carpet was drab Wilton, and had worn like iron.

It was a reassuring office. At least you felt that the firm must have been operating for some time, and Mr. Elsgood was going to miss it. He said plaintively, 'I fear I have offended Mr. Rowe.'

That he had. Probably Mr. Baker too.

He defended himself, 'It would have been more considerate to have told all of you sooner, but in the circumstances that was not possible. I did try to phone Mr. Rowe last night, three times in all, and got no reply.'

Nell said, 'He'll understand. Of course it was a shock coming so suddenly, but I'm sure everyone will understand.'

He sighed, 'I hope so. There has always been a fine spirit of loyalty here. It would distress me deeply if it should appear that I was unappreciative of that.'

It had been a happy office. Nell would be satisfied if the new man was half as courteous and considerate as Mr. Elsgood, but if he wasn't she could always look around for another job. She smiled sweetly, to reassure Mr. Elsgood that she bore him no malice for retiring, and asked, 'What about these appointments? Do we tell them that someone else will be dealing with them?

Mr. Elsgood wanted everybody told. A less sympathetic man might have left them to find out when they arrived, but Mr. Elsgood dictated letters to some explaining the situation, and phoned up others. He assured them all that the new head of the firm had an excellent record and that they would be lucky commanding his services.

All the clients sounded regretful. Elsgood and Elsey was something of an institution in Cheslyn Slade. Talking over their troubles with Mr. Elsgood had cheered many a worried soul, because Mr. Elsgood cared. He never hurried them. He wasn't a young man, of course, but he had years of experience, and a wealth of understanding.

Nell was less than happy about it herself. Her sentimental streak was making the morning poignant. As Mr. Elsgood sighed, putting down the telephone after each farewell, she sighed with him. And when Norman Rowe came back from the courts just before lunchtime, and asked with dignity if Mr. Elsgood could spare him five minutes, she wanted to say, 'Don't be too hard on him. He didn't want to sell out.

9

It's breaking his heart.'

She went into the end office where Mrs. Storey was at the filing cabinet and Joan Frisk was typing. Mrs. Storey, slipping in one file and lifting out another, said as she saw Nell, 'This is ridiculous, you know.'

'What is?' Nell asked.

'We just can't do it in time.'

Mrs. Storey, usually a stolid figure with her carefully waved salt-and-pepper hair, dark skirt, and matching twin set, looked hot and flustered today. There were tendrils of hair escaping from the neat coiffure, and a smudge of carbon paper or ink on her cheek. She said, 'Mr. Baker wants all the files right up to date. Nothing left outstanding. And it isn't as though work's stopped, you know. There's today and tomorrow to get through as well.'

Joan went on with her copy typing. 'I can't see what the flap's for. Badger's jumping out of his skin.'

Mr. Baker did not answer to the name 'Badger', but it had been his nickname for a long time, used sometimes with affection, sometimes with exasperation. He worked as hard as anyone in the office, arriving first and leaving last. Another man taking Mr. Elsgood's place was a traumatic prospect for him, and he was obviously determined to give no cause for initial complaint.

The 'Inquiries' bell rang in the corridor, and Joan got up and flipped up the hatch and said, 'Good morning, can I help you?'

The woman standing there announced succinctly, 'Mrs. Martin. Mr. Elsgood. Twelve o'clock.' It was a few minutes to twelve, and Joan said,

'Do come in, Mrs. Martin.'

Mrs. Martin was going to miss Mr. Elsgood. Her late husband had left her a wholesale confectionery business, and an adult family of three sons.

Her hobby was changing her will, which she did on average twice a year, and Mr. Elsgood always listened to her reasons and took down her instructions with flattering attention.

Now she settled herself on one of the chairs in the small waiting section of the room, grim-faced, and clutching her handbag as though it contained her fortune.

So Edwin Anthony's out of the running for a while, thought Nell. He had been the favoured son in the last will and testament she had typed.

At twelve o'clock exactly the internal phone from Mr. Elsgood's office rang to ask if Mrs. Martin was waiting, and if she was would she come along? Nell went with her. Norman Rowe was coming out of the office, and spotting Nell Mr. Elsgood said, 'I shan't need you, Miss Attlesey, run along to your lunch. Ah, Mrs. Martin, how very pleasant to see you.'

'Old battleaxe,' muttered Norman Rowe when the door closed.

Not Mr. Elsgood, surely? Nell's eyebrows rose and he said, 'Her, of course.'

'Oh yes.' Everybody in town knew that. Nell said, 'He tried to phone you last night.'

'He's just told me. We were out.' He sighed. He was a fair-haired young man with a sensitive narrow face, who looked slightly worried most of the time. 'It's a shaker, isn't it?'

He went into his own office, and Nell went back to ask Joan, 'Coming?'

'With you.' Joan finished the sentence she was typing and got up, and Mrs. Storey sighed, registering a disapproval that got a wide-eyed stare from Joan.

'I should have thought that today, with all this extra work on,' said Mrs. Storey, 'you might have had a sandwich in the office.'

Joan shrugged, 'Why should I? It's not my fault we've had a lightning take-over bid.'

Mrs. Storey sighed again, and Nell said, 'He surely can't expect everything to be perfect.'

'How do I know what he'll expect?' Mrs. Storey's voice was shrill. 'I don't know the man. But Mr. Baker's very worried, I do know that.'

Joan grinned callously, 'So's Dream-boat' – she meant Norman Rowe. 'He tried to dictate a couple of letters before he went into court this morning, and he was stammering and stuttering all over the place.' She nodded at her open note-book, with its lines scored out and over-written. 'He'll have to think again this afternoon, and I hope he made more sense for the magistrates this morning or it's hard luck on our client.'

They left Mrs. Storey looking martyred, closed the door at the top of the stairs and hurried down into the street. The offices on the ground floor were occupied by a chartered accountant at the back and an estate agents at the front. The accountant, coming in out of the sunshine as they went out, said, 'Lovely day, isn't it?'

'Lovely,' they agreed with him.

'Forecast's unsettled, though,' he told them, and they grinned at the aptness.

'You can say that again,' said Joan, and a few moments later, 'I wonder what he'll be like.'

'Late middle-aged and paunchy.' Nell sounded so sure that Joan turned in surprise,

'You've seen him?'

'No,' said Nell blithely, 'but if he's being put out to grass he's got to be past it, and if he's had a coronary he's probably paunchy.'

Joan giggled, 'Hard luck on you. Dream-boat's no ball of fire, but he's not bad to look at.'

'I'll miss Mr. Elsgood,' said Nell.

Joan sobered. 'He's a pet. I thought he'd go on for ever.' There was a brief silence for the old order changing, while the two girls threaded a path through the midday shoppers. They were both sorry Mr. Elsgood had retired, both had been content with the present set-up in Elsgood and Elsey, but they had other things on their mind right now. They were going to a party on Wednesday night, and they had decided to buy something from Polly's Place, the local boutique.

The fashions were not way out in Polly's place. If they had been Polly would have been out of business in no time, there wasn't much call for pace-setters in Cheslyn Slade. But the selection was bright and reasonably priced, and both Joan and Nell were fairly regular customers.

The girls in the shop knew them and greeted them and left them alone to sort out what they wanted to try on. Joan decided on a pale blue number, with a long skirt, a high waist and collar, and tossed back her long fair hair and looked at herself with satisfaction.

Nell tried on several dresses, settling for a red panne velvet, shimmery and short. She was a quick moving girl, petite, but with a leggy grace, and as she turned in front of the mirror Joan said, 'Will Colin like it?'

'I think so,' said Nell. 'Anyhow, I like it.'

'You wait till you've got a ring on your finger,' Joan flashed hers smugly, 'then the first thing you'll have to ask yourself is – will Colin like it? I always know which dress Harry would pick for me.'

Harry was a bank clerk, earnest and bespectacled, and Nell was not surprised that his fashion choice should be very demure. 'And it's reduced,' said Joan triumphantly. 'It's a bargain. He'll be pleased about that.'

Nell usually went home for lunch unless she met Colin, Joan went home too, but today having passed nearly half an hour in Polly's place they bought a bag of buns and three plastic-covered packs of sandwiches, and sat in the square in the sunshine to eat.

The sun was warm and Nell loved the feel of it on her face. She had a honey skin, with a skein of freckles bridging her nose. Joan, guarding her own fairer skin, leaned back in the seat in a patch of shadow thrown by the equestrian statue that towered over them – a local bigwig who had got himself involved in the Charge of the Light Brigade.

The man and the horse both looked surprised, the horse with arched neck and flaring nostrils, the rider sitting high and straight, as the traffic eddied around them.

The family to which the rider had belonged had died out long ago, the house in which he had lived was now council offices, but he might still have found his way around if he'd come back to town. The layout of Cheslyn Slade hadn't altered much.

'I think we should be getting back.' Nell yawned, the warmth making her sleepy.

Joan shaded her eyes and squinted at the clock in the church tower and protested that they still had ten minutes. But Nell was on her feet, and Joan said, 'Oh, all right then. Perhaps it is a bit mean lolling around while Mrs. Storey and poor old Badger are flogging themselves to death.' Joan was really quite fond of them both.

'Everything's got to be ship-shape and Bristol fashion,'

Nell mimicked Mr. Elsgood. 'And how about hanging out a banner for him – Welcome to Swinging Cheslyn Slade?'

'Why not?' Joan picked up her handbag and her Polly's Place carrier. 'We don't want him thinking there's no action here. What's London got that we haven't?'

Nell considered, and looked up at the statue. 'The Charge of the Light Brigade?'

'Yeah,' said Joan. 'And that's about our lot.'

In the office Mr. Baker and Mrs. Storey were still immersed in paperwork. 'Any more excitement while we were out?' Joan asked, and Mrs. Storey said tartly,

'Not that I noticed. Oh, and Mr. Rowe wants you to take in the letters he gave you this morning, for signature.'

Joan collected her notebook. 'He's got to be joking.'

'He wasn't,' said Mrs. Storey. 'He isn't finding much to joke about today.'

Joan pulled a face at Nell and went off with her notebook, and Nell hesitated, feeling almost guilty that she didn't share the general gloom. She said, 'I don't know why you should worry. This is a well run office.'

'First impressions count,' said Mr. Baker heavily. 'The next few weeks could be difficult for all of us.'

Possibly, thought Nell; a new broom after all these years, there were bound to be changes. And a three-months contract was no insurance for Mr. Baker who had probably reckoned on working here for another ten years.

She put the bag on a corner of Mrs. Storey's table that wasn't covered with papers, and said, 'We brought you some sandwiches and a bun if you're not taking a lunch hour.'

'Thank you,' said Mrs. Storey.

Mr. Elsgood was still in his office too, although he did go home to lunch, leaving Nell with Mrs. Martin's new will to type – Edwin Anthony out, Cyril Joseph in – and a property conveyance to complete.

The afternoon was like countless previous afternoons had been. There might be turmoil in the other offices, but for Mr. Elsgood it was business as usual. Nell was so used to seeing him behind that desk, a courtly old-fashioned figure, that it was difficult to imagine anyone else in his place.

She thought – I wonder if the new man will match the decor, or if we shall have a change there too. I wouldn't mind saying good-bye to the Cries of Old London.

The church clock chimed three, and the phone rang. If he hadn't seen her at lunchtime Colin usually rang during the afternoon about this time. Mr. Elsgood didn't mind, and Nell always kept the calls brief.

Mr. Elsgood was smiling as she replaced the receiver. 'A nice young man,' he said approvingly. 'You won't forget to invite us to the wedding, will you?'

'Of course I shall,' said Nell, 'when I get married. But I'm not even engaged yet.'

He twinkled at her, 'They tell me young people don't bother so much about engagements these days.'

'Some do,' she said lightly. 'Some don't.'

'We shall look out for our invitation,' said Mr. Elsgood. 'My wife will never forgive you if you forget us.'

'I won't,' said Nell. 'I promise I won't forget you.' And she went on with her typing.

She offered to work late when it came round to six o'clock, but he said there was no need, so she said, 'Good night then, see you in the morning,' and got out of the building without looking in either of the other offices.

If Mrs. Storey or Mr. Baker had asked her to help she could not have found the heart to refuse, but she could see no sense in all these frantic preparations.

A new boss, taking over at a few hours' notice, should expect loose ends. If he didn't, if he did turn out to be difficult, he could find himself a new secretary for a start, because Nell would not be begging to stay on.

She went round the back of the office into the yard that was used now as a parking lot. Stables were now garages, and Nell's bicycle was propped against a wall.

Five minutes' brisk pedalling got her out of town, and in another five she was riding along narrow winding lanes that led to farmlands and moors. To farmhouses and cottages, and to Quarry House.

The name had once meant just that. Gravel had been scooped out of the hillsides here, and from open pits; but now the hills had grown green again and the pits had formed a rather charming lake edged with ferns and fir trees.

When Nell's grandfather bought the land and built the house he had made a good living out of the gravel. But it was prettier now, a rambling house, needing a coat of paint, set in a beautiful haphazard garden. There weren't many lakes around these parts. Folk who didn't know presumed the effect had been landscaped.

As Nell turned into the gates a man who had been bent double, hacking down the rough grass with a sickle, straightened. He didn't get quite upright, he stayed a little bent, one hand on his back, and grunted, 'Knocking off time.'

Nell got off her bike. 'Hard work on a hot day,' she said.

'Weather's breaking,' he said. 'Cup of tea won't come amiss.'

They walked down the drive together, past the lake, towards the house. Ocky Corns, who had been christened Harold, was gardener here, and odd job man and family friend. He had become gardener and odd job man when the Lady shut down. The Lady was a coalmine, and Ocky had worked so long underground in the dark narrow seams that he would never stand quite straight again, always with that slight stoop.

And he carried the other mark of the veteran collier, the blue scars on the back of his hands. Blue scars and green fingers; everything he planted grew. There was a flourishing vegetable garden behind the house, and rose bushes bloomed lushly among golden gorse and purple heather.

Ocky listened and nodded as Nell chattered on about Mr. Elsgood's retirement and the new boss, a complete stranger, who would be arriving on Wednesday. 'Mr. Baker's not too pleased,' said Nell. 'I suppose he feels a new man will have new ideas, and he's set in his ways, is our Mr. Baker.'

'Always found one lawyer much the same as another,' said Ocky with contempt for the whole legal profession, and Nell launched into Mr. Elsgood's defence.

'We'll miss him, he's been very easy to work for. I felt sorry for him today, the firm's been his life.'

'Sorry for him?' said Ocky. 'Sixty-eight and pick his time?' Ocky had been redundant at fifty-two, but he smiled because the years since then had been the best years.

There was a crashing in the undergrowth and a huge black dog burst through the waist-high ferns, his coat shin-

16

ing like jet, his teeth white and strong. Muscles rippled and fangs gleamed; beautiful as a panther and daft as a brush, he sprang for Nell, and she side-stepped with the quick foot-work of long practice while Ocky held the bike.

Pedro's welcome-home was always boisterous. Nell fussed him and hushed him, and he fell in beside her, walk-ing close, the picture of a devoted guard dog.

That was probably how he saw himself. Pedro led a thrill-ing life of his own against immeasurable odds. He was forever stalking invisible enemies, not only through the garden but also through the house. It was unnerving some-times, especially late at night.

Nell wheeled her bicycle into the garage, noting that the car had gone in for servicing, and went into the house by the kitchen door. The kitchen was a big room: cooker and sink and fridge and washer taking up the wall under the window, a Welsh dresser and a corner cupboard and wheelback chairs around a scrubbed-topped table making a convenient and pleasant place for meals that didn't rate the dining-room.

The table was laid for five, and the kitchen smelled warm and spicy from freshly baked scones. The woman lifting the scones off a wire tray on to a plate was plump and pink-cheeked with a placid contented air.

Florence Hill had been baking in this kitchen before Nell was born. Ocky had his own home and his own family, but Quarry House was Flo's home, and Nell, Nell's father and grandmother, were her family.

Ocky was washing his hands at the sink and Flo said, 'Hello, had a nice day?'

'A bit livelier than usual,' said Nell.

'Oh?' Flo was pleased, something to hear over tea. She looked at the Polly's Place carrier. 'Been shopping?'

'A dress,' said Nell.

'We'll have to be having a look at that, won't we? Tell them it's on the table, will you?'

Nell's grandmother was where she usually was just before tea, sitting in the small parlour doing her embroidery. She was an accomplished needlewoman, and the piece she was working on now was an altar cloth, scarlet silk and gold thread on white satin.

'Tea's up,' said Nell, sticking her head round the door.

'I'll be along,' her grandmother called back. She had silver hair, softly waving, and a sweet almost unlined face. She had small bones and the delicate air of Dresden china. And she had a stamina and determination that could wear away a stone unless you had her measure, and even then she usually got her own way.

Her late husband had adored her. So did her son, and so did her granddaughter. It was a fair swap; she would have died for them any day, and at least they were forewarned. They knew they had a pocket-sized dictator in this exquisite old lady, who looked as though a voice raised in anger would terrify her.

Nell and Pedro went on down the hall to the room that had been a drawing-room before it became a work room. John Attlesey was a wood carver. He sat at his bench with its fitted vices, carefully stripping the bark off a bough with a file.

He had heard Nell coming and was waiting for the door to open, a man with powerful shoulders, grizzled beard and hair and a tanned skin. He looked like a sea captain or a mountaineer, the hands that held the file looked strong.

He and Nell smiled at each other. She asked, 'What's it going to be?'

'Wait and see.' He rarely knew himself at this stage. The texture, the colour, the grain, even the aroma of the wood, all spoke a language that John Attlesey understood. Wood still lived in his carvings, taking another shape but still living and beautiful.

'Tea's ready,' said Nell. He worked on for a moment or two longer, and she leaned against the work bench and watched. She liked watching every stage of a carving, although perhaps the last was the most exciting, the final smoothing and waxing when the colours and the graining were revealed and it was perfect.

Pedro was circling a sliver of bark on the floor. It looked exactly the same as countless other chips and shavings, but not to him. He had sorted this out as the enemy and was reconnoitring, snuffling nose to the ground, and hackles raised.

John Attlesey put down his file and Nell said to Pedro, 'Give over, you idiot dog, come and have your tea.'

Pedro sneezed and the enemy disappeared, and Nell held open the door for her father to go through. John Attlesey didn't walk. If he had done, with the aid of the two sticks on the end of the workbench, it would have taken him longer to reach the kitchen. He went in a wheelchair. An attack of polio in his early thirties had paralysed him, but any self-pity had long been assuaged by the fact that his hands had regained most of their strength and all their skill.

Before then he had never had a day's illness. He had been a sculptor of promise, working in marble and stone, as well as a wood carver. But that bright July the darkness had fallen.

His wife died. She and his work had been his reasons for living. He had not been able to bear the sight of the child whose birth had taken Ellen away from him. He had left her care to his mother and to Flo; walked out of the house where he and Ellen had lived, and told his solicitors to sell up everything. But within the month John Attlesey's agony was not only of the spirit. He was physically near to death with poliomyelitis.

He wanted to die. He put up no fight, but he didn't die, and when the virulence of the attack ebbed he lay helpless as a child himself in the house where he was born.

When his father told him the child had been christened Ellen he felt the first emotion to break through the numbness of irreparable loss. Anger. If he had had strength he would have shouted, as it was his voice was low and bitter. 'Not Ellen. She should never have been christened Ellen.'

His father had said, 'We're calling her Nell. She's a bonny thing. Your mother's taking it hard that you won't even look at her.'

'No!' John Attlesey had said savagely. As his father sighed and left him he had realized that his hands were clenched. Until then they had lain helpless as his legs. There was still no feeling in his legs, but his fingers flexed slightly again as he strained to repeat the response that fury and frustration had triggered.

It was hard now for him to remember that there had been a time when Nell had not brought sunshine into the room. When his mother first carried her to his side he had looked at her with leaden eyes, a doll-sized scrap of humanity, and he would never see Ellen again.

But Elizabeth Attlesey proceeded in gentle implacable fashion.

Each day she had brought his daughter to him, and his slow-growing tenderness for the child coincided with the return of life to his hands, and the promise that he would work again.

Before Nell's first birthday John Attlesey was back in his studio. He was carving in soft woods: pine, redwood, spruce. But he held her in his arms when there was one candle on her cake.

He carved oak now. Any wood. Stone, marble, was beyond his strength and always would be. A block of marble stood in the corner of the workroom, brought there before Nell was born. It had never been removed; he enjoyed the feel of it, he said; to touch it was still a delight.

But he would never release the spirit in that stone, as he did in the wood. The prisoner slept.

They were at table in the kitchen: Flo and Mrs. Attlesey and Ocky, they had started their meal. Pedro darted for his feeding bowl, John Attlesey moved into his place at the table, and Nell sat down at hers. She helped her father and herself to cold veal and ham pie and salad, and her grandmother said, 'So Mr. Elsgood's retiring.' Ocky had passed on the news.

Nell nodded, 'Mmm, it was quite a surprise, next to no warning at all. From the day after tomorrow I'll be working for someone else. His name's Stephen Harmon and he used to work in London.'

'London?' said her father, and she explained,

'The going was too rough. Mr. Elsgood says he's been ordered a less strenuous routine.' She grinned, 'He should get that in Cheslyn Slade all right!'

Her grandmother asked, 'How old is he? Is he married?'

Nell clapped the palm of her hand to her forehead. 'I forgot to ask. First thing in the morning I'll check.'

Her father and Ocky chuckled, and Flo smiled into her teacup. Nell's grandmother was incurably romantic. When Nell had announced, 'I'm engaged to Barry Russell,' she had started visualizing that walk down the aisle.

Nell had been six at the time and Barry's ruby ring had come out of a cracker, but the next ten years slipped by and her grandmother had assessed every male Nell had dated since as husband material.

As that had not been Nell's yardstick this had caused some awkward scenes, but now there was a halcyon period because Grandmother approved of Colin, although she had her moments of panic, seeing Nell still on the shelf at twenty-one.

Nell had given up arguing that times had changed. Women weren't the surplus sex any more. Today there were enough men to go round. 'A steady and reliable young man,' her grandmother would insist, 'is always hard to find,' and you couldn't deny that.

Twelve months ago Nell had reached a flash point of exasperation and told her father, 'She's got to stop it! One of these days I shall nod without listening to what she's saying, and she'll be putting an engagement notice in the local.'

Her father had smiled, 'She's frightened for you. No brothers, no sisters, a cripple for a father. She doesn't want you left alone.'

Nell never thought of her father as a cripple. No one did who knew him well. He was less mobile than some, but he had more than enough intelligence and character to outweigh any physical handicap. 'She wants you safe,' he'd said.

'What's safe?' Nell had demanded, and her father spoke quietly.

'Love. Nothing else. Caring enough to live with memories if you have to, because no one else comes near. Don't settle for less, Nell.'

She had promised herself then that she would not, and somehow after that she had found it easier to smile at her grandmother's incessant matchmaking.

She said now: 'I'm sorry Mr. Elsgood's going, but I wouldn't mind a change of job. We're all being offered a three-months' contract, but I'm signing nothing until I see how the new man turns out. He could be a horror.'

The local weekly newspaper, the *Cheslyn Slade Clarion*, was on the dresser and Nell fetched it and folded it back at the Situations Vacant page.

She ran her finger down the column. 'Bricklayer's labourer ... cook ... domestic help ... experienced hair stylist ... experienced forecourt attendant, Crabtree Garage ... secretarial ... secretary ...'

There were three possibles, but nothing that sounded like the chance of a lifetime.

Elizabeth Attlesey said, 'Flo and I wouldn't mind having you at home. This is a big house to run.'

'Speak for yourself,' said Flo cheerfully. 'I don't want her here all day, it's bad enough at weekends.'

Weekends Nell usually did enough housework in a few action-packed hours to ensure that Flo could cope for the next week. Flo and Nell managed well enough, but this was another family joke, Elizabeth Attlesey's disapproval of 'career' women, and her dread that Nell might join their ranks.

She had protested strongly when Nell had taken a secretarial course after leaving school, and it was a long time before Nell could speak about any aspect of her work without her grandmother being struck stone deaf.

Now her father demanded, 'And who does she expect to support her if she leaves work?' His mother frowned at him; he was joking, but it was not humour she considered in good taste. Nell said,

'There's that, isn't there? And I wouldn't fancy lowering my standard of living, like a dress every other week. I bought one today. Do you want to see it?'

She took her dress out of the carrier, and held it in front of her. They all approved, her grandmother with less enthusiasm than the others, although even she admitted it was a pretty colour, and asked, 'Are you going to wear it this evening?'

'It's for Wednesday, we're going to a party.'

'You and Colin?'

'Yes.'

Her grandmother smiled, 'You might ask Colin what he thinks about changing your job.'

Ocky guffawed, 'He could have some ideas at that.'

'Could he?' said Nell, and Ocky added with mock gravity,

'Like a free advert in the *Clarion*. It's his dad's paper,

22

isn't it? They ought to be able to help you find a new job.'

'Good thinking,' said Nell. 'Can I give you as a reference?'

'Turn up in that frock, lass,' said Ocky, 'and they'll not ask you for a reference.'

She was ready and waiting when Colin came. They were driving to a pub to meet some friends – nothing exciting, just a pleasant way of passing a Monday evening. Nell went out as the car stopped in front of the house, and Colin leaned across and opened the door so that she could slip into the seat beside him.

They kissed briefly. 'How's my girl?' Colin asked. It was a rhetorical question when she was plainly in robust health, and there was no need to ask how he was either, as she had seen him last night and spoken to him on the phone this afternoon.

She had a snippet of news for him – Mr. Elsgood's retirement. Colin Greer's father owned the *Clarion*. He also owned the local printing works, and the main newsagents' and stationery shop in town.

Colin worked as a journalist, and Mr. Elsgood's retirement would be worth an interview and a photograph, because Mr. Elsgood was a prominent citizen.

'I'll be along tomorrow afternoon to see the old boy,' said Colin. 'Will you fix me an appointment?'

'Say lots of nice things about him,' said Nell.

'We always say nice things in the *Clarion*, except about the Council. Who's taking over? Norman Rowe?'

'No. No one's met the new boss but Mr. Elsgood, but we're hoping for the best.' She touched the plastic wood of the dashboard and Colin smiled. Nell often brought out his protectiveness. She was scatty enough to brighten the dull days, and vulnerable in that she had had it easy all her life.

He laughed, 'He might not be getting the most efficient girl in town, but he'll be working with the prettiest.'

'Thank you very much, and what do you mean – not the most efficient? I've been doing the job for three years.'

'And you still can't spell.'

She grimaced at him. She kept a dictionary in the office. Colin had received more than one letter with a touch of

23

erratic spelling, but Nell checked for business purposes. 'Maybe not,' she said gaily, 'but I make a super cup of coffee, and that's very important in a secretary.'

Colin brought her home around eleven, and would have come in if she'd asked him. She hesitated, feeling a little unkind. The only time they had had alone together tonight had been driving to and from the roadhouse. But she was tired, so she said, 'It had better be good night, darling. Tomorrow is going to be one of those days.'

Tomorrow would be the last day before Mr. Harmon arrived, and only Joan could be relied on to keep her cool. Colin held Nell close and kissed her, and her breath quickened and her blood sang, and for a dreaming moment she kissed him back. Then she drew away. 'See you for lunch tomorrow?'

'Yes.' He was considering a follow-up kiss, but Nell's mind seemed on more mundane things, so instead he said, 'I love you,' and traced the line of her brow, nose and chin, with a fingertip.

'Love you,' murmured Nell, 'but it's still got to be good night.' She wriggled free, and out of the car, and as she let herself into the house and heard the car drive away she wondered if she did love Colin, if he loved her. And she thought it likely.

The next day started as it meant to go on, and Nell had been right, it was a day to remember.

First, the alarm didn't ring and she overslept, waking with Flo shaking her and demanding, 'Do you know what time it is?'

'Oh *no*!' Nell shot out of bed. She should have been downstairs by now.

'Your breakfast's ready,' said Flo. She went to the window and pulled back the curtains. 'And it's pouring with rain.'

Nell washed and dressed and fixed her hair and make-up at a rate that left her breathless. When she got into the kitchen she could hardly get out the words 'I don't have time for breakfast.'

'Have a cup of tea and a piece of toast,' said Flo. Nell's father was in his workroom, he was always an early riser; her grandmother came down when she felt rested. There was only Flo and Nell, until Flo opened the back door and let in Pedro.

Nell screeched. Early morning Pedro usually confined his greetings to a swish of the tail and a prodigious yawn. His bed was in the corner of the kitchen, and he had rarely left it when Nell left the house. But this morning he had taken a stroll and the cool rain had alerted and freshened him, so that he was bright-eyed and raring. Before Nell could shove him off he had patterned her skirt with monstrous muddy paws.

There was no brushing that down. She rushed up to her bedroom to change, while Flo grabbed Pedro who would have entered into the spirit of things given half a chance and galloped along with her.

On the way back, as she passed her grandmother's room, Mrs. Attlesey came out and said, 'Good morning.'

'Morning!' Nell called over her shoulder.

'Don't rush, dear,' Mrs. Attlesey's voice was plaintive.

'I'm late.' Nell jumped down the last three stairs.

'More haste less speed,' her grandmother proclaimed from the landing.

'Don't you believe it,' muttered Nell.

Flo had Nell's mackintosh and a headscarf and a large umbrella ready in the kitchen, and Nell slipped on the mac, tied on the headscarf, and looked at the umbrella.

Flo said, 'You'll be needing that as well. I went to get your bike out and you've got a flat tyre.'

'I *haven't*!'

'Flat as a pancake.'

'And there's no car.'

'And Ocky won't be here till ten so you can't borrow his bike, so you'll have to walk.'

It was half an hour's walk, the lanes were muddy and the rain came down, steady and drenching. The umbrella wasn't much help; it seemed to act as a windbrake, impeding progress, so that Nell closed it after the first few minutes and battled on, head down, comforting herself with the thought of a nice dry office, and turning on the electric fire to cheer herself up.

The streets of the town were almost empty. Nell passed one woman, who said, 'Miserable, isn't it?' as she dived out of one shop into another.

'Foul,' said Nell through chattering teeth.

There was nobody in the hall or in the corridor beyond the 'Elsgood and Elsey' door at the top of the stairs. A typewriter was clattering in Joan and Mrs. Storey's room, and as Nell took off her mac, and propped up her umbrella in the small sink of the cloakroom, she heard the phone ring in Mr. Elsgood's office.

She ran to answer it. It was possible Mr. Elsgood wasn't in yet. It stopped ringing as she burst into the room. Mr. Elsgood had picked up the receiver. He looked round at Nell, but it wasn't his eyes she met.

Another man sat behind the desk, and she met his gaze with the paralysing shock of a collision.

CHAPTER TWO

On the telephone Mr. Elsgood said, 'Ah, good morning, Mr. Redfern.'

One of the letters Nell had typed yesterday, explaining that Mr. Elsgood was leaving the practice, had been to Mr. Redfern. Mr. Redfern had a case pending; a customer had paid for a ton of best anthracite with a bouncing cheque and resisted all requests to come up with the cash.

Mr. Redfern, who knew Mr. Elsgood personally, was ringing to wish him well on his retirement and assure him that he would be sorely missed in the local Conservative club. 'Very kind of you to say so, Thomas,' Mr. Elsgood was murmuring, pink with emotion.

Nell gulped and stood still. The man behind the desk had to be Stephen Harmon. He was not supposed to be arriving until tomorrow, but no one else would be occupying that chair. He continued to look at her with slight inquiry.

She only needed to say, 'I'm Ellen Attlesey, Mr. Elsgood's secretary,' and walk up to him with a smile. But when you have just hurtled into a room and skidded to a halt it isn't easy to give an impression of poise and confidence. She felt as woolly-witted as though she had run full tilt into a brick wall. She pointed mutely to her own desk, and more or less backed into it.

That explained who she was without having to get the words out. It might also give him grounds for wondering if the natives spoke English.

Not that he'd done any talking. He'd just looked at her, watched her into her chair, and then looked down again at the papers on the desk. The whole thing could not have taken more than a few seconds, but for Nell it seemed to be in nightmare slow motion.

Her desk was clear, her typewriter to one side. Rain dripped from her chin on to the desk, and she opened a drawer to get out a tissue and dab her face. The tissue came away with traces of foundation, lipstick and eye-shadow, which must mean that the rain had merged the lot together.

Not only did the natives not speak English, but they wore rainbow warpaint when they came down from the hills.

There was a small mirror in the drawer somewhere, and she rummaged for it and blotted away with her head bowed.

The click of Mr. Elsgood's replaced telephone made her look up. He said, 'Sorry about that,' to Mr. Harmon, and to Nell, 'Good morning, Miss Attlesey.'

'I'm sorry I'm late.'

'A very rare occurrence,' said Mr. Elsgood kindly. It was. She was always here by nine unless she had a valid excuse, but as ten o'clock was his customary hour he wouldn't have known anyway.

This was a fine start with a new employer. As Badger had been saying yesterday, 'First impressions count,' and Nell's had been bedevilled. She explained, 'I had a puncture, so I had to walk.'

Rain was still beating on the window and she had Mr. Elsgood's sympathy. He sighed for her, 'And this is no kind of morning for a walk.'

Mr. Harmon said nothing until Mr. Elsgood said, 'This is Miss Attlesey who has been my very efficient secretary for some years,' then he said,

'Good morning,' pleasantly but without enthusiasm.

She was very conscious that she was looking a sight. Her toes squelched in her shoes, her face was a hot healthy glow of rain-washed tissue-scrubbed skin.

He was younger than she had expected, lean, and well tailored; straight nose, strong mouth, but the lines running from nose to mouth didn't look like laughter lines; and sitting silent beside Mr. Elsgood he conveyed an impression of intimidating intellectual superiority. Put those two in court on opposing sides and Mr. Elsgood would be pulverized, thought Nell.

Dear Mr. Elsgood, who was singing her praises, insisting that she had been his right hand, ever helpful, never failing. He meant every word, but she squirmed inwardly and wished he would moderate his enthusiasm. She didn't relish being sold, and it felt like that; Mr. Elsgood was so very anxious that Mr. Harmon should keep Nell on as his secretary.

He said merrily, 'Miss Attlesey has always been tolerant of my many failings. Her sense of humour has proved equal to more than one crisis.'

Nell was naturally cheerful, but she was sounding like the life and soul of the party, a wide mindless grin on her face no matter what. Mr. Elsgood looked at her, misty-eyed with benevolence, and said with a catch in his voice, 'Miss Attlesey has been a ray of sunshine in this office.'

'I must try not to overtax her sense of humour.' Stephen Harmon smiled, but Mr. Elsgood caught the irony and said pensively,

'This has been a very happy office.'

He had not wanted to retire, but he had known it was time he did. His wife was right, they had reached the stage where they should take that round-the-world cruise they had always promised themselves, and buy that house by the sea. He knew, and his wife knew, that he was growing daily harder of hearing, and finding routine more of a strain.

Stephen Harmon had the highest reputation. Mr. Elsgood had no fears for his clients nor for the future good name of the firm. He would be proud to hand over to a lawyer like Harmon.

When Harmon had phoned last night to say he would be in Cheslyn Slade today to see about the flat, and might he look into the office to meet his future employees, Mr. Elsgood had said certainly.

This morning he had met them, with a courtesy that should have been reassuring. He was about the same age as Norman Rowe, and they had shaken hands as Mr. Elsgood introduced them, and Stephen Harmon was a lifetime older. He had an inborn authority that made Norman Rowe seem like a gangling teenager. Alexander Baker stood ramrod stiff, Mrs. Storey's smile twitched nervously, and Joan Frisk's eyes widened like saucers and stayed that way.

Mr. Elsgood, for the first time, realized that his standards of efficiency might differ from Stephen Harmon's.

He explained when they were alone, 'They are all a little overwhelmed by the speed of events, but there is a splendid spirit here. You won't find a more conscientious team anywhere.'

Stephen Harmon said he was glad to hear it. Nell hadn't

arrived. That was unfortunate, Mr. Elsgood relied on her and without her was slightly at a loss. He had rarely before been confronted by the unopened mail, and frowned at it in the In-tray, as he offered his chair to Stephen Harmon and took the seat on which the client usually sat himself.

Harmon accepted the offer. Mr. Elsgood began to open the mail, passing over the letters with a few words of background. He was on the third letter when the phone rang and Nell came rushing through the door.

Ellen Attlesey was a bright girl, her gaiety was rooted in kindness, and it distressed him to hear Stephen Harmon say drily, 'I must try not to overtax her sense of humour.'

He heard himself sighing, 'A very happy office,' and then Nell said in clear cool tones,

'From the glimpse I've just had of myself in the mirror I must have overtaxed your sense of humour already, Mr. Harmon. Would you excuse me a couple of minutes while I make myself look more like a secretary and less like a circus clown?'

Stephen Harmon smiled again, and Nell smiled too. But if she had covered her mouth no one would have known she was smiling at all, and the same applied to him.

Two minutes, she had said, and two minutes she meant. She wiped off the rest of her make-up and replaced a minimum fast. She pulled a comb through her hair, and tried to push in a little bounce with fingertips so that it might dry into a semblance of style. As she turned from the cloakroom mirror to the door Joan came in.

Joan hadn't realized Nell was there; as she saw her she asked, 'What happened to you?'

'I was late,' said Nell, idiotically.

'I know that,' said Joan. 'Have you met him?'

'Just.'

'You were off the mark, weren't you? Late middle-aged and paunchy!'

'Way off,' Nell agreed.

'What do you think?' Joan chewed her underlip, sounding apprehensive.

'I think I'm away to a heck of a start,' said Nell. 'Mr. Elsgood's just told him I'm a little ray of sunshine.

Joan threw back her head and chortled, 'I like that!

That's sweet.'

'Sweet,' said Nell. 'Only I don't think he's the type who'll want little rays of sunshine playing around.'

They were still with the mail when she got back. Mr. Elsgood said, 'Switch on the fire, Miss Attlesey, we don't want you catching a chill.'

'Thank you,' she said. She wasn't cold, but her feet were soaked. If Mr. Elsgood had been here alone she would have taken off her shoes and propped them up to dry. In front of Mr. Harmon that was as unthinkable as stripping down to bra and pants.

She switched on the fire and got out notepad and pencil and answered the phone when it rang again. Another client to say goodbye; the day would probably be punctuated by them.

While Mr. Elsgood spoke to the caller Nell said, 'May I?' indicating the correspondence that had been opened, and Stephen Harmon nodded and pushed it across.

He got up and went to the window. It overlooked the yard and the stable-block. He stood, looking down, and Nell glanced at the first document, a Land Registry document, and Mr. Elsgood said, 'That is very kind of you,' and then, 'Thank you,' and then, 'Goodbye.'

He sighed as he put down the receiver. Each time he had sighed. Nell wondered if any of Mr. Harmon's clients had parted from him as though they were losing a friend. Of course most of the men and women who were phoning Mr. Elsgood had known him all their lives. They *were* friends.

Harmon had not turned. He was still looking down, although there couldn't be much to see except the parked cars. Nell's disjointed thoughts darted behind lowered lids . . . You won't buy a suit like that in Cheslyn Slade . . . I wonder if you are married . . . I wonder how she'll like living here after London, shopping at Polly's Place . . .

She set aside the Land Registry document. It had to be posted on to a client who had bought a cottage that had no deeds. The accompanying letter would be brief, and she could draft it herself without bothering anyone for anything but a signature. She would have done for Mr. Elsgood, but now she wasn't sure what she must do, and waited to be told.

Mr. Elsgood was pondering, chin in hand. Mr. Harmon turned from the window. 'If Miss Attlesey could be spared this afternoon I should be glad of her assistance.'

'But of course,' said Mr. Elsgood, as one might say – Miss Attlesey's services are yours. All this is yours.

'Thank you. I'll be back, say two o'clock?'

'Any time,' said Mr. Elsgood.

He looked at the door for several seconds after it had closed behind Stephen Harmon, then he went round and took the armchair behind the desk and said, 'Well, Miss Attlesey, shall we start work?'

In every material way he had already abdicated. Stephen Harmon had been introduced to the staff as the head of the firm, and would be along after lunch to sit in that chair, but Mr. Elsgood could not forgo the last few hours. Everything he did today would be completed by another man, but until lunchtime he could occupy his old place.

They dealt with the mail, and at eleven o'clock Nell made coffee in the percolator. As she unplugged and poured out she asked, 'Will you leave us this?' and Mr. Elsgood said,

'I think not. My wife has an excellent percolator, but I still feel I should enjoy my morning coffee better from this one.'

The thought of Mr. Elsgood brewing up in the old percolator and thinking of them all every morning brought a lump to Nell's throat. It would have been less pathetic if the percolator had been bright and shiny, but it was battered and tarnished.

She hoped his wife would 'lose' it and make his coffee in the gay ceramic pot from which she had given Nell a cup of coffee a week or two ago, and drink her coffee with him and keep him cheerful. Nell was sure she would. Mrs. Elsgood was a bright little body.

She asked, to change the subject, 'Is Mr. Harmon married?'

'No, he isn't.'

So there would be no Mrs. Harmon going through the racks in Polly's Place. Mr. Elsgood said, 'He is a very respected solicitor. He has a fine reputation.' Nell made a small admiring murmur, and Mr. Elsgood went on, 'He may find the period of adjustment somewhat trying. This is not

32

the kind of practice he has been used to.'

Nell could believe that. Stephen Harmon had made this office look like a period piece. It suited Mr. Elsgood, with his stiff white collars and gentle fussiness, but Stephen Harmon's complete competence – and she had no doubt of that – was going to look incongruous backed by yellowing steel engravings and the Waverley Novels.

She said quietly, 'Let's hope he does adjust.'

'He must.' Mr. Elsgood was implacable. 'That is his reason for coming here. But at first it may be frustrating for him and I hope you will all be patient and make allowances.'

He had looked fit enough, the last kind of man for pity. But he was faced with a grim situation, having to keep check on his abilities because of his health. Nell thought of her father, who had come to terms. Most people did. Life was compromise. Slowly almost everyone surrendered and succumbed. But when it happened fast it had to be worse. As it had happened to her father. As Stephen Harmon must have realized that he was not going to reach the heights.

'A little give and take,' said Mr. Elsgood hopefully.

'Of course,' said Nell. 'Where's he living, by the way?'

'He's staying at The Raven for a while.' That was the best of the local pubs. 'And then he's moving into the flat over the stables.'

The stable block had an upper storey of one-time haylofts that had been connected with electricity and drainage when the stables became garages. The building belonged to Elsgood and Elsey, the offices downstairs were rented on lease. The rooms over the stables had never been lived in, but had been used as junk dumps over the years by all the offices. The last time Nell had been up there was last winter when she had gone to check that the pipes were lagged.

She remembered the spider webs and shuddered, 'I should think he'd be more comfortable staying on at the Raven.'

Mr. Elsgood gave a prim little cough. 'No doubt, but a public house, even one as well conducted as the Raven, offers little in the way of quiet and privacy. Both of which Mr. Harmon requires.'

It would also be cheaper, living on the premises. 'He's got

a problem,' said Nell. 'Clearing out all that junk.'

It had stopped raining when she met Colin for lunch. They sometimes went to the snackbar and had soup and sandwiches, sitting on high stools at the counter. Sometimes they had the 'business man's lunch' in the café behind the cake shop. It depended how busy Colin was. Today he had time for a meal, and having skipped breakfast herself Nell was glad about that.

They took the corner table, beneath the alcove with the artificial flower display in a boat-shaped urn, and Colin chose lamb chop and Nell chose shepherd's pie. Then he sat back and looked at her critically. 'You've changed your hairstyle.'

'It got wet through this morning. It's left it a bit limp. And if you'd like to offer me a lift home tonight I wouldn't say no. My bike had a puncture and I had to walk.'

'Shame,' said Colin.

'It couldn't have happened on a better morning. When I arrived the new boss had jumped the gun by a day. He was there. He'd met all the rest of them, and I belted into the office half an hour late looking like a drowned rat.'

Colin laughed. 'Not a drowned rat, a wet kitten – I bet you looked cute. What's he like?'

'You might see him this afternoon. I asked Mr. Elsgood about an interview and he said would two-thirty do?' It would, said Colin. Nell watched the waitress back out through the swing doors from the kitchen, bearing the tray with their meal. 'Mr. Harmon will be in the office then. I'm doing some work for him this afternoon.'

She knew her job. For a while at least she should know it better than he did. Colin teased her, 'You don't look too happy at the prospect. Make a clean breast of it, tell him before you start that you can't spell.'

She hadn't realized she was looking apprehensive. She smiled, 'I've never worked for anyone but Mr. Elsgood before. Still, as Ocky says, one lawyer's much the same as another.' Except that Ocky hadn't seen Stephen Harmon.

He came into the office at two o'clock. Mr. Elsgood wasn't back from lunch, and Nell was sitting at her desk with enough pencils sharpened to take dictation from now until tea-time.

He had been with Badger and Norman Rowe. Nell knew that because she had looked in on Joan and Mrs. Storey, and Mrs. Storey had asked, 'Haven't you any work to do, Nell?'

'Right at this moment, no,' Nell had said crisply, because it was none of Mrs. Storey's business.

'He's in there.' Mrs. Storey's eyes had swivelled towards the connecting door. 'I wouldn't like him to come out and find us chatting.'

Even Joan seemed to have lost some of her ebullience. She had giggled, but kept her voice down to say, 'It's like a morgue, isn't it? You'd think Mr. Elsgood had died instead of retiring.'

Nell went back to her own office, and sharpened pencils, and re-checked the typing she had done before lunch, and waited.

Stephen Harmon had a pleasant smile, practised no doubt and professional, but it was attractive even if it didn't quite reach his eyes. He said, 'I should be glad of your help if you're free.'

It wasn't going to be dictation. He didn't have any papers and he didn't go to the desk. He said, 'It's a matter of clearing out the rooms over the stables.'

Nell swallowed slowly. 'You want *me* to clear them?'

'I want you to supervise the clearing. Mr. Elsgood doesn't want anything salvaged. Mr Connel and Mr. Savage will be along within the next half hour to see if there's anything they want. The rest will be collected at five.'

'Right,' she said. 'Who's fetching the rest of the stuff?'

'The Council refuse department. You can manage that?'

It was hardly a secretarial chore, and if she had known she would be spending the afternoon in the haylofts she would have brought dungarees, but it would make a change and she must try to keep clear of the spider webs. 'Of course,' she said.

He thanked her and the smile switched off. There was something very dismissive in the way Stephen Harmon turned from you; as though having allocated a task any problems it produced were yours. With Mr. Elsgood she would have chatted on a few moments longer, but Harmon was already on another wavelength. Communication had

35

ceased, as abruptly as though they had been talking by telephone and he had replaced the receiver.

Nell looked in again on Joan and Mrs. Storey. The door was open between their room and Norman Rowe's, and Mr. Baker was coming through with some papers. Nell said, 'If Mr. Elsgood or anyone else asks for me would you tell them I'm over in the stables?'

'Doing what?' asked Joan.

'Clearing the lofts out,' said Nell. 'He's having them turned into a flat.' There was no need to particularize who 'he' was, although this was plainly the first Mrs. Storey and Joan had heard of it. Joan gasped,

'*You've* got to clean up?'

'Not with my own fair hands. It's being collected. I'm there to wave it off.'

'That's not your job,' Joan protested.

'He seems to think it is,' said Nell.

Mr. Baker put down a sheaf of papers on Joan's desk and demanded, 'Three carbons with each to catch the afternoon post.'

The heavy rain of the morning had left the yard muddy and the outer brickwork of the stables glistening wet. Inside a flight of stone steps led to the upper storey. There was a door at the top that had never been closed in Nell's memory, one hinge gone so that it lay askew against the wall.

The place smelt dank. The windows were grimy enough to reduce broad day to twilight, and she couldn't imagine anyone turning this dump into a home.

There was so much junk: rolls of old lino, old carpets, boxes galore, chairs, tables, pictures, pots, a pram, a hat rack eerie in the shadows with dark hanging shapes. A good thirty years of stashing contained in three small rooms.

One room wasn't so small, the one you entered first. Cleared of its contents it would be a good size. Nell stood inside the doorway, switched on the dusty light bulb, and looked around her.

Not my day, she thought – half drowned in the morning, and I'm going to look like a chimney sweep by the time I get home tonight.

She moved cautiously, skirting the spider webs. Mr.

Connel, chartered accountant, and Mr. Savage, estate agent, were due any time to give their dumped property the once-over before it was carted off as rubbish.

It seemed to be rubbish all right. She couldn't see why Harmon hadn't simply had the lot cleared out, no one was going to want any of this. Although legally, to be on the safe side, it was probably wise to get permission. 'So – come on,' muttered Nell, rubbing a peephole through the grime on the window, and looking across the yard to the back door of the house.

There was nothing she could do until they did come, and she could use company. It was dreary and depressing in here, and the mud and the grey skies didn't make the outlook much brighter.

The same cars were parked in the same places, except for one that had to be Stephen Harmon's. That was against the wall of the courtyard, she hadn't noticed it when she crossed the yard. No doubt in future it would be in the garage where Mr. Elsgood's sedate saloons had rested, so long as Mr. Elsgood had been commuting one mile there and one mile back.

But that wasn't a sedate saloon. That was the sort of car Colin coveted to a point of fury, from behind the wheel of his own sports car.

You could sell that, mused Nell, and fix yourself up with a better place to live. Or was the car a status symbol? Friends and colleagues might not come down here, but they might still see the car. So long as Stephen Harmon had that he had the aura of success around him. He could travel hopefully.

One thing about a bike, you had nothing to lose. Any old banger was a status symbol compared to a bike.

Nell saw Mr. Connel step out of the house, and went from the window to the top of the stone steps to meet him. He came gingerly, looking at the mud on his shoes. He was a neat man, orderly as the accounts he worked out for a living, alone in his single-room office.

When he saw Nell he said, 'Good afternoon.'

'Good afternoon,' said Nell. 'I don't think you're going to want any of this stuff.'

He laughed politely, 'I'm sure I shan't. So far as I can

remember very little of it has come from my office.'

'Walk right up,' said Nell, 'and take your pick.'

Walking in, he peered about. 'Mr. Harmon here?' He had lowered his voice to ask, and when Nell said no he upped it back to normal pitch. 'I was surprised to hear Mr. Elsgood was leaving.'

'We all were,' said Nell.

'It won't be the same without him.' Mr. Connel shook his head, adding discreetly that he had found Mr. Harmon very co-operative, very charming, at their meeting.

'But not the same,' said Nell.

Mr. Connel shook his head again. 'A real gentleman, Mr. Elsgood.'

'Anybody home?' called Mr. Savage. He was as outgoing as Mr. Connel was reserved: red-faced, overweight, and usually smiling. The light was on and they were talking, and it was obvious someone was up here. He puffed a little, reaching the top of the stairs, and announced that he was not as young as he used to be. 'And I can tell you right away,' he said, 'I don't want any of this back.'

He gave the hat stand a nod of recognition. 'That was in one of my rooms when I moved in, and that desk over there. I soon got shut of them.'

Mr. Savage's offices were furnished in modern style, and Nell could see what he meant about the hat rack.

Mr. Savage looked at the two closed doors. 'Is – er—?' he began, and Nell said,

'No, he isn't here,' surprised that she should know what the question was going to be, and realizing that Stephen Harmon seemed to be having the same effect on everyone on the premises. They were all whispering and looking jumpy.

Worry sat strangely on Mr. Savage's jolly round face, but it was there as he asked, 'What do you think about this Joe?'

'It was quite a shock,' admitted Mr. Connel.

'I reckon Elsgood could have given us some warning.'

'Mr. Harmon seems a reasonable man,' said Mr. Connel mildly.

'He's a sharp lawyer.' Mr. Savage spoke through the corner of his mouth as though grudging the admission. 'And our rents are a gift by today's rates. We can always move, I know, but I'm used to it here, I don't want to move.'

Neither did Mr. Connel. He said, 'But the renewal of the lease has always been understood, a gentleman's agreement,' and Mr. Savage grinned at his naïvety.

'This new fellow's for the main chance first and a gentleman when it suits him, mark my words.' Having confirmed Mr. Connel's secret fears he clapped him jovially on the shoulder. 'Well, if he gets greedy there's aways something on the books, we'll *have* to move.'

'Oh, I *do* hope not,' said Nell. Mr. Connel and Mr. Savage had been working here far longer than she had, she considered them both as friends. She knew their families. Mr. Savage beamed at her,

'No sense running to meet trouble. This isn't London, is it? Not too many suites of offices wanted in Cheslyn Slade. He'll probably leave things as they are.

'Now let's see what we've got up here. Haven't been up here in years.'

He cast an estate agent's eye around, sizing up the rooms, not their contents. 'I suppose something could be made of it. I could have found him a flat, offered to, but he wasn't having any.' He scratched at a beam. 'Surprising,' he said; and sniffed along a skirting board. 'Not bad.'

Nell said, 'I think it smells pretty horrible.'

'Smells empty, my dear, but not of the old dry rot.'

She asked, 'When you put that hat-rack here, did you leave those things hanging on it?'

'Damned if I know,' he said. On investigation they turned out to be an ancient mackintosh and a bulging duffle bag. Mr. Savage took down the duffle bag and Nell said quickly,

'There's no point in opening it, is there?'

She was all for leaving it as it was, but Mr. Savage was poking cautiously at the top. 'Books,' he said, 'and newspapers.'

He brought out the newspapers, and Mr. Connel helped himself to a book. The newspapers were the colour of old parchment but infinitely more fragile. They came to pieces as he opened one looking for the property page, although he was still left with enough to compare prices of a semi-detached in Market Street nineteen years ago with a similar property he was offering today. 'Scandalous, isn't it?' he asked Nell.

Mr. Connel looked up from his bound volume to say, 'They don't produce magazines like Cornhills any more.'

'Do you want them?' asked Nell.

'No, thank you,' said Mr. Connel. He closed the book, and still holding it looked at the hat rack. 'Although it seems a pity to burn all this stuff. Even this' – the hat rack – 'painted up, I've seen them in the shops. And the desk.' He went to the desk, put the book on top and took out a drawer. 'It's sound enough. Might be some woodworm somewhere, but not too much to treat by the looks of it.'

Nell asked, 'What do you suggest I do with it?'

'The Scouts are having a jumble sale next week. They might be glad of it.'

'Well, they're very welcome. How do we get in touch?' She remembered. 'Your niece is the cub-mistress, isn't she?'

'I'll give her a ring,' Mr. Connel offered. He must have got through right away and got his niece right away, because he was back while Mr. Savage was still reading his scraps of newspapers, to say that Shirley said they'd take anything they could get. If they couldn't sell it they'd find some use for it. Please put the stuff by and the scoutmaster would collect it in his van as soon as possible.

Mr. Savage took the piece of newspaper with the house in Market Street. 'Not to show the customers, though, they might think I'm getting the difference,' and went back to his office.

Mr. Connel stayed to give Nell a hand, sorting out the items that had been reprieved. The task wasn't as grisly as it might have been. Mr. Connel had brought a window-cleaning aerosol and a couple of dusters over with him, and when the windows were cleaned and the light came in you could at least see what you were about.

The lino and the old rugs were fit for nothing but burning, but chairs could be cleaned and painted, and there was an old cabinet wind-up gramophone that might find a home. They pulled and pushed the refuse-junk to the front, putting the jumble sale load at the back. It was dirty work and Mr.

Connel was such a tidy man that Nell was surprised, and concerned for his well pressed suit.

She said so, and he said, 'This suit's due for cleaning.'

It is now, she thought, glad that her own skirt and sweater were washable. She wiped as much dust as she could off the furniture, although it was bound to look dingy until it had been cleaned and polished or painted.

There were some old pictures too, in ornate tarnished gilt frames, stacked in one of the smaller rooms. Somebody might want them, paint the frames and take out the Monarch of the Glen and kindred subjects. Mr. Connel agreed, and the pictures joined the jumble sale section.

Nell enjoyed herself. When Mr. Savage's secretary came hurrying over to say that Mr. Connel's phone was ringing Nell said, 'I can manage now. Thank you very much for your help, and I can easily manage now, we've done most of the sorting.'

It was his niece calling to say that the scoutmaster would collect tomorrow evening. 'Good,' said Nell, and looked at Mr. Connel's grubby hands, and hoped his wife would be able to shift the grime from his shirt cuffs.

He looked at their handiwork and said, 'Shirley is delighted. She says it's been very uphill collecting for this jumble sale, as St Mark's had one last week.'

'Not like ours,' said Nell, and Mr. Connel gloated,

'No indeed. I saw a hat rack like that painted red, and they were asking a ridiculous figure.'

He went back to his office, and Nell continued to dust and potter until the refuse collectors arrived and carted away the rubbish.

It was after half-five before that was cleared. She went over to the office then, glad that she had a little time before Colin should be calling to give her a lift home. She washed in the cloakroom, made up again as she had done this morning, and went along to tap on the door of Mr. Elsgood's office.

Mr. Harmon might be in there. If he was she could report that all the junk had been dealt with, and if he cared to call in the Scouts' hall on Saturday week he could see some of it jazzed up and make them an offer.

No, she thought, no cracks! She was trying to live down

that 'ray of sunshine' tab, and she was not sure he had a sense of humour.

Mr. Elsgood was there. No one else. His desk was tidy, all papers in the Out-tray. He was sitting back in his chair as though it had been a hard day.

Nell said impulsively, 'You look tired!' The words were out before she could stop them, and today they were tactless and would have been better unsaid.

He smiled at her. 'Reminiscing for that young man of yours has made me aware of my advanced years.'

'You saw Colin?'

'We had a nice long chat, but mine has not been a colourful career.' He smiled at himself. 'The only moment of glory I could recall was getting my half century in a college cricket match. I think your young man would have preferred something a little more up to date, some stirring courtroom drama.'

Nell laughed, 'You probably won't recognize yourself when you read it. If it's too stirring you can sue the *Clarion* for libel.'

'Small hope of that, I fear,' said Mr. Elsgood. He pressed down on the arms of the chair for leverage in getting to his feet, and then touched the Out-tray. 'All signed, but they can wait till morning for filing and mailing. Mr. Harmon will be here in the morning – you will be on time?'

There was no sting in that, just gentle raillery, but Nell said with emphasis, 'I most certainly will.'

Mr. Elsgood looked into the other offices as he always did if he left before six, and wished everyone goodnight. He went down to the garage and got into his car.

Time passed so quickly. Recalling the old days this afternoon it had seemed impossible it had been so long since he had been like Norman Rowe.

He drove out carefully as always, a steady and reliable driver, just as his professional record over the years had been steady and reliable. He had done what he could to the best of his abilities. And to small effect, he reflected ruefully, because he had been like Norman Rowe, but never, even after years of experience, with the brilliant and ruthless touch of Stephen Harmon.

'Did you see Mr. Harmon?' Nell asked as she climbed

42

into Colin's car for her lift home.

'Only the old boy.'

'How did the interview go?'

'Usual guff,' said Colin. ' "Cheslyn Slade's Senior Solicitor retires to the seaside, missed by his many friends, once shook hands with the Queen Mother, presented with a thingamybob by his staff." Are you giving him anything?'

'Of course we must,' said Nell.

'The copy's too late for this week's paper,' said Colin. 'We'll get a picture and run them together in next week's edition. You could present it with a nice big smile.'

'Grinning like a Cheshire cat,' she said. 'The little ray of sunshine.'

Colin grinned too, but tentatively, because Nell had sounded almost snappish.

Quite late in the evening she told her father that Stephen Harmon had turned up today. It was so late that her grandmother and Flo had gone to bed. The radio was playing some music her father wanted to hear and Nell had been half listening, half reading. When the programme ended she said suddenly, 'I met my new boss today.'

She hadn't lied so much as evaded when they'd questioned her earlier – not her father, the womenfolk; and she had spent most of the evening giving herself a bath and washing her hair. She was in a yellow candlewick bath robe now, her hair still pinned in rollers, sitting on the old chintz-covered settee, her feet tucked under her.

'Why the secrecy?' asked her father.

'Because Grandmother had a dozen more questions waiting, and I only met him for five minutes, I couldn't have answered any of them.'

'None of them?'

Nell grimaced. 'Except that he's not so old and he's not married.'

'She'd have found that interesting.'

'She needn't,' said Nell. 'He's spoken for, I'd take a bet on it. And you should see his car.'

'That's a cynical attitude,' her father's deep voice rumbled with laughter, and Nell unpinned a roller, found her hair still damp and wound it up again.

'He'd still be a knockout without the car, but you know

43

what they say, that you can tell a man's taste in women by the car he picks. So Mr. Harmon's girls are gorgeous and fast and very rich. It's too much competition for me.'

All her life she had talked happy nonsense with her father, a vein of fantasy going back to the make-believe of her earliest memories.

He looked at her now, as though assessing her chances, then he said solemnly, 'I'm afraid it is.'

'I thought so,' said Nell, 'so tell her, will you, if she gets any ideas?'

'I'll point it out.'

She eased her feet from under her. 'I think I'll go to bed.' This was a little earlier than usual for Nell, but she wanted time to spare in the morning. Ocky had mended her puncture and she intended to reach the office well ahead of Stephen Harmon. She said, 'It doesn't work with women, you know.'

'What doesn't?'

'This business of matching your transport up with your love life. I'm certainly not looking for a man who reminds me of my old bike.'

Stephen Harmon's car was not in the courtyard next morning when Nell propped up her bike against the stables. Not many cars were, as she was a good twenty minutes earlier than usual.

She wouldn't have been surprised to find the 'Elsgood and Elsey' door still locked, but someone was in, and Mr. Baker was the obvious choice. He was usually first, and he had a set of keys. He collected the mail in the hall, and delivered it on the desks of Mr. Rowe and Mr. Elsgood, but this morning he hadn't got around to that, and finding her own office still locked Nell went back to his.

'Early bird this morning,' said Mr. Baker.

'Making up for yesterday,' Nell smiled.

'It's as well. We'd all better watch our step.' He put down the last letter on Mr. Elsgood's pile. He looked as though he hadn't slept too soundly, and picking up her mail Nell said, 'It went all right yesterday, didn't it?'

He refused to be reassured. 'Appeared to,' he said, and she persisted,

'Mr. Harmon wouldn't have taken a small town practice

like ours if he hadn't needed a quiet life. Why should he want to stir things?'

'The leopard doesn't change its spots,' said Mr. Baker gloomily.

She smiled again. 'Well, it'll have to change its ways, won't it? Cheslyn Slade's no concrete jungle.'

She got a wry look in return and went away wondering if Mr. Baker knew more than he was telling about the man who was taking Mr. Elsgood's place.

She sat at her desk, opening the mail. There was nothing new, and she made notes as she put each communication aside so that she could tell Mr. Harmon what had gone before if Mr. Elsgood left it to her.

When there was a knock on the door she looked down at her watch as she called 'Come in.' There were no appointments this early so far as she knew. Half past ten was the first on the books.

The man who came in was stockily built with dark wiry hair, wearing a pained expression and workman's overalls. 'Mr. Harmon's office?' he asked.

'Yes,' said Nell. 'Can I help you?'

'I'm Morrisons the builders,' the man announced as though she had denied it. 'We're supposed to be starting on the flat over the garages this morning, aren't we?'

'Are you?'

'And the place is still full of furniture, isn't it? It was supposed to be cleared out, wasn't it?'

She had never in all her days heard of builders arriving as promptly as this. 'You want to start *now*?'

'Rush job. Bonus if we finish in time. How can we finish if we can't start?'

He had a point there. She said, 'It will all be taken away tonight. Couldn't you work round it for today?'

'Easier said than done, the place is full of it.' The door opened and Stephen Harmon walked in. 'Morning, sir,' the builder turned to him in plaintive accusation. 'I thought you said we'd have a clear field in there this morning.'

Stephen Harmon put down a briefcase on the desk and looked at Nell. She said defensively, 'Nobody told me they were starting work right away. I arranged for some of the things to be collected tonight for a jumble sale.'

'There's enough left for half a dozen jumble sales,' grumbled the builder, and that was an exaggeration.

'Can you get it out and dispose of it?' Harmon asked him.

'Well—' He was going to negotiate and Nell said meekly,

'I did promise it to the Scouts.'

'Very charitable,' said Harmon, 'although it might have come cheaper if I'd made a donation.'

'I'm sorry.' She bit her lip and looked appealingly at the builder. 'Could you carry it down and stack it in the yard?' It wasn't raining today, thank heaven. He shrugged.

'I suppose we could. Mind you, it's good working time going.'

As he left Nell said again, 'I'm sorry.'

'A misunderstanding,' said Harmon, and of course it had been. He sat down behind Mr. Elsgood's desk. She said,

'I have the post here. May I explain them to you, or would you rather wait for Mr. Elsgood?'

'Thank you.' He meant carry on, and she put down a small pile of papers in front of him, stood beside him and tried to put him in the picture.

There were a couple of contracts for house purchase to be signed by a couple of their clients; and papers relating to the probate of a will, an assault and battery charge, a motorist who looked like notching up his hat trick for speeding endorsements, and an amateur jazz group that was driving a next-door neighbour out of his mind.

Harmon listened with a brief nod now and then. It was inevitable that he should be comparing this with his previous practice and Nell had to admit, 'Nothing very exciting.' She added, 'But in a town as small as this you often know the people involved and that makes their problems important.'

'Any problem we handle is important.'

It was a bland cliché, but if he was going to live here the time would come when he would know some of their clients personally.

The motorist's young wife worked behind the counter of the main confectionery-cum-tobacconists in town, and she was expecting a baby. And if he lost his driving licence he

46

would lose his job. Mr. Elsgood was very concerned about that case.

Nell said, 'It's a friendly town. They're nice people.' She meant . . . You won't find it so bad settling down here. It might seem slow at first, but there are compensations. Cases are people here, you help friends.

Harmon said, 'It seems a charming town. Would you take a few notes, please?'

He had charm, even when he was cutting you off in mid-sentence, well in mid-subject. Silently Nell went back to her desk. From his briefcase he took out files he must have taken round to the Raven with him last night. With the first open before him he began to dictate.

She had always managed to take Mr. Elsgood's dictation beautifully. Mr. Elsgood took his time, he paused to consider, and even then he often had second thoughts. But Mr. Harmon sounded as though he was reading the whole thing from a prompter machine, and had been told to get through at the fastest possible rate consistent with clear enunciation. Mr. Elsgood sometimes mumbled. Mr. Harmon didn't. She could hear every separate word, but she could only get down about one in three.

If it had been a short note she might have relied on her memory, and risked filling in the gaps later, but after a few minutes it was obvious that she could do no such thing, and she had to say again, 'I'm sorry.'

'Yes?' He looked up. Full direct gaze was disconcerting even when you were prepared; she blinked automatically and begged, 'Please would you go a little slower, I can't get it down?'

He smiled. 'From where?'

'While we're about it,' she said, 'from the beginning, please. I should have spoken up before.'

He started again, without apparent impatience. The same phrases, but this time pausing to check that she was keeping pace with him, instead of concentrating completely on the papers on the desk. She was grateful. Few men would have avoided at least looking reproach, even if they didn't voice it. She did her darnedest to keep up, and towards the end they were getting along quite briskly. Certainly at more words per minute than she had ever been called on to record for Mr. Elsgood.

Mr. Elsgood arrived while she was typing, somewhat flustered because there was a pile of old furniture in the yard, and he hadn't been able to get his car into the garage. He had had to drive it to the public car park beside the bus station, and walk across the square.

'That was my fault,' said Nell. She gave him the message left for him, that Stephen Harmon had gone to the magistrates' courts with Norman Rowe. Then she explained why it was her fault that the contents of the haylofts were still around, and Mr. Elsgood said,

'Oh, dear me! I can quite understand you not expecting the builders to be starting this soon, but I do hope Mr. Harmon wasn't—'

Nell said, 'He was very nice about it,' and Mr. Elsgood looked relieved.

Over sandwiches at the snack bar at lunch time Colin said, 'Norman Rowe introduced me to your new boss over at the courts. He's out of his class here, isn't he?'

'Think so?'

'He got a character who pleaded guilty to using a motorcycle without proper tax unconditionally discharged. It was a pleasure to listen to.'

She said, 'I'm glad we got him off.'

'How's he compare with old Elsgood?'

'No complaints.'

'Good-looking bloke.'

'Yes.' Anyone with eyes could see that.

'Well, don't go overboard for him,' Colin smiled at her. 'You may have three months' security of employment on that contract, but I'll be surprised if you last longer than three weeks with your spelling.'

They hadn't signed any contracts yet, but Nell would. Colin, although joking, was slightly jealous. Mr. Elsgood had been practically a grandfather-figure.

She teased back, 'And you should see his car!'

The day had not gone badly. Before she left Nell checked that the Scoutmaster would be along without fail to collect that jumble this evening, then she cycled home for a meal and to get ready for the party tonight.

'Brought the sausages?' asked Flo as Nell stepped into the

48

kitchen, and she clapped her hands to her face,

'I *bought* them, I've left them in the office!' She had forgotten them; they were hanging in a carrier bag in the cloakroom, and Flo had wanted them for tea. She asked, 'Shall I go back?'

'Not to bother,' said Flo. 'It's not worth traipsing back again. We can have cold ham.'

Nell hurried through her meal. She admitted that Stephen Harmon had arrived, and said he seemed pleasant enough.

'Still looking for another job?' Ocky asked, and Nell said,

'I'll give it a day or two before I make up my mind.' She sounded casual, but she wasn't looking for another job. She would settle for the one she had. Getting to know Stephen Harmon better might be rewarding.

She was in the red panne velvet dress when Colin arrived, and as she ran down the stairs he whistled. 'That's a very inviting get-up.'

'Thank you, I'm glad you approve.'

Clear-skinned, clear-eyed, she preened gaily in his admiration. She was pleased with the dress, content with herself, confident she could hold her own against any competition tonight. Colin would stay close. If she chose to cast her net she could probably bring in other fish, and that might be fun, just for the evening, to add zest to the party.

Most of the guests would be familiar faces. The jokes would be 'in' jokes, the topics well worn. Anything new to talk about would be welcomed – like the new man in Nell's office.

In the Raven Hotel right now, she presumed. Perhaps having dinner, or in the bar, or studying more business papers in his room.

There would be no one there tonight as intriguing as Stephen Harmon. He was a stranger, that was enough to make him interesting in this small town, but even where he was known he would still turn heads. Folk would always watch and wait when he walked in, thought Nell.

She glanced up as the car passed the building that housed Elsgood and Elsey and said, 'Stop for a minute, will you?' There was a light in the upper storey. 'I left a pound of sausages in the cloakroom.'

'*Sausages?*' said Colin. 'I've heard of taking along a bottle, but why are we taking sausages?'

'Flo asked me to get them, and I forgot to take them home. Mrs. Robbins is still there, so I might as well get them now.'

The car had drawn up by the kerb and she jumped out. The front door opened when she pushed it, and so did the door at the top of the stairs when she turned the knob.

It was late for Mrs. Robbins, the cleaner. Late for anyone, except a man who had nowhere else to go. If Stephen Harmon should be here Nell would say, 'Why don't you come along with us?'

That off-chance was the real reason she had scrambled out of the car. The light was on in the corridor, and in the office at the end of the corridor that had been Mr. Elsgood's room and was now Mr. Harmon's.

He *was* still here. She could hear him speaking on the telephone, the door was slightly ajar. She didn't deliberately eavesdrop. She walked towards the cloakroom and towards the office, smiling a little because she felt that luck was with her.

He had a controlled and carrying voice. She could imagine him swaying a witness, and coming as a treat this morning to the local magistrates. 'A pleasure to listen to,' Colin had said.

She heard him laugh. So he did laugh. He could be amused. He said, still laughing, 'I can't afford her kind of salary here, my secretary works for peanuts. Come to think of it, that's about what she's worth.'

CHAPTER THREE

NELL came back and got into the car with a bright tight smile on her face. 'No sausages?' asked Colin.

'What? Oh, Mrs. Storey must have put them away. I left before she did. She must have seen them and stuck them in a drawer or a locker. It hardly seemed worth doing a full-scale search.'

She hadn't gone into the cloakroom. She had stood for a frozen moment in the corridor, then come out quickly and quietly, and the murmur of Stephen Harmon's voice had followed her. She could probably have heard what he thought about the lot of them if she had kept her head. *A set of country hicks.* And maybe they were, but this was their country. He was the foreigner, the outsider, and she had been about to ask him to come to the party because he was alone and they were friendly folk round here.

No wonder he was a good lawyer. He could put on an act that would fool anyone.

Beside her Colin was talking. She turned to look at him, and forced herself to listen, pushing Stephen Harmon out of her mind on a last wondering note . . . *I wonder what he did* pay his last secretary?

Colin was talking about tomorrow, when he was off for the rest of the week, going up to London for the Motor Show. He talked about cars, and Nell listened with a flattering concentration.

They hadn't far to go to the party. It was in a tree-lined avenue, and there were already a dozen or so cars parked outside. They parked theirs at the end of the queue and made for the brightly lit house with a front door open and the hall full of people.

Peter Beddows, their host, owned a small engineering works. Dora, his wife, was blonde and pretty, and flung herself at Colin and Nell as they came in. 'Ah, my favourite people!' She said that to all her guests. She was feverishly gay with determination to get the party going, and Peter handed them brimming glasses.

51

Colin knocked his back, and Nell carried hers carefully through the hall into the room where the buffet was laid and the guests were standing around.

There was a chorus of hellos. Everyone knew them. Joan and Bernard semaphored from the other end of the room, Joan with an arm wave, Bernard with raised hand as though he was conferring a blessing. 'I'm telling them all about our dishy new boss,' shrilled Joan.

'He's a dish,' Nell agreed ... She wouldn't sign a three months' contract. Let him find someone else to work for peanuts. A week's notice and good luck to you, she'd say ...

'He certainly gives the old place a bit of class,' said Joan.

'Think so?' said Nell. 'Now I'd have said Mr. Elsgood had class.' He had been kind, and sincere. 'A real gentleman,' Mr. Connel had said; and Mr. Savage, 'This new fellow's a gentleman when it suits him,' which was perceptive of Mr. Savage.

'The magistrates' courts are going to miss old Elsgood,' said Colin, 'but after seeing him this morning if I was in the dock I'd rather have your Mr. Harmon acting for me.'

'Not mine.' Nell took a plate and put a small sausage roll in the middle of it, and looked up at Colin, her eyes comically wide and her mouth wry. 'I'm thinking you're right, my spelling will see me off.' She looked round at them all. 'Anybody needing a secretary? I'm a fast worker, but I can't spell.'

That took the talk into general fooling. Nell got her offers, none of them genuine, and pretended to consider each; turning some down in mock horror, accepting a couple – one in the bank so that she could fix them all up with overdrafts, and another with Edwin Martin, of Martins Wholesale Confectionery, who promised her all the chocolates she could eat.

It was a noisy party, and Nell did her party piece all evening through. She joked and danced and flirted and gossiped, and accepted the compliments that came her way with a smile.

Ed Martin, a bachelor with a racy reputation, was making a set for her. Colin handed her over grudgingly when Edwin asked her to dance, but when it came to who was seeing her home Colin snapped, 'I am, mate,' and Nell said, 'That's right.'

Edwin's expression was reflective. In the car Colin said, 'I wouldn't put it past that so-and-so to try to date you while I'm away.'

Nor would I, thought Nell, it wouldn't be the first time. She said, 'Don't worry. He's not my type.'

'He's deep,' said Colin, 'and he fancies you. He might not risk phoning and asking outright, but he could very well turn up in the snack bar at lunch time, or bump into you in the street. Then, if you got chatting, you could say O.K. to a meal together or a film.'

'I could?' She couldn't. Not because Ed Martin was a danger man, but because he bored her.

'You're dizzy enough.' Colin was tolerant, as though it was an endearing failing. 'But you've got to watch his sort.'

'I'll remember that,' said Nell gravely.

They were in unlit roads; the moors and the pine trees had replaced the pavements and buildings. Moonlight shone on the pool before Quarry House as they drove down the drive. Colin said, 'I'll ring you every evening.'

'Yes, please. About what time?'

'I don't know, it depends. Does it matter when?'

'I shouldn't think so,' said Nell. 'I'll probably be here.'

Colin wouldn't be ringing just to check, he'd ring because he wanted to talk to her. But not knowing when to expect his call would mean that she would have to stay at home. She would have hurt him if she had pointed that out, he would be genuinely indignant to be suspected of suspicion.

He kissed her goodnight at the door, and holding her said huskily, 'I'll find you a new job if you do want one.'

'I might at that.' She turned to put her key in the lock. The hall light was on. As she pushed the door open they stood in brightness. It wasn't much after midnight, all the guests had work in the morning, so the party had been scheduled to finish at twelve. She said, 'Have fun at the Motor Show, and remember it's the cars for sale, not the models, and you phone me.'

'Every night,' Colin assured her. 'And remember what I

told you about Ed Martin.'

She stopped smiling when she closed the door, and went down the hall towards the kitchen looking thoughtful. It was possible that Colin had been about to propose, and she had deliberately dispersed the romantic shadowy atmosphere by opening the hall door because she didn't feel romantic. Another time perhaps, but not tonight. And if he had meant a job in the *Clarion* offices she wasn't too sure about that either.

She opened the kitchen door and took the brunt of Pedro. Then while he capered around she poured herself a glass of milk and gulped thirstily.

She heard the squeak of the wheelchair coming down the hall, and her father appeared in the doorway. 'Enjoyable evening?'

'It was the usual crowd.'

The table was laid for breakfast and Nell poured herself more milk out of the bottle, and took her glass to the table and sat down. She explained, 'Dora put on a decent spread, only I wasn't hungry. I've had things on my mind. Work. That contract. You know, three months is a long time.'

Her father sat watching her. 'You don't think you'll be happy there any more?'

Until she had heard Stephen Harmon on the telephone this evening she had been eager to work for him. Now she asked, 'Am I stupid?'

No one else she knew would have answered that without smiling and without flattery. Her father said simply 'No.'

'Colin thinks I am.' She tilted her head, resting her cheek on her hand. 'Not that he minds, he thinks it's amusing. But Colin believes I need to be put on my guard about Ed Martin. You know Edwin Martin?' Her father grunted assent. 'Well, he was at the party, and Colin thinks Ed could lure me into the woods. Because Ed is a wolf and where else would a wolf lure you?' She laughed a little. 'Only I know what Colin doesn't. That Ed Martin's a sheep in wolf's clothes and there are flocks of them.'

Her father said, 'About your job.' He could always cut through the banter and the unimportant things.

She sat straighter. 'My prospective employer is another who thinks I'm stupid.' She frowned at an invisible spot on

54

the table just beyond her clasped hands. 'I went back into the office tonight and I heard him on the phone. He said, "My secretary here works for peanuts, and that's about what she's worth".'

She couldn't pretend it was funny. The humiliation she had held down during the party hours burned in her cheeks.

Her father asked, 'What did you do?'

'I was in the corridor, he didn't see me, and I got out.'

'So now you're thinking of handing in your notice?'

She looked up, but he said no more. Nell was proud of her father, especially of his courage. She would not have had him ashamed of her for the world, and to start snivelling because she had been snubbed was the action of a spoiled child.

She said, 'I'd dearly love to make him eat his words,' and as the glimmer of a smile broke through her father's gravity, 'I finished my training with good speeds. If you don't get the practice you don't keep up your speeds. Working with Mr. Elsgood has never been full mental stretch, bless his heart.'

Of course she was not stupid. Sometimes she pretended to be. Like letting Colin think she couldn't see through Ed Martin, or couldn't control any contretemps in that direction. Like pretending she couldn't spell.

Her father wheeled himself to the fridge and peered in. 'If you didn't eat at the party how about a snack now?' Pedro's great black head raised, and his tail thumped as Attlesey brought out a cold chicken.

'You'll cop it,' said Nell. 'That's for tomorrow.'

'Who's the master in this house?'

She grinned. 'Grandmother, I'd say, although she'd die rather than wear the trousers.' She fetched the carving knife and fork, bread and pickles, and looked on while her father carved with a flourish.

They often ate after the others had gone to bed, but rarely on this scale. This had the air of a celebration. Nell suddenly felt extra alive and full of energy, as though she had taken up an exciting challenge. The depression that had lain heavy in her subconscious all evening faded away.

She had always done her work well enough to satisfy Mr.

Elsgood, but from tomorrow she was aiming higher. Her shorthand would improve if she practised. Any spare time around the office she'd do some research, and from tomorrow some homework so that she'd know all there was to know about their cases. She'd sign that contract, and then she'd hand in her notice at the end of the three months. 'I wouldn't go on working for you,' she'd say, 'for all the peanuts in the world.' A childish gesture, but satisfying.

She promised herself 'I'm going to be as efficient as that super-girl he left behind. He couldn't afford her kind of money here, he was saying that on the phone. But me – I was working for peanuts!' She breathed deep with clenched teeth. 'I'll show him!'

Her father handed her a plate piled with chicken and chuckled, 'If your grandmother hears you're becoming career-minded we'll have trouble.'

'Not a word,' ordered Nell. She fed Pedro a hunk of meat. 'Don't even let her suspect it or she'll sabotage me somehow.'

The wishbone was on the serving dish and she picked it up. She had a wish, Stephen Harmon pleading, 'You can't leave, I can't manage without you.' She said, 'It's a long time since we pulled a wishbone. Remember how it goes?'

She crooked her little finger around it and held it towards her father, who obligingly hooked on to the remainder. They twisted until the fragile bone cracked, leaving Nell with the stubbier portion. 'That's one wish that won't come true,' she said. 'When I was young I always won. How did you manage it?'

'I didn't. I thought you had the knack.'

The knack of dreams come true! She laughed ruefully, 'Well, if I did it seems I've lost it now.'

Next morning she got to the office early again, glad to find the yard cleared of jumble. She had had every-confidence in the combined assurances of cubmistress and scoutmaster, but it was a still relief.

Stephen Harmon had kept calm, but he had registered it against her. Now she was wise to him, she knew what he thought of her, and she would be wary of putting herself in the wrong again.

She came into the hall through the back door as Mr. Baker

came in through the front, and he stopped in astonishment half way up the stairs. 'My goodness, Miss Attlesey, is this getting to be a habit?'

'I'm coming round to your way of thinking.'

He unlocked the glass panelled door at the top of the stairs, and she followed him into the corridor. 'I don't want any cause for complaint if he starts comparing us with his previous staff.'

'Very wise,' said Mr. Baker.

He opened the first door first, on Mrs. Storey and Joan's room, then the connecting door into the room he shared with Norman Rowe. Nell stood in the connecting doorway, while he sorted mail, and asked, 'Do you know what the set-up was there? Do you know anything about him before he landed on us?'

'I – had heard the name.' Mr. Baker cleared his throat and Nell waited. 'He was a partner in a London firm.' They'd been told that. 'With a reputation for winning his cases,' said Mr. Baker, 'and for letting nothing get in his way.'

Nell took her mail. 'That shouldn't hurt the practice.' She flipped through the envelopes, deducing the contents of some. 'There are one or two here that could use a shot in the arm.'

'No doubt.' Mr. Baker's smile was wintry. He had hardly smiled at all since Mr. Elsgood broke his news. He had always been sober-minded, but until this week he had seemed content. Now he was scared, and it wasn't fair, for his work was his world and he shouldn't have to fear for it.

Nell said, 'You're the corner-stone in this practice. You know more about the law than either of them.' She had heard both Norman Rowe and Mr. Elsgood ask Mr. Baker's advice, and take it, and it had been sound advice. She said, 'If Mr. Harmon had a better man in his last office I'll be surprised.'

Mr. Baker blinked. He was unaccustomed to compliments. He had never minded being taken for granted because he had believed he was irreplaceable. Mr. Elsgood couldn't have managed without him, he knew that. Neither could Norman Rowe. But Stephen Harmon was a different matter.

He said gruffly, 'Thank you.' No one had ever said that before, about him being more knowledgeable than the qualified men. It left him a little embarrassed, and more than a little gratified.

The sausages were still hanging in the carrier bag behind the cloakroom door. Nell would take them home tonight, they should be all right, it was cool in here. She took off her coat and went into the office, and sat down at her desk and looked at the envelopes spread out before her.

She was less confident than yesterday. Hearing that phone call had made her unsure of herself in spite of her fine resolutions. She had been classed second-rate and she was not used to that. It confused her. She didn't know whether she was dignified with hurt pride, or spitting with fury. Even at this stage she was tempted to jump up and walk out.

Why stay to work for a man who was only tolerating you? That had been no flip remark she had overheard, that had been a lawyer's considered opinion. And her considered opinion of him was that he was insufferable – under that quiet manner all that male arrogance and sheer big-headedness. Maybe she was not providing the high-powered assistance he was used to, but he was not the kind of boss she had been used to either. This changeover was her loss as well as his.

She looked across at the big desk, and longed for the comforting presence of Mr. Elsgood, who would have thanked her for opening the mail and getting everything ready for him, and meant it.

She couldn't walk out. She'd told her father about the phone call and he'd know why she was quitting. So she got on with the job.

She opened the post. Then she went over the desk diary, checking today, writing in a couple of future appointments from the morning's mail. Mr. Elsgood had started work at ten o'clock. Stephen Harmon walked in a couple of minutes before nine, but Nell was ready.

He smiled, seeing her, and wished her good morning, and she gave him a cool 'Good morning' back, and thought – if you phone your friends tonight you'll be lucky if you have any more funny stories about your bird-brained secretary.

They dealt with the mail. It was a little disconcerting to find that he knew about all of it. Mr. Elsgood would have briefed him, of course. All the cases on their books didn't amount to so very much. But this morning Nell made no apology for lack of excitement. This was it. These were the kind of problems he would be handling from now on.

Someone still owed fifty pounds on a car that he couldn't pay. There were good reasons why he couldn't, but the debt was outstanding and his solicitor would have to contact the H.P. company and plead his case and suggest ways of getting round the impasse. Fifty pounds might be peanuts to Stephen Harmon, but it headed his list for this morning.

Nell listened while he phoned, and had to admit that he made a good job of it, getting the terms down to an amount that could be met. Mr. Elsgood would have got the same terms, she felt, but half a dozen letters could have winged to and fro before the final one that Harmon was dictating to her now.

The pace had certainly changed. There were three new cases and one regular on the diary, and they would have kept Mr. Elsgood fully occupied. During one at least he would have dished out coffee and sympathy, but with Stephen Harmon they got a straight statement of what the law could or could not do, and that meant that two of them came out having been told they would be wasting time and money if they carried on.

Nell felt sorry enough for the middle-aged spinster, whose stepmother had inherited the small family home because her father had never made a will, to take her into Inquiries on the way out and ask Joan to get her a cup of tea.

With Mr. Elsgood Nell would have gone back to her own office looking as distressed as she felt, and they would have agreed it was a sad case. But Harmon was already on the phone when she got back, dealing with something else.

The regular had been turning up for years. He liked going to law, it was a hobby with him. Right now he was having right-of-way trouble, and Mr. Elsgood always set aside a clear half hour for Mr. Thomas of Sunnybank Farm.

Stephen Harmon saw him in and out in ten minutes. At the end of which Harmon had all the relevant facts, and Nell couldn't resist saying as she closed the door behind the departing Mr. Thomas, 'I don't think we'll see him again.'

Harmon shrugged, 'He can please himself. It's a free country.'

I could tell you, thought Nell, folk don't like being bustled around here. You're going to work yourself out of business before you start at this rate.

But she said nothing. In any case he had a slab of dictation for her, she needed all her attention for that. She kept up this morning, because he paced it to what he had decided wss her rate. And it was. But it wouldn't be in a few days, she was starting her crash-course tonight.

At twelve-thirty he went, to lunch presumably; and Nell went along to Inquiries to ask, 'How did Mr. Thomas look?'

Mrs. Storey said, 'He marched right out.'

'I thought he would.'

'But then he came back again.'

'He *did*?'

Mrs. Storey said, 'He said Mr. Harmon wasn't a patch on Mr. Elsgood, but he seemed to know what he was talking about.'

'So far as the law goes,' Nell had to admit.

'What else does he talk about?' Joan was intrigued, and Nell grimaced,

'To me? Not a thing. Not a word.'

It was Joan's lunch hour too, she went home for it. In the corridor she turned into the cloakroom and looked surprised when Nell didn't. Nell explained, 'I've brought some sandwiches. Colin's away. And I'm catching up on work.'

Last week Joan would have considered that ridiculous. Now she asked, 'What's he like to work for?'

'All right.'

'I don't know whether I envy you or not.' Joan pursed her lips and shook her head. 'I wouldn't like to slip up on the job if I was working for him. I'll bet he could cut anybody down to size in no time at all.'

'He'd better keep that talent for the courts,' said Nell, and she laughed. But she spent her lunch hour typing out the dictation he had given her. When he came back it was waiting on his desk and he looked at it with raised eyebrows.

She said, 'My shorthand's rusty, but my typing's good. Bear with us for a few days and with luck you'll be feeling at home in no time.'

Without explaining her grievance that sounded fairly pointless and more than a little tactless. But he was reading the typewritten pages as though they were the only thing of interest around here, and she doubted if he had even heard her.

Mr. Elsgood looked in during the afternoon. He had said that he would be staying on for a week or two in an advisory capacity, and went through the motions of being consulted. Possibly Norman Rowe did consult him, but to Nell it was plain that Harmon needed no advice Mr. Elsgood could supply. He let Mr. Elsgood sit there, look at documents, make comments, offer suggestions.

Nell took notes. Harmon gave token attention, which fooled Mr. Elsgood all right. He left after a while, and smiled as he said good-bye, and Nell closed her notebook and looked across at Stephen Harmon, who said, 'Would you type that?'

She wanted to say, 'Why bother? You don't want it.' But if she was going to be the perfect secretary she had to keep her resentment to herself.

She made a tabulated copy with cross-indexing, and put it on Harmon's desk. It looked more impressive that way than Mr. Elsgood's hesitant humming and hahing. It looked quite a snappy report. He read it without comment except for 'Thank you,' slipping it into the top drawer of the desk.

Edwin Martin phoned Nell that afternoon. So much for Colin's assumption that he wouldn't try the direct approach. He got a brush-off more abrupt than it might have been. She would have kept any personal call as short as possible that came via Stephen Harmon's phone. She hissed, 'I'm busy, I can't talk now.'

'I'll ring later,' offered Edwin.

'I'll be busy later too,' said Nell, and put down the phone. Harmon had not raised his eyes from a transcript he was studying, and Nell muttered, 'Excuse me,' and hurried along to tell Mrs. Storey to put no more private calls through to her. 'Get the numbers, would you, and tell them I'll call

61

back?'

Mrs. Storey said yes, looking worried. 'I was in two minds about putting it through. Was there trouble?'

'No,' said Nell.

'Oh dear!' said Mrs. Storey, who didn't believe her.

Edwin phoned home that night. Was Nell doing anything tomorrow evening, because he had a couple of theatre tickets? She was, said Nell, sorry. How about next week, then? 'Ask Colin,' said Nell. 'We might make a foursome.'

'Serious, is it?'

'Deadly serious. In fact he warned me about you. I shouldn't be talking to you.' Edwin didn't realize she was laughing. He took all this quite seriously and was beginning to protest when she said 'Good-bye,' and hung up, and her grandmother who always materialized when the phone rang, determined not to miss a thing, asked,

'Who was that?'

Nell told her. Mrs. Attlesey smiled. She didn't mind Nell having admirers, the more the better. Colin was the pick of them she was sure, and she was glad that Nell appreciated that.

All the same, 'It wouldn't hurt Colin to know he isn't the only pebble on the beach,' she said. 'After all, you two aren't engaged yet, are you?'

'No,' said Nell, 'we're not. But don't you worry, everything's in hand. The moment there's a change I'll tell you.'

Her grandmother gave her the indulgent look she did so beautifully, gentle and humouring, so that everyone thought here was a woman with no will of her own. Almost everyone. Nell put light hands on her shoulders. 'And there's no need to tell Colin that Edwin phoned, because I shall tell him myself. And it's a joke, lovey, not a bit of competition.'

Elizabeth Attlesey's soft mouth drooped. She said, 'My dear, you know I never interfere.'

'Of *course* you don't.' Nell kissed her. 'And the next call should be from Colin.' As she made for the stairs her grandmother demanded,

'What are you doing, sitting all by yourself in your room?'

62

'Listening to records,' said Nell.

She was in fact practising her shorthand. She practised each night, with dogged determination, keeping it as secret as though she was practising black magic. In fact her grandmother might have considered that a lesser evil. Anything smacking of female emancipation, or threatening to come between Nell and swift and happy domesticity, was anathema to Elizabeth Attlesey.

Nell's father enjoyed himself, sharing the secret and the joke. He gave Nell dictation when the others had gone to bed, and noted with satisfaction the rate at which her speed improved even in a couple of days. Nell's job, until now, had been a pleasant way of earning a weekly wage, no more, but the prick to her vanity in overhearing that phone call had spurred her into reassessing her resources.

It pleased her father. They laughed about it, he and Nell, when she brought home a law book on Friday night to read up a reference Stephen Harmon had used, 'In the case of Dobson v. Jeffries . . .'

Nell smuggled the book past her grandmother and took it into the studio to her father and said, 'Hide this. She's after me. It's subversive literature.'

Colin phoned late on Friday. Nell went to answer the phone, leaving the book open on the settee, half way through discussing the case with her father. She was smiling when she came back. She said, 'Colin asked if I'd signed that contract yet.' Nell had signed today, they had all signed, and Colin had just made his little quip again about her not lasting three weeks. She said, 'He's bet me two cigars against a bottle of scent that within a month my contract will be torn up.'

'He's lost,' said her father.

'Yes,' said Nell, still smiling. She sat down again on the settee, picking up the book. 'He doesn't know I'm cheating. And then of course he does think I'm stupid.'

Colin had asked her each evening what she was doing and she had said watching television and reading. She had said nothing about work, except that Mr. Harmon was taking over good and proper, but so far there had been no major upheavals.

Colin was coming home tomorrow, seeing Nell in the

63

evening. The office was closed for the weekend, and Stephen Harmon had gone away. He had left a Lake District number with Mr. Baker.

Nell wondered what kind of house and what kind of people he was visiting. At the end of that first week the only thing she knew for sure was that he was in no hurry to integrate into the social life of the town. To her knowledge he had turned down three invitations to dinner and two suggestions that he might join the golf club.

There had been friendly advances, ranging from professional bodies to Mrs. Elsgood phoning to ask if he was comfortable at the Raven, and offering their hearth and home any time he needed them. He was unfailingly courteous, explaining that at the moment he was concentrating on settling in, and committing himself to nothing. And Friday evening he got out of town.

Colin was curious. Almost the first thing he asked on Saturday night was, 'How's the first week gone?'

'I told you, not so bad. I've only had a couple of days since I saw you.'

'So you have.' He looked at her fondly. 'It's seemed longer. I missed you.'

'Surely not,' Nell smiled, 'with all those lovely cars around?'

They had a meal at a roadhouse called The Cedars that put on dances at the weekend, and as she danced Nell wondered again what Stephen Harmon was doing tonight. If he was dining out, with what kind of girl? Or if he was with friends, sitting talking, was he telling them about the folk he was working with now? The secretary who had been told to supervise the clearing of a flat for the builders, and had held up the lot for a jumble sale. Who had let him dictate for nearly five minutes before she had said, 'Sorry, but would you mind starting again?'

Next week Nell saw Harmon in action in front of the local magistrates. She had been coming over to the courts regularly during the last three years. She knew the magistrates and the solicitors, the court officials and the policemen. She had sat in the small public gallery with her notebook, and outside in the corridor, comforting and calming clients. This building was like an extension to the office,

64

a great deal of their work took place here.

Nell had listened to Mr. Elsgood and Norman Rowe times without number, but today she watched Stephen Harmon, and by him Elsgood and Rowe were amateurs. It was like watching Richard Burton after the local drama club. She went back to the office feeling punch-drunk.

As she walked in Mr. Baker asked, 'How did Mrs. Watkins fare?' and Nell said,

'She *is* scared; and so was I before Mr. Harmon was half through with that horrible man. He made him convict himself.'

The case had been 'Harassment of tenant', and Mrs. Watkins, a widow, was their client. Until Harmon's cross-examination the landlord had sounded almost jovial. He was florid-faced, in a smart tweed suit, and he had chuckled at the suggestion that he was in any way persecuting the frail and elderly woman who was his tenant.

But under Harmon's quiet questions the geniality turned into blustering, and the smiling face darkened. He became indignant, then angry. It was gently done, stripping away the veneer of false affability, layer by layer, and revealing the man within as a bullying brute.

He realized too late how he was affecting his own case and stopped shouting to give Harmon a glare of pure fury, about the worst thing he could have done in the circumstances. After which Harmon thanked him and sat down, and the magistrates felt extremely sorry for little Mrs. Watkins.

'I must admit I had my doubts about our winning that case,' Mr. Baker admitted, and Nell felt a twinge of disloyalty herself. Mrs. Watkins was a fluttery old dear, easily confused. If Mr. Elsgood had been handling it Nell suspected her landlord might have laughed her accusations out of court.

She caught Mr. Baker's smile of satisfaction and thought – he's enjoying the reflected glory. She had enjoyed it herself. Of course she had. She had sat on the edge of her seat, holding her breath, revelling in the sheer professional skill of that cross-examination.

That month was exhilarating. Trying to keep up, or even a jump ahead. Nell had worked in this office long enough to know the routine procedure for most of the cases, and most of the cases were routine. When they weren't she took letters and instructions, and remembered for next time, concentrating with a singlemindedness that had never been needed before.

It was a marvellous moment when Harmon paused during dictation and she was waiting for him. He speeded up after that and she kept up, and although he showed no surprise he must have realized that this was spectacular progress.

She told her father that night, gloating. 'It was worth all the slog. He's been gearing his dictation to my rate ever since that first day, and I've let him until I felt I could get it down as fast as he could get it out.' She grinned, with more than a hint of malice. 'He'll have to gabble if he's going to get ahead from now on!'

She had scored today and it had been a sweet if secret triumph that she could discuss with no one but her father. She hadn't confided in anybody else.

She would have felt a fool telling any of her friends. Colin in particular would have laughed himself hoarse at the thought of Nell taking umbrage because Stephen Harmon's last secretary was more efficient, trying furiously to prove it wasn't true. Colin would have recounted that joke all over town, and never for a moment considered that Nell might make the grade.

His attitude would have differed from her father's all along the line. He would have been as astonished and disturbed as her grandmother to learn that Nell was getting more of a kick out of her working day right now than she was from her leisure hours.

Her leisure followed its usual pattern, with Colin as her steady date. But her working day had a new pattern of challenge where she needed her wits about her every minute.

Four weeks after Stephen Harmon took over from Mr. Elsgood the staff was unchanged. They did have their contracts of course, and they were all earning their salaries because contract or no contract Harmon expected value for money. There was none of the warmth they had felt for Mr. Elsgood, but in its place was a reluctant respect, bordering on awe. Even from Joan.

It was the same with the clients. They didn't like Mr.

Harmon like Mr. Elsgood, but they did feel that Harmon would handle their problems promptly, and if they had cases to be heard speak for them forcefully and to the point.

And he did. Nobody had any complaints there. But he went on avoiding invitations, pleading work, prior engagements. So far the excuse that he had hardly had time to settle in seemed valid, although even Mr. Savage, who had tried hard to establish friendly relations, had given up by the third week, and now simply exchanged greetings instead of issuing invitations.

The builders kept up a brisk rate and almost certainly qualified for their bonus. By the end of the month the flat over the garages was ready; walls, ceilings and paintwork stark and white.

Everyone in the office had kept an eye on the progress, and the rooms now looked surprisingly spacious. Bathroom and kitchen fittings had been brought up to date, that was the only reconstruction. And Stephen Harmon had told the landlord at the Raven he would be leaving after next weekend.

Nell went up as the builders were clearing away, for a final look around. She wondered what kind of furniture would be coming here, how the rooms would look then. Very modern, she thought, no nonsense at all; and she determined to get in somehow to see, because Stephen Harmon's choice of furniture and fittings must provide some insight into the man.

He had given no clues so far. There had been no conversation except on business matters with any of his staff. At the Raven he ate alone, and spent the evenings in his room. He was often away for the night, always away at weekends. At weekends he left phone numbers, but no other information. The staff, both at work and at the Raven, got no confidences from Stephen Harmon.

Nell had to be closest to him. She spent most of the hours between nine a.m. and six p.m. at his elbow. Professionally she was beginning to know his methods to the stage of anticipation. She could follow an instruction hardly visible to a third party, a gesture or a look. Professionally, most of the time, there was a growing affinity between herself and Stephen Harmon. But personally he was as much a stranger

67

as the first morning she had set eyes on him.

Looking around the empty flat she thought – just one picture would be something to start with. A painting he had chosen to live with could tell her a lot. So would bare walls, if he preferred them. She asked him, 'When are you moving into the flat?'

'Saturday week.'

'Is there anything I can do?'

'No, thank you,' he said, and that closed that avenue.

They were all curious, but not one of them dared ask, 'May we come and see?' and nobody, Nell included, would have the nerve to arrive at his door uninvited.

'Wait till he's gone away for the night,' Nell joked, 'and we'll run a ladder up to the windows.'

'Not me!' Joan was speaking for all of them. 'Not if I had an affidavit that he was a hundred miles away.'

The day before Harmon was due to move into the flat was a court day. Not the local courts this time, but one in a nearby town under whose jurisdiction the young man in peril of a third speeding endorsement had been flagged down.

They all felt involved in this case because they all knew Bryan Harris and Margaret his wife. She was the girl behind the sweets and tobacco in the shop just down the road, expecting her baby in four months' time, and he was a sales rep who needed his car for his job.

If he lost his licence it would be a bleak outlook. The magistrates would have considered that, and Mr. Elsgood would have pointed out the hardship, but he had pleaded hardship before and his clients had still been banned. Bryan Harris was speeding, only a few miles over the forty, because he had just been talking to Maggie on the phone and she had said she didn't feel so good.

He had been anxious to get home to her, and Stephen Harmon – as Mr. Baker recounted gleefully – practically had the magistrates in tears. The licence was endorsed but not suspended, and Maggie and Bryan were incoherent with gratitude. Back in the office everyone was delighted. Maggie's worried little face had been haunting them every time they went near the shop, and she had seized on each member of the firm for reassurance whenever a purchase was made.

Mr. Baker and Nell had been the only members of the staff, apart from Harmon, in court, and Mr. Baker recounted the whole proceedings from memory, giving an almost jaunty performance.

Nell would have liked to watch it through, she had seldom seen Mr. Baker so chirpy, but she had to get along to her own office. Stephen Harmon had driven them both back here, and walked on down the corridor while Nell and Mr. Baker had gone into the first office with the news of the magistrates' decision.

Harmon was reading a paper on his desk. Nell sat down at her own desk and felt it was a pity he wasn't sharing the general jubilation. When he looked up she said, 'It's made everyone's day. Everyone was worried for them.' It took him a moment to understand what she was talking about. She said, 'It *was* a special case. Most of us see Maggie every day.'

'Oh, yes.' He was with her; not in the involvement, but at least he knew that Maggie was Margaret Harris. She smiled,

'But you don't smoke and you don't eat sweets, so you won't have seen so much of Maggie.' He didn't smoke and he didn't eat sweets in the office. Outside he might smoke like a chimney and never stop chewing, but she doubted it. She was happy enough for Maggie and Bryan to allow herself a slight flippancy.

'No,' said Stephen Harmon.

There was a knock on the door and Norman Rowe came in. He said he was pleased to hear how the hearing had gone, Harmon agreed that it was a satisfactory decision. Norman Rowe smiled on, offering as his reason for intruding a case that had just landed on his desk. He handed over a page of notes, and Harmon said, 'This contract isn't binding. It was signed before he was eighteen.'

'Of course,' said Rowe, a dull flush betraying him. 'Yes, of course. I shall contact them right away pointing that out.'

'Of course,' Harmon murmured. His expression was bland, and he held a pencil loosely, watching Norman Rowe out of the room, but Nell sensed a seething impatience that would have broken the pencil in two if he had let his fingers clench.

She snapped before she could hold back the words, 'You're not the only one with problems. We all have them.'

Harmon looked at the door, not at her. 'His problem's himself.'

'Whose isn't?' Nell demanded. 'But of course he'd have seen that date if he'd stopped to look at it. He just picked up those notes because he wanted to congratulate you on saving Bryan Harris's licence and he didn't have the confidence to walk in without some other excuse.'

'Then God help our clients,' said Harmon wearily. He looked at Nell now. 'Amen!' she said. 'But in the meantime you do nothing for his ego. You could be his present problem.'

His impatience was turning to amusement. 'And what's your present problem? Don't tell me you've got a bruised ego too.'

'Not now my shorthand speed is faster than your dictation,' she said.

'Which you achieved at a surprising rate. How do you do it?'

'On average three hours' practice a night.'

'Why?'

She said lightly, 'Not to fall short of the big city standards.'

'What made you think you might?'

'Intuition. I should have been a seventh child of a seventh child.' ... Besides, I eavesdrop ... but she wasn't telling that ...

'I apologize if I gave that impression.' He smiled, 'Not that I'm complaining.'

'Neither am I.' She had no resentment left. She was glad she had overheard that phone call.

'About this problem of yours,' he said, 'would you like a legal opinion?'

'I don't—' she began.

'Over dinner?'

'So long as it's without prejudice,' she said, 'why not?'

And against all logic she had a feeling that the last few minutes had been the most momentous of her life.

CHAPTER FOUR

THE rest of the afternoon passed without anything else remarkable happening. Several phone calls, a couple of appointments, the pace the same, everything the same. Nell took notes and carried on with the office chores, and looked at Stephen Harmon from time to time and thought – I'm having dinner with you tonight. There's an odd thing. What on earth shall we talk about? Why on earth did you ask me?

The answer to why he'd asked her was easy – why not? She was attractive enough to be bearable facing one across a table, and even Stephen Harmon could be tiring of his own company. Every other Friday night he'd gone away for the weekend, but tomorrow he was moving into the flat. Nell had worked hard, why not give her a small reward, a free dinner?

Besides, this afternoon had spotlit the gulf between him and his staff, and maybe he felt it should be bridged. Nell was the one on hand. If Norman Rowe had stayed around Stephen Harmon might just as easily have asked him if he was free that evening. Or any of them. It was probably just a cursory courtesy to keep the staff happy.

As Nell left the office at six he said, 'I'll pick you up at half seven?'

'Yes.' She didn't ask if he knew where she lived, her address was on records anyway, but he would have to ask directions. Heading for the hills and following the lanes could become complicated if you hadn't been before.

If he asked any of the staff they'd want explanations from Nell on Monday morning. Joan would consider it most remiss that Nell hadn't told her, but there was really nothing to tell, and Nell went out of the office, got on her bike, and pedalled for home.

Her father had company in the workroom. Daniel Spencer, a small stringy man with a humorous face, who sold most of Attlesey's carvings in a crafts shop in a bigger town fifteen miles away. Nell had known him all her life. She was usually glad to see him, but tonight she had wanted a few minutes alone with her father, although she greeted him with enthusiasm. 'Hello, and how's my favourite tycoon?'

He was no tycoon. His shop was on the tourist-trade route, but so were a thousand others. He made a fair living and dealt more than fairly with those whose work he sold and could remember when that block of marble had been brought into this room, and John Attlesey had said, 'This will be for Ellen. Something superb for Ellen.'

But Ellen had slipped away, and if the stone ever changed shape the hands that changed it would not be John's.

Dan Spencer smiled at Nell, 'Still touting my wares. The panels are going well.'

Attlesey had been carving wall panels and Dan Spencer had made a show of them, on a white wall under black beams, where they caught the eye of those who peered through the window into his shop.

'Good,' said Nell. 'They are beautiful, aren't they?'

Dan Spencer always stayed for the evening, so he was sitting around the table too when she made her casual announcement, 'I'm going out tonight.'

'Where?' asked her grandmother.

'I'm having dinner with Mr. Harmon.'

Only her father failed to react. He went on eating. The rest stopped, including Dan Spencer. Nell knew what was coming before her grandmother asked, 'What's Colin going to say about this?'

Her father said, 'What's it got to do with Colin?' and Elizabeth Attlesey gave her sad and patient smile, which meant she could have shaken him. He knew very well what it had to do with Colin.

Having dinner alone with a man was a provocative situation that could easily be misinterpreted. It was one thing for Colin to realize that other men wanted to go out with Nell, and another for Nell to have dinner with one and never a mention of it beforehand. Her voice rose. 'How long has this been going on?' and she looked even more patient as the men broke into broad grins, Flo sighed, 'Here we go again!' and Nell said emphatically, '*Nothing* is going on. Just *forget* it.'

'What shall I tell Mrs. Greer?' Elizabeth Attlesey looked

pensively around as though there was a chance of guidance from beyond, and Dan Spencer asked,

'Who?' He had known Mrs. Attlesey a long time, and he always enjoyed seeing her in action.

'Colin's mother,' explained Nell's father. 'And why should you have to tell her anything?'

'I'm playing bridge with her tomorrow night.'

'Then concentrate on the game for a change.' His mother ignored him, and turned reproachful eyes on her granddaughter. 'She'll ask about you, she always does.'

'Tell her I'm very well,' said Nell, 'and I'll see her on Sunday.' She liked Colin's mother and got on well with her, and she was invited to Colin's home for tea on Sunday. It was a fairly regular arrangement, tea here or there, with one family or the other. Without actual committal Nell had got herself generally accepted as Colin's girl, and if that relationship should peter out she could expect a wearying time from her grandmother.

'This Mr. Harmon isn't married, is he?' said Elizabeth Attlesey thoughtfully.

'*No!*' exploded Nell. 'And don't you dare!' She could think of nothing more embarrassing than her grandmother, in the sweetest possible way, sounding out Stephen Harmon's intentions.

'What *are* you talking about?' her grandmother began, and Flo said,

'We all know what she's talking about. You can be the interfering old body.'

Elizabeth Attlesey closed her eyes for a moment, retaining her composure beautifully. 'Thank you, Florence,' she said faintly. 'I think I'll continue my meal in my room.' She swept out with dignity, and Flo said,

'Now I've got to take a tray up.'

'Let her go without,' said John Attlesey. His mother had always used physical fragility as a weapon and now, in mid-seventies, she was using age as well. There were times when those who loved her could have slain her, but instead they went on cherishing her.

Flo put the just-started plate of food on a tray, cut a slice of jam tart and slid that on to a smaller plate. 'She's got to eat her meals, I don't want her laid up.'

'She blackmails the lot of you, doesn't she?' said Dan.

'Lives by it,' said John.

'Always been quite a woman,' said Dan. 'Never changes' . . . Once, just after Ellen died, when John was lying helpless, hating life, hating his daughter, Dan Spencer had come to this house and seen Elizabeth Attlesey come out of her son's sickroom, her granddaughter in her arms. She had been weeping, but when she saw Dan she smiled. She had told him that John was a little tired, but coming along splendidly, and the baby was doing so well. She had talked brightly in her soft sweet voice, and all the time tears had covered her cheeks like a shining veil. He had gone home and told his own young wife, 'His mother will make John accept that child if it kills her. She's quite a woman' . . .

Nell took no chances. From just after seven o'clock she stayed closed to the front door so that she could open it herself when Stephen Harmon rang the bell. She intended to get out without hesitating, because she wouldn't put it past her grandmother to call after her from the top of the stairs, 'If Colin phones where shall I tell him you've gone?' But the moment Nell opened the door Pedro, who had been spread-eagled in the middle of the hall, leaped to his feet and charged.

If Stephen Harmon had been in the line of exit he could have been knocked for six. Fortunately he was standing to one side and the great black beast hurtled past him and stood facing the night, with its myriad shapes and sounds, barking furiously.

Nell apologized, 'He thinks he's protecting us, and he isn't a dog who stops to look around.' She grabbed Pedro by the collar, hauled him back to the house and pushed him in shutting the front door behind him, an effort that left her breathless.

'I've rarely been so pleased to be overlooked,' said Harmon.

'He makes a lot of noise, but it's all bluff.'

'He'd do well in our business.'

She got into the car beside him. '*All* bluff?'

'Only at the last ditch.'

'Even at the last ditch,' she said, 'I'd expect you to have something in reserve.'

74

'Would you?' His tone was dry and it had been no compliment. He knew what she meant – that she would expect him to use tactics others might balk at. She was glad he changed the subject by asking, 'If this is Quarry House, where's the quarry?'

'Under the water.' The pool glimmered palely in the moonlight as he turned the car, manoeuvring it around Dan Spencer's van, as they headed for the drive and the road. 'Some men strike oil. My grandfather was a gravel merchant who struck water.'

'That must have made things difficult.'

'The gravel was worked out. They weren't quarrying any more. I can't remember it as a gravel pit, it's always been a pool to me, but there are five little springs bubbling away down there, and a stream running under the hills that comes out in the River Trent.'

He seemed unimpressed by the picturesque details. 'It's a very isolated house. Who lives with you?'

The first personal question he had asked her. Unless you counted this afternoon – 'What's your problem?' – but that had been nonsense. She said, 'My father, my grandmother and our housekeeper.'

'I hope you don't tell everyone that your dog's harmless.'

Everyone who knew Pedro knew that, just as it was general knowledge that John Attlesey was disabled, and of course it was lonely. Darkness all around, the hills stretching for ever, the wind whistling through the pine trees.

Reaching the end of the drive Stephen Harmon slowed down to glance left and right. There was nothing coming. This was more a lane than a road, the nearest neighbours a quarter of a mile away. 'Aren't you scared?' girls would ask. Men would say, 'It's a bit off the beaten track, isn't it?' and of course you kept doors double-locked as a common-sense precaution at night, and opened them on safety chains if you happened to be in the house alone during the day. But it was Nell's home, and within it she had known only love and security.

She said blithely, 'The garden's beautiful in daylight. You should see our roses.' For some reason, which she found hard to explain, she felt a warm and comforting glow that had nothing to do with the car's heating system.

She pointed out Hangman's Oak, reputed to have stood six hundred years; and informed him that these moors were marked 'Cardinal's Chase' on old maps because they had briefly belonged to Cardinal Wolsey, before he overplayed his hand and lost the lot.

She gave a running commentary as they purred through the night. 'That path through the woods there, in about a couple of miles you come to Castle Ring, that was an ancient British encampment. Then there's a honeycombed hill, if you know the way off this lane, and Solomon Slee's cave. He was the hermit who knew when the world was going to end. Only it didn't.'

Nell had been reared on the legends of the hills. They had been her bedtime stories as a child, and this was easier than small talk; and if she was boring Stephen Harmon he didn't show it. He seemed amused and interested.

As she talked, at the back of her mind she went on wondering why she should feel so comforted because he had noticed that her home was vulnerable.

A smile curved her lips and she recognized it. This was how the clients looked. The ones who came in with stiff upper lips or quivering lower lips. In the end they often smiled like this because Stephen Harmon was in charge so it was going to be all right. He would take care of everything.

Well, she could hardly expect him to change the isolation of Quarry House, and come to that what was she expecting from this evening? A pleasant hour or two, no more. There was nothing to indicate that this might be a beginning. But the glow stayed and with it the thrill of expectation.

They ate at the Cedars. It was popular and the food was good. They took their seats at a corner table, Nell where she could see everyone and everything, Stephen Harmon with his back to the room so that he could see no one but Nell.

But he seemed content with the view. It was hard to realize this was the unapproachable character she had worked with for the past month. Off duty he had a devastating charm with no sign of patronage, and Nell put herself out because he had to be used to the best.

He didn't talk much about himself, except for the odd anecdote with a caustic humour she found hilarious. It was while she was creased with laughter that she realized the trout and almonds could have been bread and cheese and she would still be having the time of her life. She wasn't trying any more. She was completely relaxed. Her laughter stopped and he asked, 'What is it?'

'It is you, isn't it? You don't have a twin brother?'

'If I do they never told me.'

'Just a split personality?'

'No more than you. What happened to Mr. Elsgood's little ray of sunshine?'

Nell winced. 'Don't think that didn't chill my blood too.' She took a sip of wine. 'By the way, how much did you pay your last secretary?'

She didn't expect a reply. She got a raised eyebrow and an inquiring silence, and explained, 'I came back into the office while you were on the phone that first night. I heard you say you couldn't afford her here, and all I was worth was peanuts.'

If she'd hoped to shake him she was disappointed. Of course he was used to keeping a poker face. He said, 'At the time it seemed an equitable valuation.'

'At the time I didn't rate you too highly either.'

'But I was wrong.' He sounded serious. 'You're worth a higher wage than you're getting. You could well be worth a better job. You'd get both in a bigger town.'

'Are you firing me?'

'On the contrary, I'm admitting that Mr. Elsgood was right. You are an excellent secretary.'

She said, 'Thank you,' looking down, a little confused; and looking up to see Dora Beddows through the wrought-iron partition that divided the bar from the dining-room. Peter was at the bar, Dora was scanning the diners to see if she knew any of them. She spotted Nell and waved and Nell waved back. Dora came tripping between the tables. 'Hello! What—' She reached them, and saw that the man whose back had been turned to her did not have Colin's face. She couldn't have looked much more surprised if he had had no face at all. She blinked as though her vision might be at fault. 'Oh, I *am* sorry ... I thought ... I mean ...' She floundered helplessly and Nell said,

'This is Stephen Harmon. Stephen, Dora and—' she indicated Peter who was standing by the bar with two glasses in his hands, looking around for his wife – 'Peter Beddows.'

'How do you do,' said Stephen.

Dora gulped. She hadn't met him before, but she knew who he was and she was enthralled. Nell's cheeks were pink, and he looked every bit as distinguished as they'd said, but no one had said, and Dora was prepared to bet no one guessed, that Nell and her boss were on dinner-for-two terms.

She swallowed again, making a frantic effort to sound at ease. 'Hello there! Oh, Nell, I was going to ask you about coming over for a meal next week. Perhaps Thursday evening? Perhaps Mr. Harmon could manage Thursday too?'

Mr. Harmon, not Stephen, Nell noted. Dora obviously did not feel equal to instant familiarity. And Mr. Harmon said he regretted it very much but he could not manage Thursday. He was moving into a new flat over the weekend and next week would be rather disorganized.

Dora laughed. She understood. She had had removal troubles herself. When they'd moved into where they were living now it had been *chaos*. Anyhow, it was so nice to have met him and she did so hope he was going to enjoy living here and she'd give Nell a ring, should she?

'Yes, please,' said Nell. Dora hurried back to Peter, who was still holding his two glasses, and Nell asked Stephen, 'What happens when you run out of excuses?'

'There's always work. As my secretary you could put it around that I don't have much free time.'

'Don't you?'

He smiled at her, 'And when I do I prefer to choose my own company.'

The flattery was blatant, but he had chosen his company tonight, selecting Nell, and that had to disarm her. He said, 'I doubt if I'd have much to offer Mrs. Beddows' dinner party.'

'You mean,' Nell corrected bluntly, 'you don't think it would have much to offer you.' She could see Dora telling

78

Peter who was over there with Nell Attlesey, as they followed the waiter taking them to their table.

Harmon didn't bother to deny it. He asked, 'Who did she think I was?'

'Mmm?'

'Who did she expect to see having dinner with you?'

'Colin Greer. You've met him – the reporter for the *Clarion*. When I eat out it's usually with Colin.'

'I see,' said Harmon.

'Do you?' Her eyes danced. 'And who usually eats out with you?'

'Unfortunately no one in particular.'

The wine had gone to her head a little. Dora was so impressed that she was still staring with glassy eyes, and Nell felt idiotically happy. 'If there's no one in particular,' she said gaily, 'I'm sure it's your own choosing.'

It was the obvious thing to say even if it wasn't true, and with Stephen Harmon it had to be true. He'd never want for female company.

'You flatter me.' The words came on a note of laughter. He looked at Nell across the table, smiling, but he didn't see her. She couldn't have explained how she knew, the hardening of the mouth perhaps, but briefly and bitterly he saw another face.

Then he said, 'Doesn't Greer own the *Clarion*?' as though there had been no intruder at their table.

'His father does.'

'Are you marrying him?'

'Why do you ask that?'

He looked over his shoulder at Dora and Peter, well out of earshot. 'Your friend there for one thought you were inseparable, and I should say marriage is still in fashion in this town.'

'Not quite inseparable,' said Nell. 'And if we do marry it won't be for a long time.'

She didn't ask 'Why haven't you married?' Questions about Colin didn't bother her, perhaps because her feelings didn't go deep. At no time tonight had she wished Colin were here instead of Stephen Harmon, but he had just wished someone else in her place.

She moved from dangerous ground and asked, 'What

79

time are you moving into the flat tomorrow?'

'In the morning.'

'You don't really expect to take a week to settle in, do you?'

'If the place isn't in order before evening there'll be hell to pay. It's a reliable firm and there isn't much coming.'

'What about food?'

The cupboards were bare and the fridge was empty when she had looked around during the week. She said, 'I could bring the essentials along to get you over the weekend, or arrange for them to be delivered.'

'Thank you,' he said.

They passed Dora and Peter's table on their way out and Dora's smile was meaningful. She would have been disappointed to hear that Stephen Harmon was driving Nell right home, and taking no longer than a couple of minutes to say good night.

Dan Spencer's van was still standing in front of Quarry House, and Stephen's car drew up alongside it. Nell said punctiliously, 'Will you come in for a drink?'

If he accepted she hoped that her grandmother would not put in an appearance, and perhaps that apprehension showed, because he said, 'I'd better get back to the Raven. With luck I'm moving into the flat right after breakfast.'

'I hope all goes well.' As he reached across to open the door for her she said, 'I enjoyed myself tonight.'

'So did I.' He took her hand and held it for a moment, but there was no chance or hope that he was going to kiss her. The pressure of his fingers was a long way from a caress. It was light and firm and brief. 'Thank you, Nell,' he said, and she said, 'Good night, Stephen,' and got out of the car.

She paused at the open front door before she stepped inside the house. His face was a blur behind the window of the car. She waved as the car drew away, although he wouldn't be looking at her any more. He would be negotiating the bumps in the drive.

When she saw him tomorrow, and in the office on Monday, it would be Stephen and Nell now. There had been that much intimacy gained by their shared talk and laughter. He'd found her entertaining company, and he'd told her she was an excellent secretary, and that was fine because that was as much as she wanted. She wasn't competing any further.

Besides, she wouldn't have stood a chance. Stephen Harmon's private life was not here. It was the nights and the weekends he was away from Cheslyn Slade. The girls he met then would be right out of Nell's league.

But she had enjoyed herself. She had had a *very* pleasant evening. She went towards the drawing-room where the lights were still on. Her father and Dan Spencer had it to themselves. They sat before the dying fire with the remains of supper on a tea-trolley, and when Nell opened the door Dan said, 'Coast's clear. You can come in.'

'Time tomorrow for the cross-examination,' said her father.

'You two can joke,' said Nell gloomily. 'It's me she's determined to marry off.'

Dan stirred himself, seeing the time, and Nell wheeled the trolley into the kitchen, washed up to a chorus of Pedro's snores, and went to bed.

She slept soundly, and so far as she could remember next morning dreamlessly. Flo was in the kitchen when Nell came down. 'Have a good time?' asked Flo.

'Yes, I did.'

'Madam will have her breakfast in bed,' Flo announced. 'And she wants you to take it up.'

'When did she decide on this?'

'Last night. When she decided she didn't want any supper.'

'Right,' said Nell. She had plenty on her hands today to get through the housework and leave time to go round to the flat.

She gulped coffee and swallowed toast, and laid a breakfast tray for her grandmother with a small pot of tea, a boiled egg and one thin round of bread and butter cut in fingers.

Pedro came too. Mrs. Attlesey's bedroom door was a little ajar, and Pedro pushed it open and thrust his velvet black muzzle against her hand on the counterpane.

She opened her eyes, scolding fondly, 'Silly old boy! Good morning,' to Nell, who placed the breakfast tray on the bedside table and went to the window to draw the curtains.

She always slept with the pillows piled high behind her, so that she was sitting up already and needed to make no movement except to turn her head to watch Nell. Nell asked brightly, 'Sleep well?'

She got the answer she might have expected: 'Not very.'

'Oh dear!' she sympathized. 'Well, you stay where you are for a while. It's only just after nine, and it's Saturday morning.' She poured a cup of tea which her grandmother took with slightly shaking hands, and then sat on the side of the bed and watched her grandmother drink a little.

With soft silver hair framing her face Elizabeth Attlesey looked younger than her years, but this morning there were shadows under her eyes and her skin was translucently pale.

Nell said brightly, 'Dan said the panels were selling well. He wants another dozen. The rumour will be getting around soon that they're mass-produced.'

Her grandmother didn't smile, although she did say, 'That's nice.'

'So they should sell,' said Nell. 'They're beautiful.'

Her grandmother gave a small nod and sighed and put down her teacup. Nell picked up the tray from the table, and placed it on the bed. 'Eat your breakfast.'

'I'm not hungry.'

'Just the egg, then. I can't take this back. You know what Flo's like about waste. She'll make me eat it and I've had my breakfast.'

Her grandmother ate slowly, feeding Pedro with the bread and butter to which he was not particularly partial, ignoring the fact that he was depositing it under the bed as fast as she handed it to him.

As she ate she fired questions at Nell. 'What time did you get back last night?'

'Just after ten.'

'Did Mr. Harmon come in?'

'No.'

'Are you seeing him again?'

'I work with him, lovey.'

82

'Oh yes, of course.' She scooped out a little more egg and swallowed as though it was medicine. 'I want you to make a phone call for me.'

'Can't you make it yourself?' Nell asked. Elizabeth Attlesey loved the telephone, she could spend hours on it, but she said firmly.

'To Beattie Reynolds. You'll find her number on the pad. I was going there for bridge this evening, but I don't feel up to it.' Her tone implied that was Nell's fault, and Nell said,

'If you had a bad night see if you can get off to sleep again. Or shall I bring you the papers up as soon as Ocky brings them?'

'I shall try to rest.' Elizabeth Attlesey closed her eyes, and Nell took the tray back downstairs.

She went into the workroom to tell her father, 'Grandmother's staying in bed, and she wants me to phone and tell them she won't be going to that bridge party tonight. She says she didn't have a very good night, and then of course Colin's mother plays bridge too.'

He was polishing a panel, a tree, branches and roots making an intricate and fascinating pattern. 'I think that's one of my favourites,' said Nell. 'What am I going to do about Grandmother's phone call?'

'Leave it,' said her father. 'She'll have changed her mind by midday.'

'I'm not so sure,' said Nell. 'I'm seeing Stephen again this afternoon. He's moving into the flat over the garages. I'm taking some food round. Grandmother could well make something of that.'

John Attlesey dipped a forefinger covered with a cloth into the old tin containing his own special blend of beeswax polish. 'Is there anything to make of it?'

'No,' said Nell.

She had a busy morning. She was turning out the bedrooms, dusty and sticky, when the phone rang in the hall below. Nell came out of the spare room, and her grandmother came out of her room, as Flo answered. 'Nell!' Flo called up.

Nell hurried downstairs. Behind her her grandmother demanded, 'Who is it?'

'It's for *Nell*,' said Flo with emphasis. She exchanged a grimace with Nell, then went upstairs to Mrs. Attlesey. 'Feeling better, are you? Shall I get you a cup of coffee, then?'

'Hello?' said Nell quietly into the receiver.

'Hello,' said Colin. 'I hear you were out on the tiles last night.'

'News travels,' said Nell. 'If a meal at The Cedars is out on the tiles.'

'What I don't understand is why he should ask you out. I didn't know you were that chummy.'

She was not going to be dragooned into feeling guilty, because there was no reason why she shouldn't have had a meal with Stephen Harmon, or with anyone else. She tried to keep it light. 'I didn't ask him why he asked me, and we're not that chummy.'

'Oh, you don't have to explain to me, you're a free agent.' Colin was making a rotten job of sounding off-hand, she could practically hear him finger-drumming on the desk, and see his face, flushed and furious.

She didn't want anybody attaching too much significance to her date with Stephen Harmon. The relationship was still secretary and boss, professional and platonic. Colin had no cause for jealousy, but neither had he exclusive rights, and if Nell started reassuring him it would be tantamount to admitting that he had.

She was very fond of Colin, but they had not, to her thinking, reached an understanding where either should say to the other, 'You belong to me.'

Colin said, 'Well, if you want to get in touch you know the number,' and there was a loud click as he banged down the receiver.

Nell breathed a silent prayer for patience. She was not going to be blackmailed by him as well as her grandmother. She went back upstairs, meeting Flo on the landing. 'Colin!' she said, tone and expression conveying the message.

'I know,' Flo commiserated. She jerked her head towards Mrs. Attlesey's bedroom door. 'She's getting up. I wouldn't tell her who was on the phone and she reckons she'll have a better chance of getting there first next time if she's downstairs.'

It was a family joke and Nell smiled, admitting rue-fully, 'I don't think there'll be another call from Colin today.'

'Like that?' Seeing exasperation rather than distress Flo smiled too. 'And this isn't going to buy the baby a new frock. Back to the baking.'

While Flo finished her baking, and Nell zoomed around with a vacuum cleaner, Elizabeth Attlesey took herself into the workroom to talk to her son, getting to the point as she walked through the door. 'Nell didn't bring him in last night, did she?'

'What?' John looked up reluctantly from his work.

'The man she went out to dinner with.'

'What about him?'

'That is what I should like to know,' said Elizabeth Attle-sey. 'Nobody seems to know much about him, but from what I have heard—' she had shut the door behind her, and now she came close to her son and almost whispered in his car, 'he's the kind of man who might well turn a young girl's head.'

'Is that the general verdict?' John's eyes gleamed with laughter. 'It's lucky Nell's level-headed.'

'Nell could well be laying up heartache. He isn't married – I suppose that's something to be thankful for. At least, we think he isn't married.' That suspicion had come to her in the night. 'But as Nell's father you should have made it your business to meet the man she's working for before she began spending her evenings with him.'

'One evening,' John pointed out. 'And home at a reason-able hour.'

'So far,' said his mother darkly. 'But suppose Nell becomes infatuated with him. He's a man whose standards of conduct might be very different from ours. In Colin she has a nice steady young man. We know his family, we know how fond he is of Nell. Everything was going very smoothly there until Mr. Elsgood had to retire and this Harmon man comes along.' She sighed, as though Mr. Elsgood had much to answer for, then laid her hand on her son's arm with a comforting little pat, and a cajoling smile.

'But Nell will listen to you. It's no good me talking to her, but from you she'd take it if you suggested she should leave work.'

'*No*!' His refusal was flat.

'Seeing him every day,' his mother went on. 'From all accounts he's an impressive man, and Nell is a pretty girl. And that to my old-fashioned mind represents a perilous situation.'

John Attlesey sat heavily in his wheelchair. 'It might be a perilous situation if Nell drifted into a marriage simply because everything was going smoothly.'

'Nell,' said her grandmother, 'needs protection.'

Through the wide window he could see the heather hills, and dark clouds lying low. Once he had walked miles across those moors almost daily, finding inspiration in them for his work. They had their dangers, not least the peril of hidden crevices and gorges, subsidence of worked-out coalmines, where you could drop a stone and never hear it land.

But the hills had not crippled him. He would never walk easily again because of a virus, a million-to-one chance that could have struck in a city street, anywhere at any time. You couldn't avoid danger. While you breathed you were at risk.

His mother said, 'I only want the best for Nell.'

'You want what you think is best for Nell.'

'Someone to look after her when we've gone. Nell is delicate.'

He gave a roar of laughter. 'Nell has never had a day's illness in her life. She's tough as a pit pony.'

She looked at him almost fiercely. 'I can see you're going to do nothing about this.'

'No more are you,' he growled at her. 'Nell isn't a child. She's a woman. She's pretty, I grant you, but she's also bright in the head. A bit too bright for Colin, to my way of thinking, although I could be prejudiced there. She chooses her own friends, and I'd trust her judgment a little further than my own.' He met his mother's concerned eyes and his own face softened. 'Don't worry,' he said gently. 'She's got years ahead for finding a husband.'

'You may not worry.' She made that an accusation. 'But we're all the family Nell has, and I don't want her to be left lonely.'

John Attlesey said nothing for a while. After his mother had gone he sat, with his hands still and his eyes dark. Then he said huskily, 'Neither do I. My God, neither do I.'

CHAPTER FIVE

SHOPPING for Stephen Harmon's store cupboard had its perplexities. Nell hadn't asked if he intended cooking for himself or if he wanted a full complement of convenience foods, all packets and tins. She went first to the butcher's, then took a list into the grocer's and came out with a full basket and a bulging carrier bag.

In the yard behind the office there were a few cars but no sign of a furniture van. Either the removal men had completed their task or they hadn't arrived yet, and as it was nearly three o'clock Nell hoped hard that they had proved fast workers.

She put down the two bags to knock on the door at the top of the stairs, and when Stephen Harmon opened the door she stared first at him, and then beyond him at the room.

He wasn't that astonishing. It was just that it was the first time she had seen him less than immaculate, in anything but dark superbly tailored conventional suits, and white silk shirts. Now he wore slacks, a red thick-knit sweater and a loosely tied cravat. His hair was ruffled, and he looked comfortably untidy.

'Come in,' he said. He picked up the shopping bags, and she went in, speechless for the moment. She had been so wrong about this room. The furniture was not modern. It was functional, yes, but first and foremost it was beautiful. The mahogany knee-hole desk and armchair were Chippendale, the six chairs around the dining table were Hepplewhite.

Nell knew a little about antique furniture, they had a few good pieces at home, but the contents of this one room could have bought the entire contents of Quarry House from attic to cellars.

And these were no reproductions, there were genuine, and she couldn't pretend she wasn't impressed. She went across to a walnut Queen Anne bureau bookcase, and goggled at it. 'Are these family heirlooms?'

'No,' he said. 'I picked them up as I went along.'

'You make them sound like bargains from junk shops.' Not in this condition they weren't. These pieces had all had loving owners, they carried no sign of first aid work.

'I wish I could claim they were,' said Harmon, 'but I never had much time to spare for bargain-hunting. I find it cheaper in the long run to pay for what you want.'

'If you can afford what you want.' Nell was still looking at the bookcase. There was an open box of books on the floor beside it. Harmon had probably been putting books on to the shelves when she rang the doorbell.

He said quietly, 'There is always that condition,' and she regretted speaking without thinking. He wouldn't buy many bureaux like this on the fees he'd command around here.

She said, before she turned to face him, 'Have you eaten? Can I put away the groceries?'

'I was making coffee.' She could hear the percolator burping, now he mentioned it. 'And I brought some sandwiches along from The Raven. What have we got?'

He carried the bags into the kitchen and put them on the table. Nell took off her coat, opened the fridge door and one of the cupboards, and placed perishables in the fridge, and the rest in the cupboards as he handed them to her. She set aside the grilling steaks and a couple of frozen vegetable packs and asked, 'Can you cook?'

'Enough to get by.'

'Shall I cook these while you get on with whatever you were doing?'

'Thank you.'

The little red light clicked on in the percolator, and she poured coffee, milk for her, black for him. She did this each morning they were in the office. She'd last done it on Thursday when she certainly hadn't visualized this background for their next session.

He took his coffee with him back into the living-room, and went on putting books into the bureau. The door was open between the rooms, but Nell went quietly about her task. Everything around him right now must be reminding him of other times. To chatter would be intolerable.

Besides, she hadn't exactly been invited in. She'd offered services that were accepted, but to presume beyond would be asking to be shown the door. She hadn't been asked to stay for a meal either, but she had done the shopping and the cooking, why shouldn't she cook a steak for herself?

When they were ready she went into the living-room. The bureau shelves were filled, and Harmon was standing at the desk with an open book in his hand. He turned a page and gave it another ten seconds' attention, then looked at Nell and smiled. She asked, 'Where will you eat?'

'Over there.' At the table placed against the window overlooking the yard below. She touched the gleaming top. Her father would love the grain of this, the deep mahogany red. Harmon said, 'The plates and the cutlery are in the kitchen.'

She found them, and laid the table for two, coming in with condiments as he was looking at a small picture. An icon. The dull gold of it glinted in his hands, and as Nell looked across he held it so that she could see the strange stiff charm of the painted figure. A saint. Golden halo on hair like flame. Amber eyes in a face the colour of old ivory.

'Who is it?' she asked.

'St. Cecilia. Patron saint of music.' She was holding a lute.

'Are you fond of music?'

'Some music, but that wasn't why I bought the icon.'

'It's gorgeous.' The jewelled colours were rich as a stained glass window. She asked, 'Where are you going to put it?'

'That needs thinking about.' He placed it on the desk and she said,

'The meal's ready.'

The phone rang on the desk as they ate and Stephen got up to answer it. He said, 'Yes, I'm settled in. Everything's in order – they made a good job of the removal.'

Nell cut her steak carefully, wondering who was on the line, man or woman, friend of course, and if woman how good a friend. 'Yes,' said Harmon. 'Yes. Look, you'd better ring me later.'

He put down the phone and Nell put down her knife and fork. She was evidently in the way. He couldn't talk in front of her. She said, 'I'm sorry. Shall I—'

He smiled, 'If it had been a personal call I'm quite capable of asking you to go out of the room. It was an ex-business colleague. He sent some papers round, I haven't had a chance to look at them yet.'

'If it's work do you want any notes taken, or any typing done?'

'Overtime?'

'Something like that.' She smiled back. She would enjoy staying here for a while, even if it was work, sitting in this beautiful room, Stephen Harmon at the desk over there.

He said, 'As it happens I do work some evenings and I could use a secretary. This can be done on the phone, it's only an opinion he wants, but some time I may hold you to your offer.'

The overtime was not for the Cheslyn Slade firm, Stephen Harmon must still be keeping in with old interests.

'Well?' he asked. She was biting her lip. 'What's the problem?'

'No problem at all,' she said.

'You are also an excellent cook.'

'Grilling steak and frozen vegetables cook fairly easily, but yes, I'm a good cook.'

They finished the meal, and sat for a while with the coffee, talking about antique furniture, and the objects that had been in this room when it was a dump over the stables – and how much they'd fetched at the Scouts' jumble sale. Then they got on to a case coming up next week, and Nell was telling him what she knew about Mrs. O'Docherty who was suing Patrick her husband for assault and maintenance, and was twice his size and according to the neighbours battered him a sight more than he battered her.

'Crippen was a little man,' said Harmon. 'The neighbours all thought he wouldn't hurt a fly.'

'Yes,' Nell conceded. 'But I don't think we can bank on the magistrates remembering Crippen.'

At the knock on the door she experienced an abrupt deflation of spirits. Whoever it was they had broken up this twosome. Even if he dealt with them in seconds he wasn't going to come back and sit down again and carry on wasting his time.

Nell grimaced at the door, unseen by Stephen who was going to answer it, then she got up and began to clear the table.

'Is Miss Attlesey here?' she heard Colin ask, and nearly dropped the plate.

'Come in,' said Harmon.

Colin took three paces into the room, then stopped and looked around. 'You've made it very comfortable in here.'

'I've tried,' said Harmon.

'Good stuff,' said Colin. He made it sound like 'Good show!' He looked from the table to Nell, who had obviously been eating there. 'I've come to give you a lift home.'

'My father was going to pick me up.' At half past five in front of the office, unless she phoned through and changed the arrangement.

'I know,' said Colin breezily. 'I thought we might save him a trip.'

John Attlesey's car was manually automatic and specially designed, but it was still more trouble for him to get into the car and drive down here than it would have been for most men. Colin was grinning fixedly at her, and although she wanted to say 'No!' she did not want any sort of scene.

She caught a wry smile on Harmon's face, and knew he was aware of the glower behind the grin. He said gravely, 'Thank you very much indeed for your help.'

'It was nothing,' she said.

'It would have been if I'd overlooked it. I could have been back at The Raven tomorrow.'

She said tartly, 'But you wouldn't have overlooked it. You'd have phoned the store and they'd have brought everything round to you. So in actual fact I have done very little.'

She was irritated that he should be amused by Colin turning up here to whisk her away. She was irritated with Colin too, who was saying, 'Have you got a coat?' like a fussy nanny taking a child from a party before she becomes overexcited and starts to show off.

'I'll get it,' she said.

She put it on in the kitchen where she had left it. That took hardly any time at all, and she came back to see Colin walking towards the icon, enthusing, 'Isn't that a beauty? Is it a reproduction? How old is it?'

'Byzantine,' said Harmon. 'Don't touch it. The surface is fragile.' Colin stopped in his tracks. 'Nell, how much do I owe you?'

She said, 'The bills are in there. It can wait till Monday.'

Stephen Harmon might be dressed casually, but he could be wearing a boiler suit and he would still have the autocratic touch.

He saw them to the door, thanked Nell once more and said he would see her on Monday, and agreed with Colin that the Mercedes down there was his car, and that they gave a first-class performance. Then he wished them both good night, and closed the door.

There was a light outside that showed them down the steps, and Colin went on talking about the car. He went to it in the garage as if he was about to pat it, when Nell demanded, 'Who told you I was here?'

'Your grandmother. I phoned you and she told me.'

Ocky must have let it out. Nell had been making a shopping list in the kitchen, and told both him and Flo why. Her grandmother had been sewing her altar cloth in the little parlour at the time, and then Nell had walked down here.

Nell said with feeling, 'It wouldn't surprise me if she had a crystal ball. And wasn't it left this morning that I should ring you if I wanted to get in touch?'

'Yes,' said Colin. 'Only I've been thinking about this morning, and perhaps I was a bit hasty.' He gave Stephen Harmon's car a last longing look and walked on towards his own car, parked outside in the roadway. 'But I felt such a fool.' He was apologizing, but he still had his grievances. 'Peter Beddows telling me they'd seen you at The Cedars with your new boss. Telling me I'd got big competition there.'

'I hope you told him to mind his own business,' said Nell.

'I didn't know what to tell him. And why should you be helping to fix up the flat?'

'I offered to get the food in.'

'*Why?*'

Because she wanted to see. They all wanted to see. On Monday morning the whole staff would be wanting a detailed description of Stephen Harmon's home. They'd also want to know about Friday evening at The Cedars. Nell stood beside the car as Colin unlocked it, stiff with reluctance to discuss anything about Stephen Harmon with any of them.

She said, 'Look, Colin, as you pointed out this morning I don't have to account to you for my actions. If we're staying friends we'd better get that clearly understood.'

He straightened and turned, and she faced him. 'Here and now,' she said.

He had never seen Nell so determined. She was issuing a straight ultimatum and Colin, who had just seen the flat and the car and the man, had sense enough to know the dice were loaded.

He said wearily, 'Anything you say.' He could have told her that men like Stephen Harmon do not fall in love with, much less marry, girls like Nell Attlesey. If she got involved with him the giving would be all on Nell's side.

This was no time for warning. The warning would have to wait until she was less on her dignity and less ready to take offence. Right now all right they'd let the subject drop. 'O.K.,' he said, as she settled in the passenger seat and he put the car into gear, 'you're a free agent, I'm a free agent. Are you free for the pictures tonight?'

The film was messy. There was a great deal of highly coloured killing, and the acting was so bad it was almost funny. They had supper at a fish and chip shop, and said good night on the doorstep of Quarry House.

Holding Nell, Colin found it hard not to tighten his grip. For the first time their relationship was being threatened. Until now it had been almost without obstacles. They had known each other all their lives, gone to each other's birthday parties as children, dated occasionally for years, and exclusively for the last seven months.

Colin was very fond of Nell. Stephen Harmon was not going to take her away, Stephen Harmon wasn't even going to try, but Nell could be fooling herself. Nell was not a logical thinker. More like an enchanting idiot, thought Colin, jaundiced with jealousy, looking down into the clear young face. He kissed her, and asked against his better judgment, 'Did Stephen Harmon kiss you good night?'

Her face flamed, and he said quickly, 'All right, I know, we don't talk about him.'

94

'Good night,' said Nell.

'Tomorrow? You're coming to tea? My mother is expecting you.'

'Oh yes, of course.' Mrs. Greer was proud of her tea table, she was a compulsive trifle maker, and would be mortally offended if Nell failed to turn up without very good reason.

Inside the house Nell thought – he didn't kiss me good night. Stephen Harmon isn't the man to hand out kisses like handshakes, and I wasn't the girl he would have chosen, the one he saw for a moment, sitting in my chair, holding my wineglass . . .

Colin's mother had put on her usual spread. She imagined that because Nell was small she was undernourished, and always watched approvingly as she ate.

Nell, in his mother's opinion, was the nicest girl he had gone around with. She usually brought Mrs. Greer a small box of chocolates or a small bunch of flowers, and always said thank you before she left, and Colin's mother thought he could do worse.

He nearly had, more than once, but Nell was a born homemaker. There was no hurry at all, but when Colin did decide to get married Mrs. Greer would welcome Nell as her daughter.

Over the meal Mrs. Greer gossiped away, and Mr. Greer made occasional jokes. Nell sat where she always sat. She knew this house as well as her own by now. She could lay hands on any piece of kitchen equipment, and she knew best china from everyday. She could have moved in and run this home without any confusion.

Mrs. Greer said, 'It's a bit early to start thinking about summer holidays, but Father and I were wondering if you'd like to come to Benidorm with us next June.' They had friends with a villa, and always spent some of their summer holidays there. Colin went along too. Last summer Nell's holiday had already been fixed before she and Colin started dating solidly.

She hadn't thought ahead as far as next summer, but Mrs. Greer had. Nell said, 'That's kind of you.'

'I can't see Colin leaving you behind,' Mrs. Greer smiled, and Mr. Greer guffawed,

'I can't see Nell letting Colin go without her. All those girls sunbathing.'

'*Father*!' said Mrs. Greer, sounding shocked.

'June!' said Mr. Greer. 'That's the month for brides. We always get so many wedding pictures in June we can hardly get anything else in the paper. Why don't you two make it a honeymoon?'

He was teasing Nell, as he always did, and she always played up to him, but today she thought – they *are* kind, I do like them, but they like me because they think I'm the girl Colin is going to marry. To them I'm not 'Nell Attlesey', I'm 'Colin's Nell.'

Colin said, 'Yes, well, let's see how it goes, shall we, before we start fixing dates? There's plenty of time.' He could have meant the date for the holiday or the date for the wedding, but in either case it was left at that.

As Nell said good night and thank you to Mrs. Greer she decided she must not come here so regularly. She must stop letting so much get taken for granted. She needed breathing space. Anything else would be unfair to Colin as well as herself.

In the car he asked, 'What evening are you free?' the sarcasm very slightly veiled, and Nell ended up with one date for the following week instead of the usual average of three, and no mention of seeing her at lunchtime tomorrow.

Colin had decided to play it cool; his self-esteem was ruffled. He'd take someone else out, and let that get around, and see how Nell liked it.

Next morning before she left for work Nell went into the workroom. The carved panel of the tree was finished, and John Attlesey was sketching the idea for his next, a swordfish. Nell asked, 'Is the tree promised to Dan?'

'Another twelve panels are, but none specifically. Why?'

'I'd like to show it to Stephen.'

'Is he interested in carving?'

'I think he'd like it.'

John Attlesey shrugged his broad shoulders. Nell had told him last night what was in the flat. He said, 'A man who puts an early Roman Empire icon on his walls has sophisticated tastes. This could strike him as pretty crude.'

She said indignantly, 'It is not! It's wonderful carving.'

'Of course,' said her father, smiling. 'I'm just reminding you that we're all entitled to our opinions. If Stephen Harmon doesn't like it don't take it personally eh?'

Nell grinned, 'That will be his misfortune. Why should it cast me down? I don't suppose he's got a genius in the family.'

'There aren't many of us about,' said John Attlesey.

She parcelled up the panel and balanced it across the carrier at the back of her bike, reaching the office safely, and getting upstairs and into her room before anyone else, except Mr. Baker, had arrived.

Joan came early too this morning, making a rare exception because she had heard about Nell's Friday evening and wanted to know what was happening.

She knocked before entering, and had some papers in her hand, excuse in case Stephen Harmon was there. When she found he wasn't she gabbled out her questions, 'Hey, is it true? Were you having dinner with Mr. Harmon? When did he ask you?'

'Friday afternoon.'

'And you never said a *word*!' Joan looked as though she was trying to pierce a veil and see the real Nell. The Nell she knew wouldn't have been dated by Stephen Harmon. Joan couldn't even imagine it happening. But in the past four weeks Nell had worked like a beaver, and they had seen little of her in the outer office. She had been with Mr. Harmon almost all the time, and this was surely the surprise of the century, something going between Nell and Mr. Harmon.

Her train of thoughts was obvious and Nell said desperately, 'We only had a meal together. It was like a celebration. It had been a good day, Bryan Harris keeping his licence.'

'A good evening too, I should think,' said Joan.

The door opened and Harmon walked in and Joan flushed as vividly guilty as though she had had the petty cash in her hands. She couldn't even say hello. She shot out, almost tripping in the doorway, and Stephen Harmon watched her go.

He knew they had been discussing him. Nell said, 'It's a small town. Not much happens round here. And we were eating out on Friday evening, and that's something to talk about.'

'Do you mind being talked about?'

'No. Do you?'

'Not in the least, unless it keeps Miss Frisk's mind off her work. She lacks the mental capacity to cope with more than one thing at once.'

She had to protest, 'Joan is a very smart girl.'

'You've got to be referring to her clothes, not her I.Q.'

'You'd find it hard to replace her. She knows the work.'

'Who's talking about replacing her?'

'You don't sound very satisfied with her.'

'So long as Norman Rowe is. She is, thank God, his secretary, not mine.' He added drily, 'It would be criminal to disturb them. They make a unique partnership.'

She had only opened the first letter of the mail. He picked up the rest and she said, 'It could be an occupational hazard of being a lawyer.'

'What could?'

'Not really liking people.'

He considered, or pretended to. 'You know,' he said, 'you're dead right.'

She had to smile too, and let the charm wash over her. 'Have we got a minute before we get down to work? I'd like to show you something.' The panel was beside her desk, and she ripped off the brown paper. 'What do you think of this?'

He took it from her and carried it to the window. The polish was mellow, hour after hour of hand-rubbing had brought out the grain and the colour, and the carving was clean and beautiful.

He said at last, 'I like it very much.'

She had known he would, although she did not realize until she relaxed how tensely she had waited the verdict. She said, 'My father carved it. That's what he does for a living – wood carvings.'

'Will he sell it?'

'You could ask him.' She had been going to say, 'It's a present for the flat,' but the words stuck and she knew she would make an awkward job of the giving.

'Will you get him for me?' On the phone. She dialled and it was engaged. She sat it down, and said, 'I'll try again in a few minutes.'

Stephen was still looking at the panel. 'I'd like to meet him. Will he be home this evening?'

'Yes,' she said. 'You don't need to phone for that. When will you come, and I'll tell him when I get home.'

She told her father when she got home, 'He likes the panel. He wants to meet you. You don't mind, do you? He wants to ask the price, for one thing.'

John Attlesey chuckled. 'I always wanted to meet a man who can afford to eat his dinner off a Hepplewhite table. We might make a killing.'

'I doubt it,' said Nell gaily. 'I think he'll know the market value.'

'You shouldn't have told him it was new. We could have drilled a few wormholes in it and said it came from an old manor house.'

'He's a trifle too hot on the cross-examination for that. I wouldn't care to spin him a yarn.'

'Just our luck! The first patron of the arts we get our hands on is a sharp-eyed lawyer.'

They laughed at each other. Nell said, 'I knew he'd like it.' Her laughter died away, but her eyes were shining, and her father's eyes narrowed, watching her. He said, 'I didn't realize you were hocking it. I thought you were giving it to the man.'

He often gave away carvings that Dan Spencer could have sold for good money, because money was not John Attlesey's criterion of success. He was an artist, labouring to create beauty and meaning, not to amass a fat bank balance.

Nell said, 'I suppose I was, only I'd told him you were a wood-carver and he asked was it for sale and –' she gestured vaguely, 'it suddenly seemed like an apple for the teacher, a present for sir. I suddenly felt he'd prefer to pay.'

'Then we'll oblige him,' said her father.

'And please try to keep Grandmother away.'

'I suppose as a last resort,' said John Attlesey, 'we can always lock her in the cellar.'

Elizabeth Attlesey was not sure whether all was well or not. Nell had had tea at Colin's yesterday, come home after her grandmother had gone to bed and gone out before she got up. She restrained herself when Nell came back from work today and, after a smile for everybody in the kitchen, rushed off in the direction of the workroom. That was customary. Her grandmother didn't follow, or call after, although she was burning to know if Nell had had lunch with Colin, and if she was going out with him this evening.

When Nell came back she would ask her. There was no sense in worrying. It only made you feel old and ill. Elizabeth Attlesey's heart had a freak flutter. She had been examined by specialists as a young woman when it was first discovered and told she did not have a weak heart. The occasional mis-beat need cause no concern.

But lately, when she let herself get upset, the fluttering seemed worse. She hadn't mentioned it, although on Friday night it had frightened her, and she had resolved to go quietly about the things that had to be done. If only Nell was settled, at least wearing an engagement ring, then Elizabeth Attlesey felt she could relax happily, and probably last for years.

'No, lovey,' said Nell. She hadn't had lunch with Colin, it had been a busy day, and she wasn't going out tonight.

'I'm expecting a visitor,' said John. 'A business call.'

'Anyone I know?' asked his mother.

'No,' she was told.

Flo said, 'Telly for me, and my feet up,' and Elizabeth Attlesey decided it was television for her too, sitting under the standard lamp in the drawing-room so that she could carry on with her embroidery.

Nell sat with them until the doorbell rang, when she said, 'I'll get it.'

Pedro was in the workroom tonight with the door shut, so there was no immediate trouble from him. Nell said, 'Hello, do come in,' and led the way through the hall as quickly as she could without breaking into a trot.

Harmon followed with long strides, and she held her breath until they had passed the drawing-room door. It was impossible to explain, 'Someone in there will ask you if you're sure you haven't a wife hidden away, if she gets the chance.'

Maybe he'd put her speed down to the fact that the heating wasn't too good in the hall, and she was hospitably hurrying him to where a fire was burning.

She opened the workroom door and John Attlesey said, 'Mr. Harmon?' He sat at his desk, with one hand on Pedro, his touch reassuring the dog that this was a friend and not the Enemy. Pedro growled deep in the stomach, but swished his tail at the same time, and as Nell came in a little ahead of Stephen Harmon the growling died away.

'Good evening,' said Harmon. He came across and the two men shook hands. If they came as any surprise to each other neither showed it. John Attlesey had been prepared, Nell's talk had given him an accurate portrait, but the burly bearded man in the wheelchair might not have been Harmon's preconceived notion of Nell's father. If he had a preconceived notion, if he had given it any thought.

'Sit down,' said John Attlesey.

The desk was big and battered. It was where he worked out his designs, and now it was littered with sketches of swordfish, drawn on white paper with a thick-leaded carpenter's pencil. There were a couple of chairs in the workroom, apart from John Attlesey's wheelchair, wooden and straight-backed. Harmon took one, Nell the other. Harmon said, 'I want the panel. How much are you asking?'

Attlesey told him. He wrote out the cheque and handed it over, and Attlesey said, 'My daughter tells me you collect icons.'

'Only one. That hardly qualifies me as a collector.' He looked at the block of marble at the other end of the workroom. 'Do you work in stone too?'

'I did, once,' said John Attlesey. There were no curtains in this room. The big windows had old-fashioned roll-blinds, fitted when it was a drawing-room forty years ago. They were never pulled down, and now the night was a black background to the block of white marble. 'Wood is my material now,' said John Attlesey.

There wasn't much of his work around, as Dan had come to collect on Friday, but there were a few pieces in varying stages. Some abstracts; some recognizable shapes: the cowled figure of a woman with the grain of the wood making a straight pale line on eye level which somehow suggested a careworn face; a bull with massive head lowered, ruggedly hewn. The bull was no larger than a small log for burning, but the effect was both massive and menacing.

John Attlesey pointed out the equipment he used, the tools of his craft, and Harmon picked up the cowled figure, noticing how the grain gave folds to the drapery, and asked, 'Is your work mostly commissioned? Do you know what you'll make of each piece before you start on it?'

'No, he doesn't,' Nell answered, enthusiasm firing her. 'You have to be emotionally, not commercially, involved to carve something like that. The old pagan idea of trees having spirits had some truth in it, because wood *is* a living thing. He spent hours turning that' – the bull – 'over and over, glaring at it, but it's right, isn't it? That was what it was meant to be.'

John Attlesey grinned, 'Ah, there's a grand mystique about it. We always observe the ritual.'

'Don't we all?' said Harmon.

Attlesey nodded, 'Yes, you and I have something in common in our trades. I strip down the wood and you strip down the perjurers. Both of us seeking the heart of the matter.'

'But when I reach it,' said Harmon drily, 'it's rarely a thing of beauty.'

'Human nature,' growled Attlesey, 'rarely is. Give me a hunk of wood any time. Have a drink?'

Stephen Harmon stayed for about an hour. Most of the talk was about local geography, places a newcomer should be seeing around here, some of them on the moors. John Attlesey spoke as though he still visited all of them often, instead of going only when a car could get near, or a wheel-chair, and the going at the end was not too rough for a man who needed two walking sticks.

The two men could not have looked or sounded more unlike, but they seemed to enjoy each other's company, and when Harmon said he must leave Nell went with him to the front door.

As they walked down the hall Harmon said, 'He has a powerful talent.'

'I think so,' said Nell.

'Is he satisfied working here, in these primitive conditions?'

'A woodcarver's tools are fairly primitive. What do you think he should have, a desk like yours and an icon on the wall?'

'I feel he should have reached a wider market.'

'He's happy enough with the market he's got.'

The drawing-room door was open, and Mrs. Attlesey sat with the golden light from the lamp falling around her, and her embroidery in her hands. She called as they passed, 'Nell!'

'In a moment,' Nell called back, and went on, saying good night to Stephen, who showed no desire to linger, and closing the door as he went out to his car.

But when she turned back her grandmother had come out of the drawing-room. 'Who was that, dear?'

'Mr. Harmon. He wanted to buy one of Father's panels.'

'Did he? He's very handsome.'

John Attlesey came along in his wheelchair. He said, 'It was only a carving he wanted. I offered him Nell, but he said he'd prefer a carving.'

His mother said severely, 'Don't be facetious, John,' and swept back into the drawing-room, and Nell scolded,

'Stop teasing her.' She was interested to know, 'What did you think of him?'

'The last man I'd have expected to find taking over a practice like Elsgood and Elsey.'

'I told you, health reasons, Mr. Elsgood said.'

John Attlesey's grizzled brows met. 'Then he belies his looks.'

He hadn't confided in Nell about that. Nor about anything else, although their one dinner date had given a lot of people the wrong idea.

They were at the county courts all next day, and Nell came back to the office to find a note on her pad that Dora had phoned. She waited until she got home to ring back, she could guess what the call would be about and she didn't feel she could handle it in front of Stephen or any of the staff.

'How about Thursday?' asked Dora. 'Any hope of persuading him to come along?'

'Stephen Harmon? Not me, I've got no influence.'

'Another time, maybe. Does this mean you and Colin have really split?'

'No, it doesn't. I'm going out with Colin tomorrow.'

'Are you?' That seemed to astonish Dora. She said with frank envy, 'I think he looks marvellous,' and she didn't mean Colin.

All the staff at Elsgood and Elsey had taken it for granted that Nell would be marrying Colin, and Mrs. Storey's mouth was disapprovingly down when she cornered Nell in the cloakroom on Wednesday. 'I've known you a long time, Nell, and I'm going to speak plainly. I hope it won't go to your head that Mr. Harmon is paying you some attention, because I think it would be a real shame if you and Colin Greer broke up. I've always thought you made a lovely couple.'

'He isn't paying me attention,' Nell protested, knowing she was wasting her breath. In this small town if a man took a girl out to dinner that was attention.

Her date with Colin didn't mend matters. They went to a Chinese restaurant, and Colin sulked beneath the banter so that almost everything he said came out barbed. He even managed to get an edge on, 'More fried rice?'

On the way home he stopped the car on Spion Ridge, which was high and pine-sheltered and romantic by moonlight. Only there wasn't a moon tonight. He held Nell in his arms and told her masterfully, 'He isn't your type.'

'You mean Stephen, of course. I suppose I can't get it into your head that he has nothing to do with—'

'No,' said Colin, 'you can't.' He stopped her words with a kiss, and she melted for a moment, because he smelled disarmingly familiar with an after-shave lotion she had given him; and she was fond of Colin, and the warmth and the closeness of him stirred her, tingling until her toes curled.

She could have floated away on cloud five, except as always for the thought – don't settle for anything less, Nell. Was this all? Was this enough?

She drew back, and Colin said savagely, 'Do you hold him off?'

She couldn't feel angry, it was too ridiculous. 'You play the prude with me,' said Colin. 'You always have. But I shouldn't think that goes down with Stephen Harmon. He's a man of the world if I ever saw one, and I'll bet the women he knows—'

'So do I,' said Nell. 'My goodness, yes.'

'What do you think you've got that they haven't?' Colin demanded.

'A shorthand notebook,' said Nell. 'And rattling good speeds. You're not going to believe this either, but Stephen Harmon's interest in me is simply and solely because I am as efficient a secretary as any in this town.'

'You?' Colin jeered. 'You can't even spell.'

'Enough to get by,' said Nell. 'I assure you. Anywhere.'

Colin left without suggesting another date, and neither did Nell. She'd said she wanted breathing space, and now it seemed she'd got it.

She countered her grandmother's concern with gay determination, refusing to put any drama into the situation, because there was no drama. Nell was busy, and everything was fine. Nobody had quarrelled with anybody, and Mr. Harmon hadn't asked her out again, but if he did she would remember that Mr. Harmon was the stranger but Colin's family were the friends and neighbours.

Nell was busy. All day long. She wondered as the weekend came round if Stephen would suggest their spending some of it together. Those walks over the hills, for instance. He'd seemed interested enough when her father was talking about them, and some of the places weren't easy to find. Nell walked the hills with Pedro enough to qualify as a guide, and some time during Friday she thought she might bring up the subject.

But when he came in on Friday morning he asked her, 'Are you doing anything special tomorrow evening?'

'No.'

'I have a couple of friends coming for dinner. Would you act as hostess for me? If your fiancé doesn't object.'

'Colin is not my fiancé,' said Nell, 'and why should he object? and yes, I will.' She would like to meet the friends. You can know a man by the company he keeps. Or kept.

He told her, 'Anthony Tyler and his wife Carole. He's a stockbroker. They've been up north on holiday and they're calling on their way home. Perhaps you'd arrange for a meal to be sent over from the Raven.'

'I could cook a meal.'

'There's no need. If you give them the menu they'll provide it.' He smiled. 'But I would be grateful if you'd help dish up, and look decorative.'

'What do you want on the menu?'

He shrugged, 'Oh, anything. You know the kind of thing.' The phone rang and he answered it, and that was his business, and hers today obviously included a dinner party for Mr. Stockbroker Tyler and wife.

She went round to the Raven and asked the cook what she suggested. Not much fancy cooking was called for at the Raven, it was usually simple straightforward fare, but the cook could cook and she was pleased to provide something a little out of the ordinary run. Especially as Mr. Harmon had talked terms before he left. Duck casseroled in red wine could be brought round and finish simmering in the kitchen of the flat.

Nell wore a plain sleeveless dress in avocado green, with a yellow silk scarf. Ocky drove her down, using her father's car, and she was at the flat before the food.

The carved panel was on the wall, she noticed, and she smiled at it as an old friend.

When the real guests arrived the table was laid with silver candlesticks and dark blue candles Nell had brought, and she was sitting with a glass of sherry in a deep high-backed chair.

From the doorway voices mingled in greeting and inquiry. A man was saying, 'Stephen, we couldn't miss the chance of seeing you.' A woman was asking, 'How are you? How *are* you?' 'Fine,' said Stephen Harmon. 'And you?'

Mr. and Mrs. Tyler were doing nicely, thank you. Nell saw that without waiting to hear it. They looked very affluent and quite young. He was a little overweight, his face a little florid, but her face and figure were almost good enough for a model's.

Carole Tyler was blonde, with neat features, and blue eyes skilfully made up so that they seemed bigger and bluer than they were. She stood inside the doorway, facing the room. 'Well, this is a blessed relief. From the view outside we didn't know what to expect.'

Stephen said, 'I'm not exactly on the breadline.'

She noticed Nell, getting up from the chair, and said 'Hello?' making it a query.

'Hello,' said Nell.

Stephen did the introducing, and as he poured drinks Nell could feel their eyes considering her. Her professional status had been explained, but she knew that when they got back into their car to continue their journey they would ask each other, 'What do you think? She looked very much at home, didn't she?'

She returned the smiles and asked about their holiday, and got an account of it all through the Lake District from Tony Tyler, while Carole gave Stephen a string of messages from people whose names meant nothing to Nell.

She had no idea who they were talking about most of the time. How could she have? So she stayed quiet, and tried to look decorative. That was what she was here for. Although Carole Tyler in her model suit of cinnamon suede had a good start on Nell's little number from Polly's Place.

Anyhow, the duck was good. 'Delicious!' said Tony, who seemed to enjoy his food. 'Did you cook it?'

Nell disclaimed credit, smiling, 'It was sent over from a hotel.'

'Do you have a hotel in this town?' Carole asked.

'Not four-star,' said Stephen. 'You'd call them pubs.'

'It's a very small town, isn't it?' Suddenly Nell wanted to deny that, because it was a town, long established and thriving. This woman made it sound as though she was referring to a hamlet of one farm and two cottages.

'Small,' agreed Stephen, 'but we make a living.' He was laughing at her, but her expression stayed serious and puzzled.

'I still can't believe you'd settle for this.'

'Who needs the rat race?'

. . . You do, thought Nell. She had learned that much in five weeks of working with him, that he thrived on a challenge and hated to lose. And yet now he was sounding like someone who had settled for the undemanding life.

'I envy you,' said Tony. 'What's the sense in killing yourself? Taxes take it anyway. What we could see of it it seems very pleasant around here.'

But Carole still looked at Stephen. 'Is your office really in that little Victorian house?'

'The top storey.'

Nell leaned forward with some indignation. She was about to say that the premises might be modest but business was brisk, and Stephen Harmon already had a reputation as the best lawyer for miles around.

Across the table she met Stephen's eyes . . . Forget it . . . Don't argue . . . it isn't worth it . . .

She was a very good secretary. She could interpret a look. She closed her lips and sat back. It was a touch of telepathy, an awareness like a magnetic pull. She looked at his hands, and then again met his eyes, and it was as though he had reached across and held her hand, and she felt her heart thump.

The setting had much to do with it. She was playing hostess here. In a few minutes she would carry out the dishes from this course and bring in the sweet course and the coffee. She and Stephen Harmon were entertaining friends, but she was doing her part as 'overtime' and the feeling that she was 'home' was sheer pleasurable self-indulgence.

When she went into the kitchen for the coffee, Carole Tyler followed her; she had everything to hand so that she simply put down the tray she was carrying on the table, and began clearing it and reloading. Carole said, 'You have got things organized.'

There was a cheese board, and Nell opened the fridge for the orange-and-curaçao ices, and laughed, 'I didn't prepare any of this either. It all came from the Raven.'

'How is Stephen?' asked Carole.

'Fine,' said Nell. 'As far as I know. You've just seen him and asked him. Don't you think he looks all right?'

'He'll never stay here,' said Carole.

'That I wouldn't know,' said Nell. Something cold like loneliness blew through the warm kitchen. She asked, 'You know him well?'

'Oh yes,' said Carole. She thought again. 'If anyone can say they know Stephen well. His old firm are Tony's solicitors, and Tony's father's. And socially of course we've always seen a lot of him. I must say when I heard he was leaving the practice I never thought the change would be this drastic.'

108

Nell said, smiling tightly, 'You sound as though our clients pay their bills with a couple of rabbits they've poached,' and Carole Tyler giggled,

'They don't, do they? I'm sorry, I'm being tactless. But you should have seen Stephen's last flat, and his office. He was the youngest of the partners, but he was the legal eagle in that firm until he was warned he had to slow down.'

'I can believe it,' said Nell.

Carole picked up the smaller tray, with the ices on. In the doorway she looked back over her shoulder as though about to say something more. She didn't, but she looked at Nell for a moment as though she was sorry for her, before she pushed open the door and went in.

The Tylers stayed so late that they decided at ten o'clock to ring through to the Raven and see if they could put up for the night. With that settled they stayed another couple of hours, and it was midnight before they said good-bye.

Nell put on her coat while Stephen went down to see them into their car and direct them to the Raven. Mrs. Robbins, who cleaned the office, and was coming for a couple of hours in the morning to do the washing up, and Nell looked around feeling an unaccountable urge to tidy a little.

She suppressed it. And the longing to flop and revel in the luxury that the party was over. You only did that in your own home, or with dear and comfortable friends, and this was not her home and Stephen Harmon was not a comfortable friend.

When he came back he thanked her. She said she had enjoyed it. 'Tired?' he asked. She said not at all, although she realized that she was now it no longer seemed necessary to stay bright-eyed and alert. He laughed, 'Carole does repeat herself. It gets monotonous if you listen. Shall we get you home?'

'Please,' she said.

In the car, when they reached the hills, she asked, 'Have you taken any of the walks my father was telling you about?'

'There hasn't been much chance.'

There hadn't. She said, 'Tomorrow is Sunday.'

'Today is. It's twenty past twelve. Where do you

recommend?'

'Well now—' They turned for Quarry House, into the drive. 'If it's a view you want the highest hill is Spion Ridge. Then—' She had been about to describe the walk she took Pedro most Sundays, but as the powerful headlamps bathed the front of Quarry House she shut up abruptly.

There were lights here and there, which she had expected. But she had not expected Colin's car parked in front. He must be very determined to see her to wait this late, and she had a sickening foreboding that she was in for a very unpleasant scene.

CHAPTER SIX

As Stephen Harmon's car drew up alongside Colin's Nell said, 'Thank you,' and had her fingers around the handle so that the moment it stopped she could open the door. She said, as she turned to get out, 'Good night, I'll see you on Monday.'

'I hope so,' said Stephen. 'As a matter of interest are you escaping from my clutches or hurrying to see whoever it is who drives that car?'

She had been about to leap like a scalded cat, but certainly not because she anticipated having to fend off Stephen Harmon, and well he knew it. She said, 'Was I almost in your clutches? There's a sobering thought.'

'And an interesting one. Whose car is it?'

'Colin's.'

'I thought it might be. Do you need a character reference for this evening?'

'No, thank you, I can cope. But I feel I could be in for an embarrassing five minutes and it might be better if I walked into the house alone.'

'You're sure? I don't embarrass easily.'

'I do,' said Nell. 'It's me I'm thinking about.'

The drawing-room faced the front of the house, they must have heard Stephen Harmon's car arrive and leave again, but Nell got her own key out and let herself into the hall and nobody came to meet her.

She opened the drawing-room door and met Pedro. The television was in the closing pangs of a late thriller. Flo sat on the settee, Elizabeth Attlesey in an easy chair, and Colin sat in the carved wooden armchair without cushion or padding as though determined to make his waiting as martyred as possible.

Pedro slobbered his usual adoration, and over his head Colin glared at her. 'Ah well,' said Nell, patting Pedro, 'somebody loves me.'

Flo asked, 'Nice folk, were they?'

'Very,' said Nell. 'Hello, Colin, don't tell me the film was so absorbing you couldn't tear yourself away.'

Colin said stiffly, 'I stayed because I wanted to see you.' If he'd smiled when he said that she would have smiled back, but he went on glaring and she said,

'And now you've seen me, and it's late, and I'm off to bed, so good night, all.'

Her grandmother's 'Nell!' was gently reproachful, and Nell went across to her and kissed her cheek.

'You're looking tired yourself, lovey.'

This was very late for Elizabeth Attlesey, and it wasn't the movie that had kept her up, it was Colin sitting there simmering. She said, 'Colin wants to talk to you, Nell.'

And I, thought Nell, have something to say to Colin. She said, 'All right, you get along to bed. Don't you think, Flo?'

'I do that, ' said Flo. 'If I'd had my way she'd have been in bed hours ago, but you know what she's like.' She got up herself and turned off the television. 'Load of rubbish they put on.' She said her good nights, told Nell, 'Your father's still in the workroom.'

'I seem to have kept the whole house up,' said Nell.

'You didn't keep me up,' said Flo cheerfully. 'And your father's working, or was ten minutes ago. Are you coming, then?'

'Good night, Nell,' said her grandmother. 'Good night, Colin.' Her blue eyes searched Nell's face. They had been beautiful eyes, blue as harebells, but tonight they looked faded and desperately weary, and she turned to Flo for a supporting arm to get her out of the room and up the long staircase.

Nell sighed. She was frail. It was worrying. She said, 'Whatever you wanted to say to me, Colin, could surely have waited till tomorrow.'

'How do I know you'll be in tomorrow?' Colin demanded. 'I thought you'd be here tonight.'

'You could have phoned.'

'I could, but I didn't. I've brought you something.'

She didn't want to sound ungracious, but she didn't want Colin to start buying her presents, competing with gifts. 'Oh dear!' she said.

He opened the small box he had taken out of his pocket.

'If it doesn't fit you we'll have it fixed.'

A *ring*! Opals and sapphires in a wide gold band, old-fashioned and quite charming, and Nell stared at it aghast.

Colin said, 'It was my grandmother's, my mother wants you to have it. Do you like it?'

'It's beautiful.' Nell put both hands behind her back. 'But I can't take it.'

'I suppose I could get you a modern one if you'd rather.'

'*No*! Not any sort of ring. I'm sorry, but no.'

'Because of Stephen Harmon?' Colin did not look or sound in the least loverlike. He was offering her his grandmother's ring, but the spur to his declaration was jealousy, and even if Nell had been head over heels in love with him she would have been wary of accepting.

As she was not in love she said, 'Because I don't want to get married yet. To you or to anyone.'

'I'm the only one who's asking you,' said Colin. 'Whatever you talked about with Harmon tonight I'll bet it wasn't marriage.'

'No, it wasn't.'

'And that was a fine tale – a dinner party, two other guests arriving out of the blue.' His ringing derision indicated that he had been brooding about this ever since he arrived here and heard where Nell had gone.

She snapped, 'And what do you think it was? An orgy for two under the icon?' She wasn't helping anything, but she was tired and it was late, and a man who proposed to a girl looking as though he would like to shake her until her teeth rattled deserved all he got.

Colin's temper took light. He roared at her, 'I wonder you bothered to come home at all. While you were about it I wonder you didn't stay the—'

Pedro raised his head from the hearthrug. His growl began soft and gained in menace as his hackles rose and his teeth bared. Colin stopped shouting and stared. He had always thought Pedro was harmless, but Pedro was a powerful dog and at that moment he looked lethal. His muscles hunched and Colin croaked, 'Is he—'

He *was* going to spring. Nell flung herself at him, clutching fur with both hands. 'You'd better get out, and quick.'

She was having a wrestling match with Pedro, who knew exactly who the Enemy was right now, and would have had him too if Colin hadn't moved fast.

Nell heard the front door slam and the car start up before she loosed her hold and Pedro's snarls subsided. 'You,' said Nell, 'are a surprising old boy.'

It had left her breathless. She went into the workroom where her father was sitting by the embers of the fire, reading. She took the chair opposite and said, 'You knew Colin was here, I suppose?'

'With ring,' said John Attlesey.

'Why didn't you tell him to go home?'

'He wasn't offering me the ring. I see you're not wearing it.'

'Did you expect me to be?'

'No.' He smiled at her. 'How did you handle it?'

She sighed, 'First I said no. Then I asked him if he thought this evening had been an orgy under the icon, because that seemed to be his impression. He didn't think that was funny.'

'It sounds a riot to me,' said her father. 'How did it go? What were they like?'

'She couldn't get over how Stephen had come down in the world. I should have seen his last office, she said, and his last flat. She doesn't think much of Cheslyn Slade.' She scratched Pedro's ear. 'Back to Colin. Pedro went for him.'

'He *did*?'

She nodded, 'Mmm. Colin was yelling his head off that he wondered I'd bothered to come home at all tonight, so Pedro was defending my reputation. Wasn't that clever of him?'

No one had ever shouted at Nell before. John Attlesey reached across to pat the dog. 'Highly moral, and what did Colin do?'

'Pedro meant it,' said Nell. 'It was all I could do to hold him back. And Colin ran.' Her smile slipped out and John Attlesey's grin was broad.

'You certainly got your point across, setting the dog on him!'

'And after this,' said Nell, 'how can Grandmother ever

play bridge with Mrs. Greer again?'

The light was still on in her grandmother's room, and the door was open. Nell had not been optimistic about her chances of getting to bed without telling Elizabeth Attlesey whether she was now engaged to Colin, but she sighed when she saw the light.

John Attlesey insisted on negotiating stairs night and morning, with one stick and the rail of the sturdily fashioned banisters. At the bottom of the stairs he said, 'Shall I go in and tell her to get to sleep, she can hear all about it in the morning?'

'No,' said Nell, 'I'll do it.' She grimaced, 'I think I'll leave out the bit about Pedro.'

'Please yourself,' her father chuckled, 'but that was the bit I enjoyed most.'

Nell stood in the doorway and said softly, 'Asleep, love?' Her grandmother opened her eyes, and Nell went and sat on the side of the bed. She said, 'I don't love Colin. I can't promise to marry him, can I, not loving him?'

Elizabeth Attlesey said, 'He loves you.'

'I don't think so,' said Nell. 'He wants me wearing his ring so that he can tell me what to do.' She smiled, 'And I don't want that. Especially from Colin.'

Elizabeth Attlesey's lips trembled and tightened, 'Your trouble is, Nell, you don't know what you do want. You've never had to fend for yourself. You're letting a lifetime's security slip through your fingers, and you can smile now, but the time will come when you'll need security.'

'Will I?' Nell wondered.

'All these months,' her grandmother wailed querulously, 'it's been no one but Colin, and everyone thought you were made for each other, his mother, *everybody* thought it, and then as soon as he asks you to marry him you discover you don't love him.'

Nell ventured, 'Better now than later.'

'I don't know what's the matter with you. I don't know what you expect.' Her grandmother plucked at the sheet with nervous fingers. 'You couldn't get a more eligible young man than Colin, a nice family, with such good prospects.'

Nell began to laugh because her grandmother sounded so

mercenary. She wasn't, she was one of the most generous women alive. It was just that she wanted a cushioning prosperity for Nell against loneliness.

Nell laughed, and Elizabeth Attlesey shivered listening to the laughter. Colin Greer had seemed so suitable, but Nell had sent him away, and now Nell was treating it as a joke because everything was a joke to Nell. She couldn't understand that she wouldn't be young and strong for ever. At her age Elizabeth had been married three years. A long time ago, a long long time ago.

Elizabeth Attlesey began to weep. For the girl who had once been younger than Nell and who was now so old that it hurt her to breathe. She bowed her head into her small cold hands and wept.

Nell watched with mounting concern. She knew that her grandmother could use tears as easily as tantrums to get her own way, but this time there seemed no design about it, the tears seemed genuine weakness, and Nell said, 'It's all right, don't cry, please, *please* don't cry.'

She gently took her grandmother's hands from her face and eased her back on to the high pillow, shocked at the grey skin, the suddenly sunken eyes.

This wasn't acting. She was ill. Nell said, 'Lie still,' and went fast to the door. Flo's room was next to Elizabeth Attlesey's and Nell went in.

The light was off, but if Flo was asleep she woke the moment Nell touched her and asked, 'What's the matter?'

'I think Grandmother's ill. I'm calling the doctor.'

'Are you sure?' Flo was out of bed before Nell was out of the room.

'Sure enough,' said Nell. 'I daren't chance it.'

The doctor was an old family friend. Her call woke him and he lived ten minutes' car journey away, but he was at the door in less than a quarter of an hour.

It wasn't pretence. Elizabeth Attlesey lay like a waxen doll, her breath laboured, her pulse an erratic thread. Her son and her granddaughter by her bedside would have promised her anything in the world at that moment, but she had no strength to ask, hardly strength enough to keep a tenuous hold on life.

The doctor needed no more than one searching look, and

a moment of holding the limp wrist. She was past realizing he was here, or that he was giving her an injection. She lay still with closed eyes, but gradually her breathing eased so that although it was a drugged sleep it was sleep and not death that was claiming her this time.

Flo stayed beside her, while Nell and her father went downstairs with the doctor. 'She should be all right now,' he said.

'It was a near thing, wasn't it?' asked John Attlesey. Dr. Andrew Kirby nodded,

'Very near.'

'What do we do?' Self-reproach was tearing at Nell, her face was white and set, and the doctor smiled encouragingly.

'There's a great deal we can do now that we know she has a heart condition. She must have her bed downstairs – she shouldn't be climbing stairs. Strenuous physical activity and worry of any sort are right out, but that shouldn't be much of a problem, should it?'

He knew she would be cared for. Flo was a good nurse and everyone in this house loved Elizabeth Attlesey. 'And the pills,' he said. 'She's going to rattle with pills from now on, but if she takes them and behaves herself I wouldn't be surprised if she lives to a hundred.'

Nell managed a wan smile and Dr. Kirby produced pills and prescriptions and told them, 'She'll be dopey with the drug for a few hours. She must have complete rest for a week, and I'll look in again in the morning.'

Nell left him and her father talking and hurried back upstairs. Flo was sitting by the bed. In the bed Elizabeth Attlesey opened her eyes as Nell bent over her and whispered, 'I'm all right now.'

'Shush!' Nell put a fingertip on her lips. 'Go to sleep.'

'Did I give you a fright?' There was a gleam in her eyes, although her voice was so faint that Nell and Flo had to lean closer to hear.

'You did,' said Flo, 'so you can rest easy,' and Elizabeth Attlesey slipped back into sleep with an unmistakable smile.

They both looked at her for a few moments more, then at each other. Flo said, 'I suppose—'

'It was the real thing,' said Nell.

'Yes,' said Flo. 'She always did have this queer heart flutter.' The strain of a freak beat over seventy years had weakened the heart at last. The attack had been real, and almost a killer.

Nell said, 'She is going to be all right. We have to make sure she takes the pills, that she doesn't get overtired or worried.'

Flo tucked back a lock of soft silver hair that had fallen across Elizabeth Attlesey's brow, with a deft and tender touch. 'You turned him down, I suppose?'

'Colin?' As Colin had said, he was the only one who was asking her. 'Yes. The mood he was in I think he'd rather have hit me than kissed me. Some proposal!'

Flo laughed silently and ruefully, 'And she doesn't have to be worried. I don't know, it's like giving her a licence to print her own money.'

There wasn't much sleep that night for any of them. Elizabeth Attlesey slept best, that was mainly the drug, but it was incongruous next morning that the one who had so nearly died should look the best of the bunch.

Wearing a fluffy pink angora bedjacket, propped up with pillows, she swallowed her second pill of the day and said she thought she would be able to get up for an hour this evening.

'Oh no, you don't,' said Flo. 'Not unless your bed goes down with you. We're having no more shocks like last night's, thank you very much.'

Over breakfast, in the kitchen, Nell said to her father, 'I'm in a spot, aren't I? She got herself really worked up about Colin and me, that's what started it.'

He said quickly, 'Now don't get blaming yourself for anything. The condition was there long before last night. We can be thankful the first attack came when we could get a doctor to her quickly.'

They were forewarned now and forearmed. Nell turned the honey pot round, looking at it with furrowed brow as though her problem was there. 'The doctor said no worry. She's only got one worry on her mind, this fixation for getting me settled. She *is* worrying about my turning Colin down.'

'I should be worried if you hadn't, said her father. 'And somehow we've got to get it across to her that times have changed.' Nell's honey skin was pale so that her eyes seemed darker than usual, and too big for the oval of her face. He smiled at her. 'Even at the ripe old age of twenty-one Colin isn't your last hope.'

She laughed with him, 'Hooray for that,' and winced as pain stabbed behind her eyes.

'Why don't you go back to bed for an hour?' He knew she had insisted on Flo going to bed, and spent the night herself in the chair by her grandmother's bedside, and that she had been tired when she came home.

'I'd rather go for a walk,' she said. 'I think it's fresh air I need.'

Before she left the house she looked in again on her grandmother. It was hard to believe in the trauma of last night seeing her now, revelling in her role as the interesting invalid. The Sunday joint was in the oven, Nell had prepared the vegetables. Flo was sitting at the window in the bedroom, keeping an eye on the invalid.

'Have a nice walk, dear,' said Elizabeth Attlesey, just as she always said on a Sunday morning when Nell took Pedro over the hills. And then, 'Is Colin coming to tea?'

'No,' said Nell.

'Oh,' said her grandmother. 'You went there last Sunday, so I thought he might be.'

Hardly! Nell wondered for a moment if her grandmother had forgotten the events immediately before her attack, but then Elizabeth Attlesey said sweetly, 'Well, I think it's up to you, dear, to phone him this morning, because you were a little hasty last night. There's no reason why you and Colin shouldn't go on being friends, is there?'

That sounded like modern thinking, but it wasn't. Nell said, 'We'll see.' She couldn't argue. She mustn't do anything today to agitate that capricious heart.

Flo said sympathetically, 'If I were you I'd make it a nice long walk.'

Most Sunday mornings Nell took the same route across the heather hills, following a half overgrown track that skirted the ruins of one of the closed-down coalmines and then meandered into the Valley of the Springs.

It was beautiful and peaceful and usually deserted, and this morning peace was what Nell needed. When she reached the valley there wasn't a soul in sight, and she walked slowly watching the bubbling clear crystal water, while Pedro chased rabbits and motes in the sunlight and his own tail, splashing in and out of the streams, crashing through the bracken.

Nell sat on a big flat stone and threw pebbles for Pedro until he flopped panting beside her. Then she just sat. The hills always gave her peace. She could always draw strength from their solitude. Her headache had melted away, and she would get back home more refreshed than if she had gone to bed and slept away the last hour.

She frowned instinctively when Pedro gave a little bark and she saw a man coming over the hill. Then she gasped, because it was Stephen Harmon and this was an almighty coincidence.

He had already seen her. He came towards her and she stayed where she was until he was near, then she said, 'Hello.'

'Hello.'

She said, 'Friend,' firmly to Pedro – after last night it seemed advisable to point that out – and Pedro got up and paddled back into the stream on the track of a minnow.

Stephen said, 'I should have brought a compass. I never expected to find you.'

'How did you?'

'Your father told me where you were heading, but I'm more at home with my roads numbered. Still, the colliery was a big help.'

'That's what's left of the Lady. The Cobbler and Earl Grey are around too. What's left of them, they're all closed down.' She looked up at him. 'Was it a business call or are you taking a walk?'

'I'd come to apologize for the embarrassing five minutes I landed you in last night.'

'Five minutes!' She remembered saying that, and, 'I can cope.' She laughed wryly, 'That turned into the longest five minutes of my life!'

'What happened?'

'Did my father tell you anything?'

'No.' If she hadn't seen Stephen Harmon again until tomorrow morning in the office she would probably have said nothing herself, but here there were no distractions, no phones ringing, no other people with more pressing problems. She said,

'This is going to sound quite ridiculous.'

'Try me.'

'My grandmother is an old-fashioned lady. She reared me, my mother died when I was born, and she has one ambition – to see me married. Because she imagines that if I don't have a husband to provide I shall die of malnutrition.' She laughed, because it was ridiculous, 'How about that?'

He didn't laugh. He asked, 'And last night?'

'Colin asked me to marry him. I said no, and my grandmother got into such a state she had a heart attack.'

'I'm sorry.'

'We didn't even know she had a weak heart.'

'How is she this morning?'

'Oh, better. She's on pills now and she'll have treatment, but you see she mustn't worry, we mustn't let anything upset her, and I don't know what I'm going to do because she's going to fret herself to death because I won't settle down, and it's so *stupid*, isn't it?'

Nell had had no sleep, and she had had a grim night, and she could see no easy solution to her problem. She said, '*Isn't* it stupid?' and gulped on the lump in her throat.

Harmon reached down to take her hand and lift her to her feet. 'Is she set on Greer, or is it that he represents security?'

'It's security. She thinks that if I don't marry I shall be on my own some day, and she'll never believe I could earn more than a pittance.'

'She's wrong there.' He still held her. 'As your employer I'd raise your salary rather than lose you.'

The lump was still in her throat. A bird fluttered overhead and she could hear Pedro splashing somewhere along the stream. 'She's wrong on the second count too,' said Stephen Harmon. 'You'll never be alone, unless you want to be.'

Nell had always made friends easily, but she wondered

now if it would be possible to have good friends and still be alone. Carole had said, 'He'll never stay here,' but how would Carole know?

Stephen asked, 'Shall I talk to her?'

'To my grandmother?'

He was the only man in a position to say that Nell had security in her own ability, that she could command a more-than-living wage. Perhaps he could also reassure her that Nell was lucky in friends.

She said, gaily and gratefully, 'You could pretend she was chairman of the bench.'

'You expect a professional performance?'

'If I've got the best lawyer in town acting for me, of course.'

'Thank you.'

'Thank *you*,' she said, the feeling that he would cope so strong that the weight of worry lifted like a physical relief, leaving her light as air.

The sun had been out all morning, but suddenly it was bright enough to dazzle so that she blinked as she smiled, and asked him, 'Isn't it beautiful here?'

'Very. Here. The derelict coalmine was something of an eyesore.'

But the coalmines had always been part of the hills. Nell took them for granted. Even rust and decay failed to make an impact when you saw them so often. And this valley was a beauty spot.

They walked on the shingle and the soft marshy turf back to the track that zigzagged to the top of the hill. Pedro loped ahead and as they began to climb Stephen said, 'I had the impression that you were considering marrying Greer, although I think you said not for some time.' He turned to look at her. 'Have you decided now that it's never?'

She went on climbing, giving a small nod as her reply. She had thought they might marry some time. She had thought they might be in love. But last night when Colin offered her that ring she had known she would never wear it.

'What changed your mind?' He used just that tone of cool query in court. She gave her attention to the track, the grasses were rough, the stones loose. Without looking at him she could imagine his expression matching his voice, and she wondered if he was anxious she shouldn't be counting their relationship closer than it was.

She said crisply, 'I didn't change my mind. I wasn't asked to make up my mind before. When I was I decided I could do without marriage unless there was a pretty overwhelming argument for it.'

'What would you call an overwhelming argument?'

She considered as she finished the climb. By the top of the hill she hadn't come up with a better answer and she said, 'Caring for someone so much that you can live with memories if you have to, because no one else comes near.'

'I wish you luck.' He spoke so cynically that she swung round, startled. 'With your memories,' he said.

His face was the trained mask hiding his thoughts, but she knew that the memories where Stephen Harmon lived were bitter. He smiled at her as she looked at him, his eyes following Pedro hurtling suddenly into the bushes. 'Has that dog ever caught a rabbit?' he asked.

She took the cue, talking gaily. 'Not up to now, but today he has a new image. Last night was drama all round. Colin lost his temper and shouted, and Pedro went into action. Pedro has never hurt a fly before – well, perhaps a fly – but last night he stood up for me in a big way, so a little respect is called for.'

Stephen laughed. 'I'm glad you told me. I'll remember when I next feel like shouting at you.'

'I suppose it could have been bluff again, but I believed him.' She grinned, 'And so did Colin. He didn't even stay to say good night, I think he felt there was nothing left to discuss. As my father said – you get your point across when you set the dog on somebody.'

'I can't think of a weightier argument. By the way, does your father share your grandmother's opinions?'

'Very rarely,' said Nell.

On the way back she stopped to gather a sprig of white heather. It grew in a copse a little way off the track, not easy to find unless you knew where to look. Ocky had shown her where it grew. Once he had passed it each day on his way to the Lady. Lucky white heather, but it hadn't kept the pit from closing.

She said, 'For my grandmother. The specialist comes to see her today.'

'It must have been a bad night for you.'

'Yes, but it could have been worse. Now, if she'll only be sensible.'

'Let's go and talk sense to her,' said Stephen Harmon.

The doctor had been while Nell was out and announced that he was satisfied. Elizabeth Attlesey was allowed visitors, friends might look in. She must rest, but if they made her week of inaction too boring both her doctor and her family knew her capable of nipping out of bed and coming downstairs. The prospect of visitors would keep her in bed, smiling bravely.

There had been a number of phone calls already, and Flo was working on a rota so that there would be a change of face each day.

Nell went up to the bedroom and put the white heather in a tiny vase on the dressing table. 'A bit more white heather, the last was getting dusty. How are you feeling?'

'Not very hungry,' said her grandmother. 'Don't let Flo put too much on my plate.'

'I won't. I'll do you a lovely dainty tray, with a rose on the napkin. Would you like a visitor?'

'Who is it?'

'Stephen Harmon. He called this morning, we've been to the Valley of the Springs.' Nell spoke casually because keeping Elizabeth Attlesey placid was part of the treatment. Even so that would have been enough to spark off the questions if Nell hadn't gone straight to the door and said, 'You can come in,' to Stephen, waiting outside.

He only stayed for a few minutes, and he was an ideal sickroom visitor: calm, charming, apparently concerned for the patient. In those few minutes he also managed to get across how fortunate he considered himself having Nell working with him.

When her grandmother said, 'You're very gallant,' he said,

'Never in business matters. Nell's efficiency is outstanding.'

He didn't labour the point, but everything Stephen Harmon said carried conviction. That was the lawyer, all that practice in the courts, and Nell hoped he meant it.

He declined an invitation to lunch – he had to get back for a phone call, he said – and when Nell took up her grandmother's tray Elizabeth Attlesey greeted her with, 'This makes it no better, Nell.'

'Come again?' Nell wasn't following.

Glowing among her pillows Elizabeth Attlesey shook an admonitory finger. 'You were very unkind to break poor Colin's heart like that.'

'Colin's heart isn't broken. If it's damaged at all it's the tiniest little dent.'

'And flippancy is not becoming.'

'Sorry,' said Nell cheerfully. She put the tray on the bed and picked up the glass of water. 'One blue pill before lunch.'

Her grandmother swallowed the pill, needing a little cough to get it down. 'I don't condone it,' she said. 'Not for one moment. But I do understand it just a little, now that I've met Mr. Harmon.'

'You saw him at his best,' said Nell hastily. 'He can be tough as old boots.'

'A charming man,' her grandmother continued as though she hadn't said a word. 'I hear he's been very successful since he took over Mr. Elsgood's practice.' She beamed at Nell, and Nell tried again.

'Stephen Harmon's interest in me is that I'm a good secretary. I know my job and I do it well, and that he appreciates. It's purely business, and that's how I want it to be. Try to understand, lovey, I like having a career and standing on my own feet and being independent.'

'That was what was wrong with Colin,' announced her grandmother.

'What was?' Nell couldn't help asking.

'You need a masterful man,' said Elizabeth Attlesey, as she applied herself to her soup.

That afternoon Dr. Kirby brought along the heart specialist, and had his own diagnosis confirmed on every point. With rest and reason, by taking the drugs they prescribed and avoiding stress and strain Elizabeth Attlesey could have years of useful life ahead of her.

She smiled at everyone and promised she would do everything she was told; she felt better already, almost her old self again.

For safety's sake for the next few nights it was decided that Flo's bed should be taken into Elizabeth Attlesey's room, and for this week at any rate Ocky's wife would come along and give a hand.

As she and Nell started to fold up her bedclothes Flo said, 'She's looking like the cat with the cream. You haven't been daft enough to promise her anything, have you?'

'You couldn't mean like promising to get married?'

'I should hope you wouldn't go that far. I should hope you've had more sense than to promise you'll go on seeing him.'

Nell said, 'She hasn't got her sights fixed on Colin any more. It's Stephen Harmon now. She says I need a masterful man.'

'What do you say about that?' asked Flo.

Nell laughed, 'What's the use of saying anything? She doesn't listen. Anyhow, it's taken her mind off Colin, and Stephen Harmon won't take it seriously.'

'That's all right, then,' said Flo. 'So long as you wouldn't rather he took it seriously.'

Nell picked up a couple of pillows in both arms. 'Now you're being daft,' she said.

All the same she felt a little awkward next morning. As soon as he came into the office Stephen asked her how her grandmother was and Nell said, 'She's coming along beautifully.'

'I'm glad. Any other developments?'

'Not a word from Colin, and not another word about him from my grandmother.'

'Good.' He raised an eyebrow. 'Is it good?'

'Oh yes,' said Nell with emphasis. 'Although it will take her a little time to appreciate that a girl might prefer earning her own living. She is an old-fashioned lady.'

The morning was – as all mornings seemed to be since Stephen Harmon took over – busy. At midday he was still dictating, past the time Nell usually took lunch. Half way through the memo he glanced at his watch. 'I'm sorry you're ten minutes late. Does it matter?'

She'd finished meeting Colin, and she hadn't told them to expect her home midday. She said, 'I can eat later, any time.'

'I'm heating up a tin of soup. How about sharing that?'

'All right. Where is it?'

'In the kitchen. Where would you expect it to be?'

In the kitchen, in the flat. It ended in Nell heating the soup and making the toast and coffee.

She wasn't complaining. She enjoyed this more than she would have enjoyed wandering down to the snack bar, and possibly bumping into Colin. The surroundings were infinitely better, and the company.

Stephen Harmon was the most stimulating company she had ever come across, and in the unfair way of things she knew that he was available only as a companion. He had memories, not good ones, but they were in his bones. There wouldn't be much sense in getting overfond of a man who never gave you a second thought when you were out of sight.

Colin phoned that afternoon, and got himself put through to Nell's office. A client had just left and Harmon answered the phone and handed it to her without speaking. Colin said, 'I've just heard about Mrs. Attlesey – how is she?'

Nell told him. Colin said he was sorry. Nell said that yes, it was a worry, but she was much better.

'What are you doing tonight?' Colin asked. That was magnanimous of him, after Pedro, but Nell was beginning. 'I don't think it would be a good idea –' when Stephen Harmon said,

'Tell him you're working late.'

'Am I?' she mouthed. He shrugged. She said,

'I'm sorry, but—'

'I heard,' said Colin. 'Like the dinner party for four, is it?' He put down the phone and so did Nell, rather more slowly.

She said, 'That did it. Am I working late?'

'I am. Are you available?'

It was work, although nobody believed it. Nell rang home and spoke to Flo, who said that everything was fine and they'd expect her when they saw her, and have a good time.

The work wasn't for Elsgood and Elsey. It was a brief for a barrister in a union solicitor inquiry. A member's claim for industrial injury had not been filed in time and the big guns were out. No one had asked Elsgood and Elsey to handle that one.

She typed her notes on Harmon's typewriter, and when he said 'Excellent', having read them, she said 'Is this for your old firm?'

'Yes.'

'You haven't finished with them?'

'One keeps one's hand in, but I'd rather you didn't discuss this.'

'I'm hardly likely to.'

He grinned, 'I know it. You're a treasure and a model of discretion. Now, shall we eat?'

They went to the Raven. It was the nearest. You walked through the bar to the little dining-room, and most of the regulars recognized Harmon from his four weeks as a lodger, and several knew Nell. And nobody thought it had been work this evening, they all thought that Nell Attlesey and the new lawyer who'd taken over from Elsgood were getting on like a house on fire.

That was hardly the way of it, but lunch together became a pleasant habit. Evenings together too, usually working, but a couple of times they did a theatre, and they covered a fair portion of the countryside by car, and some more of the moorlands on foot.

The gossips had a field day. Joan for one was convinced there could only be one reason why Nell refused to discuss her dates with Stephen Harmon. From time to time Joan would say, 'I only hope you know what you're doing,' in tones of dire foreboding, but the affair was platonic.

The first time Stephen kissed Nell good night she stiffened for a moment, holding her breath, but the kiss asked nothing and altered nothing, nor did the ones that followed it. And if Nell had said, 'We spend those cosy evenings in Stephen's flat dealing with a stack of legal work,' who would have believed her? Still less if she had said, 'And I enjoy it.' But after three years of Elsgood and Rowe there was a never-failing exhilaration in watching Stephen Harmon at work.

Nell had been his secretary for nearly three months when she met Sir Charles Fenby, head of Harmon's last firm. He came into the office one afternoon while Stephen was out, although due back any time.

He was expected, and Nell had a large envelope to hand over and instructions to offer him a glass of sherry and keep him happy.

She poured the sherry; and produced the envelope, representing several hours of typing last night. Sir Charles was an impressive figure with silver-grey hair, who looked benevolent but had shrewd eyes under grizzled brows.

The eyes were on Nell as he snapped the locks on his briefcase, and smiled and said, 'I've heard about you, Miss Attlesey, you mustn't let Mr. Harmon work you too hard. He does sometimes forget that those who toil for him are flesh and blood and not so many machines.'

She was working hard, but it wasn't bothering her. She smiled back, 'The pace has certainly speeded up here since Mr. Harmon took over, but I'm not finding it too much. I enjoy it.'

'No doubt,' said Sir Charles drily. 'All the same, don't let him monopolize all your time.'

No? Why not? she wondered.

CHAPTER SEVEN

NELL said, 'Sir Charles doesn't think Stephen's going to stay here.'

She was in the workroom that evening. She had entertained the family at tea with a description of Sir Charles Fenby's progress like visiting royalty when Stephen Harmon took him through the offices and introduced them all. She had made it amusing by exaggerating details, like Mrs. Storey furtively dusting a chair before he sat down on it in his beautiful silver grey suit that matched his hair.

She didn't mention what Sir Charles had said to her until she was alone with her father. Then she said, 'He said I mustn't let Stephen work me too hard.'

'Very considerate,' said her father, pondering between quarter and three-eighths of an inch chisels for the panel in hand.

Nell said, 'I think he was warning me in a roundabout way not to expect too much from the job for too long.'

Her father put down both chisels. She said, 'He was on his way to their northern office and he'd got a briefcase full of documents, and I'm sure he was going to discuss some of them with Stephen.'

Attlesey suggested, 'Cases he was dealing with before he left?'

'He hasn't settled here.' She spoke slowly, giving the evidence as it had presented itself to her, the pieces fitting like a jigsaw. 'He's accepted no invitations, he doesn't want to get involved in anything outside the office. And in the office, our room — you've seen it, it looks like the year dot — if Stephen was going to be behind that desk for the rest of his working life he'd have had that room apart before now. But he hasn't bothered to change a thing.

'Then the downstairs offices — I typed their new leases this morning. The rents have gone up, but not all that much, they've both got another five years of tenure that they'll sit out, which means he doesn't visualize bigger premises, although the way business is going we should be needing them by this time next year.

'Carole Tyler said he'd never settle, and Sir Charles doesn't think he's going to stay either.'

Her father said, 'I'm inclined to agree with them.'

'But he has to slow down. That was his reason for coming here.'

John Attlesey shrugged and selected the smaller of the two chisels, and Nell said impulsively, 'You adapted when you had to and you're content. Why can't he be?'

'Content?' growled Attlesey. He unclenched his hands on the workbench so that the little wood-carving chisel rolled from his fingers. 'If these could carve that,' he looked across at the block of white marble, 'the risk of dropping dead wouldn't stop me.'

Nell said wretchedly, 'Sorry, love.'

'Don't be.' Her father picked up the chisel again and smiled at her. 'There are compensations in being knocked out of the race, you can always tell yourself you'd have won. But I don't think Stephen Harmon's out of the running, and I don't think it's likely he'll stay here indefinitely.'

'Neither do I,' said Nell.

She couldn't ask him. If she had done he wouldn't have told her. He told her very little, in spite of what everyone thought. When the talk was not on business matters they covered a good wide range, but they never came within a mile of soul-searching. All Nell knew about Stephen Harmon could have been common knowledge. Except perhaps that his parents were dead and he had no other relatives.

Elizabeth Attlesey was soon up and about again. She was following doctor's orders, resting every afternoon in the small parlour downstairs that was now her bedroom, taking her pills regularly. She used the settee with her feet up in the drawing-room in the evenings, instead of an armchair, and looked very delicate and quite exquisitely helpless.

She was not of course in the least helpless. She was strong-willed enough for implacable self-discipline, remembering the terror of that choking darkness; and from now on she would deal with her weak heart as she dealt with her family, as something to be humoured but never allowed to get out of hand.

Stephen Harmon had looked in several times, bringing Nell home in the evenings, never staying for long, but each time managing to get in a word of praise for Nell's business acumen, so that her grandmother was finally being edged into a grudging pride.

She was always pleased when Nell was admired, and if a man like Stephen Harmon enthused over efficiency it couldn't be utterly unfeminine. He seemed to approve of it, although Elizabeth Attlesey had spent a lifetime pretending to be sweet and simple and getting her way by wiles.

'I saw Mrs. Greer today,' she announced, on the Friday evening of the week of Sir Charles's visit. She had been shopping that morning. 'I was in the teashop and she came in. She tells me that Colin is seeing a lot of Dorothy Murray these days.'

'That's right,' said Nell. Dorothy worked in the stationer's shop that fronted the *Clarion* offices, so Colin had always seen a lot of Dorothy, but in the weeks since Nell declined his grandmother's ring Colin seemed to have taken a block booking on Dorothy's free time. Nell had heard it from a dozen different sources.

She had also heard that Colin bore no malice. He thought she was bedazzled out of the few wits she had by an experienced man. Colin was sorry for her, but would not be around to pick up the pieces.

Nell had seen him, once in the street and once in the library, and both times he had looked at her more in sorrow than anger.

'Dorothy is going to tea on Sunday,' said her grandmother.

'Lovely,' said Nell, 'and Mrs. Greer can make a trifle.' In the cut-glass bowl in the middle of the table. Just as it had been all those Sundays when Nell had gone to tea, except that Dorothy would be sitting in the chair where Nell used to sit. 'I wonder,' mused Nell, 'if she'll be invited to Benidorm.'

Her grandmother said with slight asperity, 'It didn't take *him* long to find someone else,' and her father grinned,

'Don't sound so disapproving, Mother. What did you want the man to do? Blow his brains out?'

On Sunday morning Nell went to Solomon Slee's cave

with Pedro and Stephen. It was a blustery day, with clouds scudding across the sky, cold enough for Stephen to need a reefer jacket over a thick sweater, and Nell to wear a red, hooded coat.

They went by car until they reached the path through the woods. Then they parked on the grass verge and walked under the fir-trees stirring the damp scent of fallen pine needles. Pedro raced between the trees, drunk with the scent of tangled trails, treeing a squirrel that hurled down a pine cone at him, and taking it amiss that neither Nell nor Stephen stopped to hurl one back.

Beyond the wood they came to a plain and then the hills, and Nell said, 'We're nearly there.'

The highest hill had caves, and the one at the top was where Solomon Slee had made his home for twelve months a hundred years ago. It had a good view. That was all it did have. It was very cramped, and even with ferns and hanging heather screening it it must have been horribly draughty and damp.

Solomon had lived on a smallholding until he announced that the world was due to end and took himself into the hills, coming down most Saturdays to stand in Cheslyn Slade's little square, proclaiming his message. By the time the hour came he had a following of several hundred. But when the hour went and the world continued to spin the followers fell away, and Solomon's explanation that he was only out by a few months appeased none of them. He came down himself eventually, when the second date failed him too.

'But here they stood,' said Nell. 'On the top of this hill, waiting for the world to end. And the odd thing is that when it didn't they were mad with poor old Solomon. Not one of them seemed grateful to be still alive.'

There were no crowds now. There was no one but herself and Stephen Harmon, and a shadow panting in the shadows that was Pedro.

Stephen smiled, 'They felt cheated. They must have expected quite a show.'

'Well, it wasn't Solomon's fault. Anyone can get a date wrong.'

'Twice?'

'So he wasn't so good on his calculations. Perhaps he'd

got the century wrong. If he did the end could be due any time.'

'The way the world's going it could.'

She pointed out landmarks – you could see three counties from here – then they left Solomon's cave and walked down the hillside. As always Pedro rushed ahead, this time chasing a bird. Without wings he stood no chance of catching it, but the speed he produced could have been a preliminary to take-off. It was a scorching rate. The rest by the cave had restored him and he went at full stretch, oblivious of anything but the bird, already over the wood and vanishing fast.

'If he catches that bird,' said Stephen, 'what shall you do with it?'

Just before the trees Pedro crashed into a patch of waist-high ferns. They didn't deter him more than a few seconds. He lowered his head and charged on. Nell said, 'Should I tell him it's got away? He's going to be very disappointed when he comes out of the rough.'

Pedro howled and the howl faded. One moment his gleaming black body was clearly visible, the next he had gone. Nell gasped, 'No! Oh, please – *no*!'

She began to run, stumbling in her haste, calling the dog's name in rising panic. Stephen kept pace and reaching the ferns caught her arm. 'Nell! Wait!'

'He's fallen. It's the pits, old shafts, and where the pits have pulled. It can happen. It's subsidence. You've seen the notices – Beware of Subsidence.' She tried to drag her arm away, but he still held her.

'I've seen them.'

'It can happen.' It was a rare occurrence but always a danger. Moors that were undermined by subterranean miles must be perilous. You walked with care. Areas of special risk were specially marked, but fresh flaws in the earth's crust could always develop. She croaked, 'We've got to get him out.' She wouldn't let herself remember that they said some shafts were bottomless. It couldn't be true.

Stephen said, 'Stay here,' but she followed him between the ferns until they reached the fault, a gaping black hole. The ground seemed firm where they stood and Nell called, 'Pedro!' going down on her knees and peering into the gloom.

She heard him whimper and she almost wept with relief. 'He's all right. He's alive. He sounds more frightened than hurt, doesn't he?' She began to drag off her coat.

'What do you think you're doing?'

'I've got to get him up. It can't be far down, I can hear him.'

'You don't know that he's on the bottom. Anyone dropping into that without seeing where they're going could be dropping off a cliff.'

'Have you got a light?'

'No.'

'Then someone's got to drop without seeing, haven't they?' He dug into his pocket. 'Car keys. There's a rope in the boot and a torch in the glove compartment. Fetch them.'

'You go.'

'And leave you here?'

'I'd promise—'

'And break your promise the moment I was out of sight.' Pedro's howl came up like a banshee. He wasn't far down, and if he was on a ledge she could have crouched beside him and held him until Stephen got back. He said, 'You're wasting time,' and she snatched the keys and ran.

She ran sobbing and praying. She had lived with those 'Beware of Subsidence' notices all her life. She had seen buildings pulled crazy by the pits, the earth faults here and there, but she had never seen this happen, a living thing vanish into the ground.

Pedro was near human, loving and loony. Suppose before she got back there was one more whimper and Stephen would tell her, 'I'm sorry, but he was on a ledge, he slipped.'

If that happened she would say, 'Damn you and your cold-bloodedness! If you'd let me go down, if you'd gone down yourself, we'd have got him out. You wouldn't take a chance for a dog, would you? Nor for anybody. Not you. Not *you* . . .'

She got the torch and she got the rope, and she ran until she fell sprawling, nearly wrenching her ankle on a trailing root. That made her more careful, a little slower and surer coming through the trees.

Once out of the wood she could see Stephen, but she daren't call, the sound of her voice might reach Pedro and panic him. Stephen came to meet her. 'He's all right. Give me the rope. If it reaches from a tree all the better, if not I'll have to hold it and you'll have to go down.'

He fastened it around the pine nearest the hole, as Nell ran to the seam and looked by the light of the torch.

She said, very distinctly in a voice unlike her own, 'Pedro, good dog, good old boy, all right now.' She wasn't breathing, the beam shook and Pedro went on whimpering. She whispered, 'Stephen, look . . . .'

He knelt beside her, putting a hand over hers to steady the torch. He said, 'If there's a patron saint for four-legged imbeciles he's working overtime this morning.'

Pedro was about six feet down, on a ledge hardly wide enough for his huddled form. Below him the seam widened and the beam hit the shining blackness of mud or dark water.

Nell said, 'St. Francis,' with chattering teeth.

Stephen fastened the rope around his waist. 'Then ask St. Francis to stay with us a few minutes longer.'

She couldn't smile. She said lunatically, 'Be careful,' and held the torch in both hands and forced it into steadiness.

'With respect to St. Francis,' said Stephen, 'why the hell couldn't you have had a poodle?'

Pedro was a big dog, all bone and muscle. Nobody was going to bring Pedro up under one arm. Stephen lowered himself hand below hand, on the rope, until he reached the ledge. He called up, 'There's no spare over, so I'm going to fasten the rope round him. I can keep on the ledge until you lower it again. Can you pull him up?'

She screamed, '*No!*'

'You can't?'

'You can't take the rope off. You could fall.'

'I can get a finger grip.'

She babbled, 'Please don't. Please, Stephen, don't. I tell you what. We can't get Pedro up yet, I can see that, so you come up and one of us will stay and one will go for help. You. Because of the car. I swear I won't try to go down. I can see I couldn't. We need some more rope, and someone else to help pull.'

She daren't look. She closed her eyes as she pleaded and he said, 'Try it now. I'll shove him as far as I can.'

She dropped the torch beside her, and took the rope in both hands. She shouted, 'Don't try to help me. Just hold on. I'll get him up.'

She gritted her teeth and hauled, walking backwards, digging her heels into the ground, throwing all her weight on the rope, terrified by the prospect of a swinging, panicking Pedro sweeping Stephen from his foothold.

Even when Pedro's great black head came above ground she couldn't grab, she had to go on pulling until she landed him like a floundering fish, and then she ran back yelling, 'Stephen?'

'Chuck the rope down,' he called.

'I'll chuck him down.' She worked feverishly to get the rope off the dog. The knot was hard and tight and Pedro was rubbed raw beneath it, but either from exhaustion or because he sensed Nell would go berserk at resistance he lay still, growling but showing no teeth, although she must have been hurting him.

She threw down the rope and picked up the torch to hold the beam on it. As Stephen reached the top he said, 'Get away from the edge, it could crumble. We'd better notify the authorities right away.'

She stretched towards him, gripping his sweater, yanking frantically, and he said, 'For God's sake, woman, will you do just one thing you're told? Get back, will you?'

Anyhow, he was out, dragging her from the edge, which still seemed firm enough. She was shaking like a leaf. It was over. He was out, safe, and her eyes burned and tears ran silent and scalding down her cheeks.

He put an arm around her as though she was a frightened child. 'Easy there, we made it. It's all right now.'

'I know,' she said, 'I do know,' teeth biting her lip into whiteness. 'I promise I'm not going to have hysterics on you, I was just so scared you'd fall. It's water down there.'

'I wasn't likely to fall. I did pot-holing and mountaineering in my student days, there was no danger.'

That was utter lies, and she would say so when she was over the reaction of relief. Nell was not given to tears. She blinked hard, and he said gently, 'Don't cry, Nell. Nothing's worth that. Nothing and no one.'

'You are so wrong.'

'I could be. It wouldn't be the first time.'

She must have used all her strength, lugging out Pedro. Now suddenly her bones seemed to be melting and her heart was thumping so loudly that Stephen must hear it. She was still in his arms and he was looking at her with an expression of puzzled tenderness.

Then he smiled, 'If this had happened a hundred years ago they'd have been sure it was the beginning of the end.'

'What?'

'Solomon Slee.'

'Oh – you mean the ground opening?' She looked back over her shoulder. Pedro was limping towards them. She said, 'It darn nearly was.'

'Who carries him home?' asked Stephen.

Luckily Pedro was more winded than wounded, although he snarled slightly as Stephen bent over him to check.

Nell leaned against the nearest pine tree, watching. She was feeling stronger herself. When Stephen Harmon was no longer holding her the stiffening came back into her spine. It hadn't been exhaustion, it had been his arms around her that had turned her to putty.

And he hadn't been unaffected. She was sure that for a moment he had been undecided whether to smile and say something light and impersonal, or draw her hard against him. She said, as he petted Pedro, 'I'd better stay here, hadn't I?'

Someone might come this way and walk through the ferns: hikers, children playing on the hills.

'You'll be all right?' he asked.

'Of course I'm all right. I was never at risk.'

He straightened, unsmiling. His eyes met hers and held them steadily. Then he said, 'That could be debatable.'

From that first morning, when she had rushed into Mr. Elsgood's office and found herself meeting those cool eyes with a turmoil of inexplicable shock, Stephen Harmon had disrupted Nell's life so that nothing had ever been the same again.

She wondered if she had known then on some deep level that this was the man she wanted. She knew now, and that for all his memories he had a tenderness for her that might grow, that must grow. She said, 'Should we debate it?'

'Some time I think we should.'

'Some time, then,' she said. 'Sit, Pedro.' Pedro was flat out, so that command was unnecessary.

Stephen said, 'Keep that dog where he is, tie him to a tree. And don't you go near the subsidence. Don't walk around at all, stay right here.'

'Yes, sir.'

'I don't want to lose a good secretary.'

Joy sparkled in her like the bubbles in champagne. 'I don't intend that you should,' she said.

By the time Nell and Pedro were delivered back to Quarry House it was well into the afternoon. She had thought Stephen might stay if only to avoid the trouble of preparing a meal for himself. Saving Pedro from subsidence had been time and energy-consuming. But he didn't. He would see her tomorrow, he said.

The rest of the day she spent quietly, like any other Sunday when she stayed home. She washed her hair. She baked a cake. She had a long phone call from an old school friend, married now and running a village store in Oxfordshire with her husband.

They kept in touch, but it was some months since their last chat and Roz started off, 'How's Colin?'

'Healthy as ever,' said Nell, 'but that's water under the bridge.'

'Oh? Who's new?'

'There's no one in particular.'

There was Stephen. This day was like no other because there was Stephen, and she was closer to him today than yesterday and tomorrow was coming. She slept with dreams, anticipating.

At nine o'clock precisely next morning the phone rang on Stephen's desk and Mrs. Storey said, 'Nell? The *Clarion* want to speak to Mr. Harmon.'

'He isn't in yet. What do they want?'

'Hang on,' said Mrs. Storey, and sixty seconds later as though this probably made more sense to Nell than it did to her, 'It's about the subsidence on the hills and the dog he rescued.'

'We'll call them back,' said Nell.

The phone clicked while Mrs. Storey dealt with that, then buzzed again, and Mrs. Storey asked, 'What subsidence, and what dog?'

Nell had come straight into the office from the cloakroom this morning, and now she gave an account of what had happened yesterday morning, belatedly playing it down. Stephen, she knew, would not want to talk to the press nor to anyone else about the dog he had rescued.

Nell had talked at home, and that meant that Ocky had gone home and told his family, and Flo had been out for the evening visiting a W.I. crony, and Nell's grandmother made on average two telephone calls every day. Yesterday, with news to tell, it could have reached double figures.

At the time it hadn't seemed to Nell to matter. It was true, Pedro would have gone for ever if Stephen hadn't saved him. But now she wished she had kept the drama to herself, or limited it to her father.

The *Clarion* came out weekly, filled with weddings and funerals, Council business, and any human interest stories they could find. Subsidence dangerous enough to get itself floodlights and a police patrol was bound to rate photographs; and an account of local lawyer rescuing local dog would be sure fire.

When Stephen came in at five minutes past nine Nell was just putting down the phone from talking to Mrs. Storey. She had her hand on the receiver and an apprehensive expression, and he asked, 'Trouble?'

'Well – the *Clarion* rang. About yesterday.'

'What about yesterday? It's the Ministry of Works they want. Or the Forestry Commission.'

'They want to know about you getting Pedro out.'

He swore softly. 'Did you tell Greer?'

She said indignantly, 'Of course I didn't! I don't even know if it was Colin who rang, Mrs. Storey took the call. But I did tell Flo and my grandmother and Ocky, and that's how it got round, I'm afraid. I'm sorry. What do we do now?'

'Do what you like, but don't involve me in any sob

stories.'

'What do I say? I can't deny the whole thing.'

He said briskly, 'If you've already said the animal fell in you can't deny that. Tell them we both pulled him out, and as you're prettier and younger than I am you'll take a better picture.' And that matter was dealt with. 'Now—' He picked up the mail. Now to work. He was out this morning, and they went through the correspondence, and a couple of other things Nell would be handling before lunch.

Then he made three phone calls, called in Norman Rowe and discussed a family court hearing today where Rowe was standing in with the parents of a fourteen-year-old accused of driving away a car, and finally picked up his briefcase and said, 'I should be back around one.'

Nell nodded. He grinned suddenly, 'If Greer calls for an interview don't overdo the melodrama, and don't go off to lunch with him.'

'Not on your life,' she said gravely. 'On either count.' The magnetic pull of attraction was so strong that she swayed very slightly towards him as he came across the room to where she sat. He put a hand on her shoulder.

'If I'm late, wait for me.'

That could have been said any time in the past weeks, but this was the first touch that was nearly a caress. She stared down at the typewriter keys after he had gone and thought – the memories start here.

Then she went on with her typing. She made three mistakes in the next line and had to scrap the letter and type it again, but once started she carried on and there was plenty of work to fill the morning, no time to wonder if the good memories had started for Stephen Harmon too.

Mrs. Martin was making another will. Mr. Elsgood had taken her instructions for the last on his last day here. Stephen Harmon had left it to Nell. Nell could cope, of course; all Mr. Elsgood had provided was a sympathetic ear for her complaints against her family. But she wasn't likely to confide in Nell and she took her seat grim-faced. Nell did her best to cheer, inquiring about Mrs. Martin's health – she looked and was robust – offering a cup of coffee, which Stephen Harmon would certainly not have done, but after announcing that she took three spoons of sugar Mrs. Martin did unbend a little.

She changed the names around again in her will, asked after Nell's grandmother, shook her head gloomily at Nell's good report, and wondered if Mrs. Attlesey had made a will.

'I don't know,' said Nell.

'We should all be prepared,' said Mrs. Martin. She drained her coffee cup and stood up. 'I can see myself out.'

She should know the way, she'd been here often enough, but Nell went with her to the door at the top of the stairs, and wished her 'Good morning' there.

As Nell turned back Joan, who had been looking through the 'Inquiries' shutter, shot out of the office and headed for the cloakroom, beckoning Nell to follow her.

Nell did, completely at sea. Joan shut the door and hissed, 'There's a Miss Conway to see Mr. Harmon.'

'Is there?' Nell didn't know Miss Conway, but anyone could see Mr. Harmon who came along and asked, so what was so momentous about this?

'You should see her!' Joan sounded breathless. 'She's fantastic!'

'Who is she?'

Joan looked guilty, as though she was sorry about this but couldn't help finding it exciting. 'She's a friend. She says.'

Joan believed there was a rival here, and possibly there was, and no ordinary competition either from the sound of it. But Stephen wasn't expecting Miss Conway, and he wasn't needing her. He was having lunch with Nell because he wanted to have lunch with Nell, and tonight or tomorrow he would hold Nell in his arms again, and when he kissed her this time the world would stop.

So let's see what we're up against, she thought.

Joan was getting the information out fast now. Miss Conway had arrived ten minutes ago, and said she recognized them all from what she had heard about them, naming them, so it seemed that she did. At the moment she was talking to Norman Rowe, who had never seen anything like her before, and was stuttering like a machine gun.

Nell tried to laugh, 'What *is* she? Sophia Loren's understudy?'

'If her hair wasn't red,' said Joan, 'she could be.'

This one didn't need to be anyone's understudy. She was there in her own right, up among the mind-blowers, the most breathtakingly beautiful girl Nell had ever seen. She was tall, slender, swan-necked, with a mane of flame-red hair, and a face of such matt perfection that Nell felt as though the freckles on her own nose were conspicuous and ugly as warts.

When Joan opened the door of Stephen's office and announced, 'Miss Conway for Mr. Harmon,' making it sound like a dirge, Nell managed to smile, but her heart was lead and she tasted ashes.

This was no casual acquaintance. This was the girl of Stephen Harmon's memories. She had a close and potent claim, and she stepped into that room as though she could own it.

Nell said, 'Good morning. I'm expecting Mr. Harmon back any time. Won't you sit down?'

Miss Conway looked her up and down, missing nothing, and not reckoning much on what she saw. 'So this is our Miss Attlesey.' Her voice had a seductive huskiness. 'And I've heard such a lot about you.'

From the Tylers, or Sir Charles? Or had she heard about Nell from Stephen? Miss Conway was laughing, so what she had heard had been amusing.

She took Stephen's chair behind the desk, and leaned back and looked around, blowing softly between pursed lips as though this passed credence.

Nell remembered Carole Tyler saying, 'You should have seen Stephen's last office.' Looking around his present one Miss Conway couldn't believe her eyes. If she got up and read the titles of the books in the glass-fronted bookshelves she might well have hysterics. The Waverley Novels for Stephen Harmon!

Nell said, 'Mr. Harmon shouldn't be long.'

'Mr. Harmon?' Miss Conway's eyes were amber, the whites blue-white, with a thick fringe of smoky lashes, and gold shimmering on the brow bones. She opened her eyes wide, and stared at Nell. 'But surely it's Stephen by now?'

Those lashes had to be false. No one grew lashes that

long. If Nell was going to stay cool she had to stay detached. She said, 'Excuse me,' and put a sheet of paper into her typewriter and opened her notebook.

'Not Stephen in the office, perhaps,' continued Miss Conway, 'but you think of him as Stephen, don't you? I mean, you *are* in love with him.'

'Now why should you think that?' Nell asked pleasantly, as soon as she managed to unstick her tongue from the roof of her mouth.

Miss Conway said, 'Come off it, honey-chile. After the two I met out there working with Stephen must be delirious for you!' She got up and went over to the Cries of Old London. 'Cherries,' she carolled. 'Ripe and red cherries. Knives to grind, bring out your knives to grind. I suppose it could all be Freudian.' She looked back at Nell. 'And would you have a drink around?'

'I'll make some coffee.'

'A jokey girl!' Miss Conway gave her husky laugh. 'I need something stronger than coffee, honey-chile.'

Nell opened the cupboard that contained a bottle of sherry and a bottle of whisky. Mr. Elsgood had occasionally raised glasses with a client, but the only time hospitality had been dispensed here since Stephen Harmon took over was when he'd kept Sir Charles waiting.

Miss Conway reached past Nell for a glass and the whisky bottle, and poured herself a stiff measure. 'This I need. I heard it had to be seen to be believed, but I still don't believe it. Though I must say I adore his little team.'

'How nice of you to say so,' said Nell. 'If you should want water with it there's a tap through the first door on the left.'

Miss Conway raised the glass, her eyes were the colour of the liquid. 'Good luck.'

'Thank you,' said Nell, and began to type.

Miss Conway drank a little, then went back to her chair and drank a little more. 'What does Stephen do around here when the shop shuts?'

'He works most evenings.'

'And you work with him?'

'Sometimes.' Nell typed on, making more clatter than was necessary.

'That's very good,' Miss Conway applauded. 'Up to even Stephen's standards, I should say. Poor Miss Attlesey, it's horrid to think you've been wasting your time.'

'Oh, I wouldn't say that,' said Nell. These amendments to Mrs. Martin's will were looking like code. But she pounded away, ignoring errors, as though she was producing work of impeccable quality. The typewriter would have to jam before she would let Miss Conway see that she was falling to pieces.

CHAPTER EIGHT

As soon as Stephen comes through that door, Nell promised herself, you can get up and get out. She couldn't watch when he saw Miss Conway waiting for him, because she might see something in his eyes that could break her heart. But until he came she must stay.

Stephen's desk was clear of clutter. The out-tray had been emptied and the papers due for the in-tray were still on Nell's desk. There was an ashtray, which he didn't use; a Victorian pen-and-ink stand with empty glass inkwells and a couple of ballpoint pens; a notebook by the phone and the desk diary of appointments.

Miss Conway picked up a ballpoint and doodled for a few minutes on the notepad. Then she reached for the desk diary and Nell said, 'I'm sorry, but I'm afraid that's confidential. Would you care for a newspaper?'

'I'd love one,' drawled Miss Conway. 'How kind.'

Nell opened the bottom drawer of the desk into which Stephen Harmon usually dropped his morning paper. There would be others, providing lighter reading in the other offices, but she was reluctant to leave Miss Conway here alone. Goodness knows why.

Miss Conway spread out the newspaper, and Nell typed and she read for another couple of minutes, until the tap on the door.

'Come in,' called Nell.

Mrs. Storey had a nervous smile for Miss Conway before telling Nell, 'The *Clarion* are here. You didn't phone them?'

'No.' Nell had been putting off the interview, although she knew it was to come. 'Would you send them along, please?' Even if the reporter turned out to be Colin it would be less of a strain than sitting here, waiting for Miss Conway's next barb.

'Colin Greer,' said Mrs. Storey quietly. Nell gave the smallest of shrugs. 'I'll tell them,' said Mrs. Storey.

Miss Conway asked sweetly, 'Is this confidential? Shall I

wait for Stephen in the corridor?'

'It isn't a client,' said Nell, although she wished she could have sent Miss Conway along with Mrs. Storey.

Harry Irving, a youngish man with receding hair and a fair moustache, one of the *Clarion's* two photographers, arrived with Colin. The first person they saw when they walked into the office was Miss Conway, behind Stephen Harmon's desk, with her flaming hair and her exquisite face, and both men stood and stared.

She was used to being stared at. Her amber eyes were luminous as she smiled, and Nell felt like shouting 'Oy!' because it seemed unlikely that either man would notice her for some time. But she lacked the courage and meekly made the introductions, 'This is Colin Greer and Harry Irving from our local newspaper. Miss Conway.'

Miss Conway extended a long slim hand, and they both bounded forward to take it. She said, 'Celia Conway, a friend of Stephen's.'

Harry reached her first. Colin had paused to give Nell a look that demanded, 'Didn't I tell you?'

'Are you just visiting our town?' Harry Irving was asking.

'A surprise visit.'

'I'd welcome a surprise like you any day,' said Harry promptly, and was rewarded with Celia Conway's husky laugh,

'Why, thank you.'

'When are you expecting Mr. Harmon?' Colin asked Nell.

'Any time.'

'I was told that twenty minutes ago,' said Celia, gay as a lark. 'He really must be arriving soon.'

He had told Nell to wait for him, not to go off to lunch with Colin. But he hadn't known then that Celia would be waiting. Nell felt desolation wrap her like freezing fog. She said, 'You're here about the subsidence?' and her voice came shrill.

'Ah yes,' Harry Irving reluctantly took his eyes off Celia. 'That's a big hole in the ground out there. We've just been getting some pictures.' He explained for Celia, 'On the moors, it's the old coalmines, the ground falls in every now and then. It did yesterday when Miss Attlesey and Mr. Harmon were out walking.'

Celia's perfect brows arched. 'The ground fell in? This sounds fascinating. What happened then?' She appeared to be waiting with bated breath. Colin produced his notebook, sat on the edge of Stephen's desk and asked,

'What did happen, Nell? Just tell us in your own words.'

Whose words did he think she might be using? She said, 'We must have passed quite near before. It was hidden by high ferns and the dog ran into them.'

'And slipped in?' prompted Colin.

Celia drew breath sharply. 'How ghastly!'

'He landed on a ledge,' said Nell. 'We got him out easily enough. And then I stayed to warn anyone who came that way and Stephen went down to the police station.'

'How did you get Pedro out?' Colin persisted. 'The ledge seems a long way down.'

She said firmly, 'Not the bit Pedro landed on. He almost scrambled out on his own.'

'But I think it's terrifying,' said Celia Conway. 'You could all have been killed. I shall certainly make Stephen promise to keep off those horrible hills.' She spoke as though it was a foregone conclusion that he would do as she asked, and no one doubted it.

Nell asked, 'What's happening up there now?' Harry told her,

'They're closing it by blasting this afternoon, a special team from the N.C.B. We should get another good picture then, and we thought perhaps one of you and the dog?'

Celia gurgled, 'And Stephen?'

Harry sucked in his lips. 'I can't see that being on.' He had seen Stephen Harmon in the courts; he could by no stretch of the imagination visualize him posing for a heart-warming doggy shot.

'How do you know if you don't ask?' Celia's lovely mouth was quivering with laughter, and Nell said,

'You'd be wasting your time, I can tell you that.'

'Can you?' Still smiling Celia turned to Nell. 'You do know a lot about Stephen. It must be all this overtime, and the rambles over the moors.'

Harry produced his camera and began fiddling with gadgets, Colin got up off the edge of Stephen's desk and cleared his throat in some embarrassment. Celia was teasing Nell and probably both men felt sorry for her. Anyone with eyes knew that Nell Attlesey's chances were nil against a girl like Celia Conway.

Harry bustled a little, looking and sounding the enthusiastic professional. 'Yes, well then, I'll take a shot of you here; then perhaps I could call at your home and get one of you and the dog?'

'Do you need two pictures?' Nell asked.

'Local secretary. Action at the typewriter.'

No one could blame Celia for grinning at that. She said, 'Oh, I do think you should get Stephen in action too. He can look very dynamic addressing the bench.'

'I've seen him,' said Harry, who was nobody's fool, 'and I think he'd look pretty dynamic addressing me if I asked him. O.K., Miss Attlesey? Put your hands on the keys, will you, and turn your head this way.'

Stephen walked in. His office seemed very full. He looked at Celia with raised eyebrows and just the right mixture of surprise and welcome. 'Hello, what brings you here?' She could have been a client, and Nell wondered just what it would take to shake Stephen Harmon's control of a situation.

'Guess,' said Celia, with a sweep of her incredible eyelashes and a smile that made nonsense of business relationships. Stephen smiled too, then he turned to Harry and Colin. 'And the gentlemen of the press, what can we do for you?'

Nell said wryly, 'They're about to take an action shot of me at the typewriter.'

'Carry on,' said Stephen.

Harry took a couple of photographs, while Colin and Celia Conway watched, Colin standing stiffly, Celia with elbows on the desk, chin resting on her latticed fingers, and flame red hair spilling over her shoulders.

'You wouldn't – ?' Harry began tentatively.

'No,' said Stephen.

'No,' said Harry, 'of course not. Thank you very much, sir.' There was no sarcasm in that. This was Stephen

Harmon's office and Stephen Harmon's secretary, and Harry Irving had been relieved to find Harmon amenable when he walked in on them. Harry asked now, 'All right if I come round some time this evening, Miss Attlesey, for a picture of the dog?'

Nell met Colin's eyes as she looked up. Colin was not a malicious man, but in spite of himself triumph glowed beneath his skin, and she said brightly, 'Oh yes, the dog should certainly be at home.'

Good-bye then, they said. As he said good-bye to Celia Harry added, 'I should like to take a picture of you, Miss Conway, some time. I have seen pictures of you, haven't I?'

She laughed. 'Did you buy the soap, that's the question?' So she was a model, not a top-line one or Nell would have remembered seeing her, although with that face and figure she surely could be.

'Do you mind?' demanded Harry in feigned indignation. 'Don't I look like a feller?'

The laughter went with them. When the door closed no one was laughing. Nell pretended to be going through the papers on her desk. Stephen said to Celia, 'Would you mind using this chair?' and she came round his desk, and took the client's seat.

As he emptied his briefcase she said, 'First things first still. You always had your priorities right.'

'If I remember,' he said, 'so did you.' Nell got up and took a couple of steps towards the door before Stephen's terse, 'Nell,' halted her.

She turned and his glance indicated the chair she had left. She went back to it. Celia said softly, 'Sit down if you must, you could learn things.'

'Couldn't we all?' said Stephen. 'What do you want?'

'A good lawyer, maybe.' She sounded as if she was smiling, Nell couldn't look. 'Or maybe a good man.'

'A good lawyer, perhaps,' said Stephen, 'but you've come to the wrong address for a good man.'

Nell wasn't there. She was non-existent, a shadow, a gnat. These two were alone. Celia's voice took on a tenderness. 'I've missed you, Stephen.'

'I'm surprised to hear it.'

'Are you? I've had a few surprises myself today. Like you in the backwoods here, getting press coverage because a dog fell down a rabbit hole. That bunch out there: the one who stammers, *he's* your assistant? and how about Whistler's Mother in the lilac twin set?'

Stephen said drily, 'I'm glad you were entertained, but the show's over and we do have work to do.'

'You can't be that busy, darling, and please tell Little Nell to go away.'

Stephen got up. 'It's been a pleasure to see you, Celia, it's always a pleasure to see you, but not in office hours.'

'I'll wait.'

'Not here.' He lifted her to her feet, and she stood close, holding the lapels of his coat, smiling up at him.

'Of course not here.' She was a tall girl, she only had to tilt her head back a little way. 'So give me the key of your flat. I still have the old one around, but I suppose it's a different lock.'

Nell got out. This time Stephen didn't call her name. She went into the cloakroom and stared at herself in the speckled mirror in utter helplessness.

How many light years was she from being able to say 'Give me the key' and knowing Stephen would smile at her? The memories might have been bitter, but everything about that girl was exciting. She had an aura of glamour as though she came from another planet.

'What does Stephen do here when the shop shuts?' she'd asked. He works. He walks over the hills. Oh, there's never a dull moment. We have a ball out here in the backwoods.

Celia Conway had found it all screamingly funny. She had been laughing herself sick ever since she arrived. Nell felt sick. She had a pain in her chest that hurt when she breathed, and when she held her breath. She wanted to go home. It was lunch time, she could go home for an hour. Except that her father would see something was wrong and he mustn't know. Not until she had a little hold on herself and didn't start crying like a child.

There was nowhere she could go for a while. Certainly not into any of the offices, and if she left the building Colin could be waiting. He had wanted to say 'I told you so' so badly that it would be a charity to let him. His little triumph

151

would come, she couldn't dodge him for ever, but not yet.

She shut her eyes, but she could still see Stephen giving Celia Conway the key to the flat, and she felt as bereft as though both her man and her home had been taken from her. Neither had ever belonged to her, but she was as lost as though, until this hour, she had had them all her life.

Mrs. Storey came in, saying as she opened the door, 'I thought you hadn't gone past. Mr. Harmon wants you.'

Nell gulped. 'Where is he?'

'In his office. He rang through to see if you were in ours.'

Nell breathed deep. 'Is Miss Conway—'

'Gone,' said Mrs. Storey, with complete grasp of the situation. They had either had the Inquiries hatch up or the door ajar, keeping an eye open for departures. Nell thought wildly – I'll bet Joan's postponed her lunch hour today.

She went back into the office. Stephen was at her desk, going through the papers. If he had read the gibberish in the typewriter he didn't remark on it. He said irritably, 'Where the hell have you been?'

'To the cloakroom.'

'What's this about?' It was about a phone call connected with a case. He nodded as she talked, then he asked, 'What did you tell the *Clarion*?'

'That Pedro fell in and got himself out.'

'Good. Come on.'

'Where?'

'It's lunch time.'

'I know, but—'

'But what?'

'Miss Conway.'

'Are you eating or aren't you?'

'Yes.'

They went to the Raven. They sat at the table they usually sat at and talked about work. How Stephen Harmon's morning had gone, how Nell's had, stopping short at the moment in time when Celia Conway had made an entrance. Nell lasted until half way through her sweet course, an uninspired Peach Melba. By then she had reached the end of small talk, and said without preamble, 'She's very beautiful.'

'Very,' Stephen agreed.

'Is she staying around?'

'I didn't give her the key to the flat, if that's what you mean. It might not have been good for the firm's image.' He was laughing at her, and she asked,

'How about the image for your last firm?'

'We catered for a sophisticated clientele.'

She tried to sound blasée. 'Did you live together?'

'She has a very attractive flat of her own.'

That was no answer. In court Stephen would never have let that slip past. Celia at least was giving the impression that they had had an affair, and the attraction between them was still there. All the same he had been surprised to find her here today in his office. Nell asked, 'Is this the first time you've seen her since you came here?'

'Yes.'

'Why?'

'Because I'm not in Celia's orbit any more. Have you finished?' He meant the meal. He'd finished the questions, he was answering no more. She looked at the melting ice cream and the raspberry jam, and put down her spoon. 'Yes,' she said, 'I'm through.'

All afternoon in the office Stephen handled everything with complete competence, and no sign of strain. He seemed as relaxed as ever, but Nell was a tumult of hope and fear, telling herself – They may have phoned and written, but they haven't met for more than three months. The weekends and nights he was away from here he wasn't with Celia. He came to the Raven at lunchtime and wherever she went it wasn't to the flat. There must be so much competition for a girl like that and Stephen isn't competing, he said he wasn't.

But then she would remember their first date, when Stephen had looked at her across the table and seen Celia It was Celia he had wanted sitting there. It was Celia he wanted. 'I've missed you,' Celia had said. He was out of her orbit here, but suppose she said, 'I've been so alone without you'?

Where was she now? Nell wondered. Would they meet tonight? If they did, even if they said good-bye again, Stephen would have his memories of Celia brightened and quickened.

153

Nell took each task that afternoon as it came, step by step, or she would have made chaos of everything. Each minute that wasn't filled the hopes and the fears darted at her. It was a long afternoon, but she dreaded it ending when she would say, 'Good night, then,' and he would say, 'Good night, see you in the morning.'

Just after half-five when he finished dictating a brief he said, 'You can type that out tomorrow. Are you doing anything this evening?'

'No.'

'Would you do some work for me?'

'Yes. Will you fetch me?' From home, about half past seven. That was what he usually did, and this time Nell could have set it to music.

He said, 'Of course,' and she thought – there's no of course about it. The thing that seemed inevitable tonight was that you would be with Celia. I don't know why you're not, but I'll do the secretarial chores, and eat my supper, and pretend that Celia never came.

She phoned the *Clarion* when she got home and spoke to Harry Irving. 'I won't be home this evening, but if you do want a photograph of my dog I could drop one into your office in the morning.'

'Thanks,' he said. 'Just got back from the blasting. The subsidence went right down into an old shaft. Your dog was lucky.'

'He was lucky,' Nell agreed.

She told the family that the *Clarion* had called for the story. Flo and her grandmother were intrigued at the prospect of Pedro in the paper and promised to go through drawers and cupboards for snaps of him. There were plenty about. He was usually at the fore of activity, from garden shots of Ocky's prize blooms to Nell's twenty-first birthday party.

She told her father about Celia. It would already be in the gossip grapevine. She told him because she told him most things and because he had the gift of keeping life in proportion.

She went into the workroom and said, 'We had a very glamorous visitor today – a model, a friend of Stephen's.'

'More glamorous than Mrs. Tyler?' Nell had described

154

the Tylers and Sir Charles in detail as she met them. She said now,

'She was a knock-out. She took your breath away.'

'He certainly mixed with the beautiful people.' John Attlesey went on with his work, tapping a chisel with a light sure touch, each tap moving it by the merest fraction.

'This one had been special,' said Nell. Her father looked up at her and her reaction was reassurance, 'And a right so-and-so under the skin. She made no bones that she felt she'd come slumming.'

He smiled with her. 'I'm working tonight,' she said. 'Stephen's collecting me.'

'I'm working too,' said her father. 'Don't get upstage about it.' She had sounded smug and he knew why. She said,

'And tea's up.' He sat for a moment, looking at her, still smiling. Then he said,

'You get your looks from your mother. It's a mercy you don't get them from me.'

'Oh, it is,' she said gaily. 'Especially the beard.' She had always known that she was his cherished daughter, but she had never realized before that he saw her as beautiful.

She was not. Her mother had been, unless the photographs lied, but not Nell. And yet John Attlesey, who had such clear sane vision in everything else, saw her as beautiful and the equal of any girl alive.

She thought – you are so biased, my dear one; and loved him for it, and wished she could see herself in the same rosy light.

Stephen collected her and took her to the flat. As usual Nell sat at the desk with the typewriter and Stephen sometimes sat, sometimes walked around dictating to her. Then, while she got the papers into order, he went into the kitchen and switched on the percolator.

As she straightened her back from completing her task she asked, 'What would you do with your evenings if you weren't still working for the old firm?'

'Lord knows. Take up booze or billiards.'

'There isn't much else to do out here in the backwoods,' she said.

She heard him laugh. 'How about potholing?'

'Not after this afternoon. They blew it up and filled it in.'

'That can't have improved the scenery.'

'It'll grow over. There'll be a valley instead of a plain beneath Solomon Slee's cave, but the grass and the gorse and the heather will grow. Our house once stood in a sand quarry.'

Someone knocked the door knocker. Stephen came from the kitchen and asked, 'Are you expecting anyone?'

'No.'

'That narrows the field.' He went to the door and the knocker that was clattering again.

Celia's husky voice was unmistakable. 'Surprise? Oh, don't say you weren't expecting me this time.'

Nell turned in her chair as Celia came in, and Celia waved airily towards her. 'Hello, little Nell, still working late?'

She didn't seem to expect an answer. Immediately she gave the room all her attention, smiling as the Tylers had done. 'Well, this is more like old times. I see you brought the nicest pieces.'

'Of course,' said Stephen.

She drifted around, looking, touching: chairs, bureau, desk; her glance sliding over Nell as though she was in a different time dimension. Almost everything here Celia had known in another setting, every piece had memories she shared with Stephen, and she was so right among them. This was her background, the beautiful best of its kind.

She's come home, thought Nell, as she stood at the window by the Hepplewhite table. It was easy to imagine her sitting there, in candlelight, her slender fingers playing with the stem of a wineglass. It was not Nell's table, and it was ridiculous to feel jealousy for a table, but Nell was blotting from her own mind a picture of Stephen sitting beside Celia, taking her hand and drawing her towards him.

'This is new.' Celia paused beneath the carved panel of the tree. That at least was Nell's. She had brought it, her father had carved it. 'My icon!' cried Celia, and turned from the carved panel so quickly that her hair swung back as she moved to where the icon hung, crooning with delight. 'How lovely to see it again!'

Celia . . . St. Cecilia of the flame hair and the amber eyes . . . 'Some kinds of music I like,' Stephen had said, 'but that wasn't why I bought the icon.' He'd bought it because of Celia, and he was protective and possessive of it. 'Don't touch it!' the command in his voice had stopped Colin dead. Five minutes later Colin had practically marched Nell away, and Stephen hadn't cared about that, but Celia's icon must not be haphazardly handled.

Now Stephen put a brandy glass on the desk beside Nell and asked, 'Would you mind seeing to the coffee?'

'But of course.' Of course she would go into the kitchen if she was no longer required at the typewriter. Coffee should be served; Celia might care for coffee.

Nell took her brandy with her and closed the door after her – if she hadn't someone would have done. The percolator was glugging and there was food in the fridge and the cupboards. Was she expected to serve supper for three or supper for two? Or would Celia prefer to get her own?

It was a large brandy and she drank half in burning gulps, for medicinal purposes. She needed an anaesthetic. Then she sat down and watched the dark brown liquid in jerky fountain through the heat-resistant glass of the coffee pot lid.

It was several minutes before Stephen came in to ask, 'Is it ready?'

'And waiting.' She put the pot and another cup and saucer on the tray which he carried into the living-room.

Celia was sitting under the icon. The chair was comfortable, but so were others, and she had probably chosen that one by design, Nell decided. She looked devastating, her slim legs curled beneath her, over her head on the white wall the jewelled colours of the icon reflecting and emphasizing her colouring.

Celia poured the coffee, and Nell said, 'Black, please,' although she usually preferred white, and having handed her a cup Celia proceeded to ignore her once more, talking only to Stephen.

He made no attempt either to draw Nell into the conversation. He asked Celia about her work. She dismissed it as 'a bit of a bore of late', but even her grimace was beautiful. She wanted to hear what Stephen was doing, she gave him messages from old friends and recalled places he knew.

It was like the talk when the Tylers came to dinner, except that all of it was shot with deeper meaning. It was what was not said that mattered, the memories that glowed in Celia's eyes and that kept Stephen's eyes hooded, so that it wasn't like the Tylers at all.

Nell was thinking – I'll have to say good night, I can't pretend to be deaf and dumb much longer, when to her surprise Celia said, 'I'd better be on my way,' and uncoiled herself in a single fluid movement like a ballet dancer. 'You'll look into that little matter for me, won't you?' she asked Stephen.

'Of course.'

'I still can't see you staying here.' She looked directly at him and shook her head, then she turned to give Nell a mocking little smile. 'Goodbye, little Nell. Watch that Stephen doesn't gobble you up, I wonder he hasn't before now.' And she went through the front door and Stephen went with her.

Nell drank the rest of her brandy. When Stephen came back she said, 'Miss Conway goes beautifully with the icon.' He sat down again in his chair. 'And with all the furniture,' said Nell, feeling muzzy and miserable. 'In fact it could be said that Miss Conway completes the collection.'

'That's a perceptive way of putting it,' he said drily. 'She is rather a collector's piece, but a little too pricey for me these days.'

'I'm sorry.' It had been the brandy talking. 'I'm not used to great slugs of this stuff. Please may I have some more coffee?'

He poured her black coffee. 'Don't be sorry, this is comedy stuff. Get that down.' He looked around, his gaze staying with the icon. 'As you say, she goes well with it, but not so well with the rest of the set-up.' He smiled without humour. 'Could you see her as the wife of a small-town lawyer?'

'No.' Nell drank her coffee slowly, but she was cold sober.

'Neither could she.' He looked as calm as though he had been asked for a legal opinion on a technical point. He held his glass and his hands were steady. 'When I had to come down here we called the wedding off. Celia's always been used to the best.' His smile was ironic. 'She saw no reason for changing her life-style because I had to change mine.'

Then why hadn't she stayed away? Nell admitted grudgingly, 'She did come looking for you.'

'She's amusing herself.' He seemed cynically amused himself. 'I'm no longer husband material, but we could still be good friends.'

She bit on her lip as she asked, 'Would you accept that?'

'I very much doubt it.' He put down the brandy glass on a table beside his chair. Nell noticed that he had drunk none. She said softly,

'And then of course she doesn't believe you're staying here as a small-town lawyer.'

'So she said.'

'Neither do I.'

He leaned back in his chair, looking at her speculatively. 'Why not?'

She went through the evidence for the argument. When she finished he said, 'You've made your point. I don't intend to stay in Cheslyn Slade indefinitely. But for obvious reasons this is in confidence.'

The business reasons were obvious, and this was almost a joke although Nell didn't feel like laughing. He didn't need to tell her it was in confidence. She was not likely to spread the news that it might be worth Celia's while to wait and see, because Stephen Harmon could still be heading for the heights.

She said, 'I understand,' and thought it wasn't fair, none of it was fair. Celia Conway was bored and so she had decided to look Stephen up again. She must have trampled his pride in dust and that would take some forgetting, but – oh, she was beautiful and she had come looking for him and for all his cynical detachment he had once asked Celia to marry him, he had wanted Celia for ever.

Right now he didn't like her much. Nell thought – you like me, I'm glad I'm the one you like, but I wish I knew how to make you start wanting me.

With Stephen she wouldn't know how to start. She sat

stiffly, overwhelmed by the surge of emotion that made her a stranger to herself. Yesterday she had been defenceless in his arms, and if he reached for her now with any word of appeal or need she could fall into his arms again.

But he wouldn't. Not now, and hopelessness brought her to the edge of tears so that she turned her head and put a hand before her eyes.

He asked, 'What's the matter?'

She tried to say, 'Nothing,' sounding stiff and stupid. Heaven knows she was stupid, but how do you compete with a girl who has everything?

Stephen touched her shoulder and she cowered away terrified, not of him, of herself. He said wearily, 'You're not thinking of what Celia said just now, are you — that I'm likely to try seducing you? In the circumstances that would be a piece of moronic arrogance.'

It would, using Nell to blot out the loss of Celia. Even so she ached to run fingertips over the furrows of his brow and the deep hard lines of his mouth. But he needed no solace and she kept her fingers clenched and managed to smile and shake her head. 'It's the black coffee getting to the brandy, making my head swim, nothing personal. And I don't believe what anyone says who calls me Little Nell.'

He agreed, 'It doesn't show much discernment.'

'Anyhow,' she babbled on, 'a pass is usually reckoned a compliment, so long as the man will take no for an answer.'

He returned smile for smile. 'I assure you, I never used force in my life.'

'Lucky old you, lucky in love,' she said with the frantic gaiety of nervous tension and then, hearing herself, 'That was a fool thing to say.' It stripped her of flippancy and he asked quietly,

'Has this nonsense embarrassed you?'

'No, I spoke without thinking. I do that. It's a bad habit.'

'Come on,' he said. 'Let's go and find ourselves a meal.'

'All right.' She stood up. 'Where?'

'Anywhere you like.' He meant anywhere away from this flat, because of the clinging perfume, soft and warm and exotic, that was still in the air; because he had seen again how exactly amber eyes and flame-coloured hair had matched the icon. Nell felt if he had been alone he would have got into his car and driven fast, heading for nowhere in particular, just going a long way through the night under the dark sky.

As he was not alone he took Nell to The Cedars. The dining room was usually half empty on Monday nights and tonight was no exception, but the food and the service were always good. Nell worked hard to entertain, and no one could have guessed from Stephen's manner that the girl with him was not the girl on his mind.

He always got glances from other women. There was no one they knew here tonight, but several females at other tables eyed him appraisingly and thought that Nell was lucky. That should have been funny too, tonight was getting its quota of quirky humour, because this had been as unlucky a day as Nell had ever known.

Back to square one, sitting at a table at The Cedars with a man who was out of reach. Very like the first time they had come here on that first date, except that now Nell knew the face of his memories, and that was no comfort when the face was Celia's.

Celia had no idea how superb her timing had been. If she had waited another week she could still have been an irresistible rival, but at least Nell might have had the right to put up some sort of fight.

If Stephen told her tomorrow, 'I'm marrying Celia,' she could only say, 'So you both changed your minds?' She couldn't ask, 'How about me?' because it was none of her business who he married. He'd never pretended he felt anything but friendship for her.

But he would have done. Given time, the tenderness in his eyes when he looked at her yesterday would have grown. Luck! thought Nell, as a thin girl with a fat man looked across at her with frank envy, what have I done to get luck like this?

When she got home her father was the only one of the family still up. She told him they had gone out for a meal. 'It was a good meal,' she said, 'I enjoyed myself.' She went through the pile of snaps of Pedro that Flo and her grandmother had rooted out. Some were good for a smile and a

'Do you remember . . . ?' She chose one and asked, 'What about this? and her father said, 'That should do.'

She put it in her handbag and yawned and stretched and said it was late. It was, and her father said, 'You'd better go up.' She wondered if she had chattered too brightly. She had said nothing about Celia turning up again at Stephen's flat, but her father was looking thoughtful as though somewhere had struck a warning note.

'Good night,' she said. She was less tired than she pretended and she lay awake for a long time.

She had no claims on Stephen. She shared his confidence only because he needed her silence. She would have liked to speak to him again tonight, to phone him because she knew that he was not sleeping. In that flat the perfume would linger. But Nell's voice wouldn't help him, and it wouldn't help Nell because he would answer the phone hoping it was Celia.

Unless Celia had already called. Her throaty voice with the laughter in it. 'Good night, Stephen, I hope you've taken Little Nell home. It must be deadly dull down there, but the girl's in love with you and you don't want trouble with the natives.'

Celia would be calling, because Stephen was 'looking into something' for her. She'd reminded him just before she left the flat, although she could only have asked him a few minutes earlier. He'd said, 'Of course.' And what was that? Nell wondered.

She took Pedro's photograph in for Harry Irving next morning, getting down town ten minutes early to allow herself time, and also because she knew that Colin rarely arrived before nine and she hoped to miss him.

The newsagents and stationers' shop was the frontage of the *Clarion* offices. You went right through the shop to the counter at the far end if you wanted to put an advert in the newspaper or buy any photographs. The door behind the counter led into the editorial offices, the photographers, and the printers.

Several people were buying newspapers, and Nell stood around waiting for an assistant to come to the *Clarion* counter. Dorothy Murray, whom Colin had been dating lately, studiously ignored her. Dorothy probably felt she did have claims; she'd been to tea on Sunday, hadn't she?

Don't worry, love, Nell could have said, even if you have heard about the fantastic girl who came looking for Stephen I promise you I'm not looking for Colin.

She had been into the offices several times, just through the door there, but the public were not expected to walk in, so she stayed where she was and after a few minutes one of the women, not Dorothy, said, 'Can I help you?'

Nell handed over the envelope. 'Would you give this to Mr. Irving, please? He is expecting it.'

'Rightyo,' said the woman.

Nell was almost out of the shop when Colin came in. She gave him a quick smile with a 'Hello' and tried to get round him. He blocked her way.

'Where are you going?' he asked.

'To the office, of course.'

'I'll walk with you.'

She didn't want him walking with her, but it was only across the green. Walking briskly she would be there in the time it took to say 'No,' emphatically enough to make it stick.

So she went on walking and as soon as they were out of the shop Colin said, 'I think you ought to know that Stephen Harmon was going to marry Miss Conway.'

'I do know,' said Nell.

'Oh! Know anything else about her?'

Nothing that was for telling. She tried to look superior to gossip and would have fooled no one. Colin announced, 'She's related to half Debrett. She was deb of the year a few years back. She's travelled around and she's done some modelling. They were due to marry the month after he came down here, only it was called off.'

'Where *did* you do all your homework?' Nell asked.

'Harry remembered seeing photographs of her. She's a bit of a celebrity. If she's going to be visiting regularly she'd be worth a story. We got the background data from an agency.'

'That was handy,' said Nell. 'But I doubt if her visits will be that regular.'

They were almost across the green. Colin said, 'Face facts, Nell, didn't I tell you?'

'Did you? I don't recall you mentioning Celia Conway.'

'I said Harmon was out of his class here. She's his class and she wants him back again. You only had to see the way she looked at him.'

'Then she gives up easily,' said Nell savagely, 'because she's gone.'

She said that to shut Colin up and give herself time to get into the building before he got his breath back. She didn't believe it for a minute. She knew that Celia would be here again very soon.

It was courts this morning, and something of a bustle. Nell went straight into her office and only came out with Stephen to go across to the magistrates' courts.

Over there there were things to deal with. Such as the mother whose son had announced he was a rat-catcher and got twenty-five pounds from the owner of a local café to clear the premises.

The café proprietor had never seen any rats but had handed over the money, and after that had never seen the 'rat-catcher' again either. The police had tracked him down, and Stephen Harmon was representing him, and his mother was determined to watch the proceedings from the public gallery.

They were gipsy stock and tough, and Stephen's instructions to Nell were to 'sit by her and keep her quiet' because if mother gave the magistrates a piece of her mind it was unlikely to help the case.

'I'll do my best,' said Nell. She went into the public section with Mrs. Lane, who had been warned, hoping for the best. If Mrs. Lane did decide to speak up Nell didn't fancy her chances of holding her down.

As Mrs. Lane settled her bulk on one of the public benches Nell saw the other occupants of the gallery: a sprinkling of interested parties in the cases that were being heard this morning, uniform in their drabness; and Celia Conway in such vivid and elegant contrast that the whole thing could have been posed for a glossy magazine.

CHAPTER NINE

CELIA smiled, seeing Nell, and Nell's lips twitched into the semblance of an answering smile, but she knew that her eyes were dark and desperate. She felt desperate. Did Stephen know that Celia was here? Did it matter whether he did? He would, as soon as he stepped into the courtroom.

Everybody in the public gallery was aware of Celia Conway, although most of them had their own troubles. Most of the heads were half turned towards her, and as Mrs. Lane looked around it was Celia who gripped her interest. 'Who's that?' she demanded. 'Wonder what she's here for?'

Nell said nothing, and Mrs. Lane, who still did a bit of fortune-telling on the quiet, announced, 'She's got a lucky face.'

That was a safe bet. 'I'm sure she has,' said Nell.

Mrs. Lane behaved herself. She was no trouble while the case was being heard. Her son got three months, which with his record was fortunate, a fact she appeared to appreciate. 'He's a lovely speaker, isn't he?' she said, referring to Stephen Harmon, as she and Nell walked out of the public gallery.

Celia came out too. Stephen had seen her, of course. He had looked across in brief and quizzical recognition. He wasn't expecting her, Nell registered. He didn't look this way again, but once a case started he always concentrated entirely on the men and women who mattered: the bench, the clients, the witnesses.

As he came into the corridor with Mr. Baker now Celia stepped past Nell and went towards him. She said 'Oh no, oh *no* . . .' as though she was answering the question whether she considered this little court was Stephen Harmon's scene, or if she had ever before heard him deal with anything like the case of the phoney rat-catcher.

Stephen said, 'I'll see you back in the office, Nell.' Mr. Baker had papers, Mrs. Lane had something to say, Celia had a hand on Stephen's arm, and Nell turned and went.

Colin had been at the press table. He must have seen Celia too. That would have made his day.

Nell went back to the office. Joan was in Nell's room, writing on the scribbling pad beside the phone on Stephen's desk. 'Three numbers to be called back,' she said. 'How about the pictures tonight?'

Joan hadn't suggested going anywhere for weeks, not since Nell began to spend almost all her spare time with Stephen. Before then they had sometimes made up a foursome with Colin and Bernard. Now Joan was rallying round. That was kind. Not over-tactful, blurting it out with such a worried look, but kind.

Nell asked, 'Can I tell you later?'

'Sure,' said Joan. 'Oh, and – er –' she touched a sheet of paper, lightly and quickly as though it was hot, 'a note from Mr. Slater, about a house.'

Elsgood and Elsey handled the legal side of most of the property deals that went through Slater's Estate Agency. They were usually routine mortgage and conveyancing. But Joan scowled at it.

'Anything else?' asked Nell, taking the frown for concentration.

'That's the lot,' said Joan.

Nell picked up Mr. Slater's note as Joan left and read, 'Believe Laburnum Cottage to be given top priority, please contact.'

The phone numbers were two from local solicitors and one London number for 'Mr. Harmon personally'. Perhaps Mr. Slater's top priority should be dealt with first.

Nell went downstairs into the bright little front room that was part of the estate agency. A young couple were studying photographs and details of property on the walls, and one of the staff, a motherly-looking woman, was leaning over the counter encouraging them. 'Yes, it's a sweet little bungalow,' she was saying as Nell walked in. 'Reasonable too, because it's a nice district.'

She smiled at Nell. 'Laburnum Cottage,' said Nell.

Mrs. Mason lifted the flap in the counter and went on smiling. 'Go on in,' she said.

Into the next room where there were desks and most of the work was done. 'Laburnum Cottage,' said Nell, to the man and the typist.

'Ah,' said the man, 'Mr. Slater's handling that himself.' He got up and tapped on another door, and stuck his head through and said, 'Miss Attlesey, about Laburnum Cottage.'

'Come in, Nell,' sang out Mr. Slater. He beamed on her as she came in and invited her to sit down. Always hearty, he seemed heartier than ever this morning, bonhomie putting a high shine on his big red face.

He had the roneo leaflet for Laburnum Cottage to hand. 'Now this we were told would be a cash sale, subject to surveyor's report, and Mr. Harmon would be arranging the survey. Now it's a rush, and they want everything through as quickly as possible.'

If they had cash in hand why not? But Stephen hadn't mentioned a surveyor's report for Laburnum Cottage. Nell asked, 'Who's the purchaser?'

'A Miss Conway.'

'Oh!' She looked at the leaflet.

'She came in yesterday afternoon, looking for a suitable property for a weekend cottage. A friend of Mr. Harmon's, I gather?'

'Yes.'

'A delightful lady.'

'Very,' said Nell. 'I think Mr. Harmon does know about it, but I'll have a word with him as soon as he comes over from the courts.'

'Splendid! It's a sound little property. Vacant possession, of course. They could move into it next week.'

'That should be soon enough,' said Nell.

She phoned the two local numbers from her own office, and got the gist of their problems. Then she began to type out the brief from yesterday's dictation. Stephen arrived after about twenty minutes and asked, 'Everything in hand?'

'Three phone calls.' The notes of the two, and the numbers of the personal one were on his desk. 'And Mr. Slater wants to know if we've arranged for a surveyor to see Laburnum Cottage.'

'He'll collect the key this afternoon.'

'So Miss Conway will be with us for weekends?'

'Unless we find subsidence or a compulsory order pending,' said Stephen. He asked for the London number, answering laconically and making notes. Business for the old firm, except that Elsgood and Elsey were the old firm, the ones that didn't feature in Stephen Harmon's plans for the future.

As he put down the phone Nell asked the question that didn't seem real, although it was going to affect all of them, 'What do we do here when you move on, put up the shutters?'

'What?' He'd heard, but he'd been thinking of other things. He didn't wait for her to repeat it, he said, 'I'll get in a man to take over. Rowe couldn't cope on his own, but with another solicitor, and with Baker, of course, they should manage well enough. 'It won't be for some time.'

Did he think that was reassurance? She said, 'I'll look forward to meeting him. I'm getting a rapid turnover of bosses these days.'

'You can't stop here.'

'What do you suggest I do? Emigrate?'

'I suggest we talk about it when the time comes. In the meantime—'

'I know,' she said. 'In the meantime I don't talk about it at all. It must be nice to be able to buy yourself a weekend cottage like calling into a boutique and picking up a sweater.'

'It must,' Stephen agreed. He reached for the notes on his desk, and she went on with her typing.

At half twelve the phone rang and Nell answered it. That was as well, as it was for her. Joan said in elaborately casual tones, 'Oh, hello, I wondered if you'd come and help me choose a pair of shoes as it's lunchtime.'

Mr. Baker had told them Celia was in court, or someone had. Joan thought that Celia would be lunching with Stephen today. Nell said, 'It's Joan. Can I go to lunch?'

'Of course,' said Stephen, and the lovely habit of weeks snapped without even eyes being raised. He picked up the phone as she went out.

Nell got to the cloakroom before Joan and put on lipstick, surprised that she managed so well. There was an eerie feeling about, as though the clock had slipped back. Joan came in. 'I'm ever so glad you're coming, I like a second opinion, then if Bernard doesn't like them I can say – well, everybody else does.'

Shoes, of course, they were buying. Nell asked what sort she was looking for, and Joan went into a description of style and colour, and would probably come out with something quite different. She usually did.

'Dreamboat's lost a letter,' she announced, giving Norman Rowe's office door a scornful glance as they passed by. 'I typed the darn' thing and put it on his desk and he swears he's never seen it. Well, who else could have had it? I'm not doing another, it's four pages long.'

We're allies again, thought Nell, the secretary-birds united for a giggle. She said, 'Did Badger tell you our rat-catcher got three months? Considering he did six last year for a similar caper I think he meant it when he thanked them.'

Joan laughed, her laughter very slightly strained . . . And did you hear that Celia Conway was with us, and afterwards she put her hand on Stephen's arm and smiled at him, and he said, 'I'll see you across at the office, Nell' . . .?

They found some shoes that were near enough to what Joan wanted, and in the doorway of the snack bar Joan stepped ahead for a quick survey. Colin wasn't there, and she looked round at Nell with a grin of relief, then made for the far end of the counter, and sat protectively between Nell and the rest of the room.

They chose salad rolls and glasses of milk, and gossiped like they used to do, and suddenly Joan said fervently, 'Nell, I'm glad.'

'What about?'

'Now don't get mad,' Joan sounded as though she half expected Nell to start screaming, 'but we all knew how it would end, and I'm glad it's come sooner rather than later. Mr. Harmon's clever, but – well, he is a stranger, isn't he? You're better off with somebody like—' she hesitated and Nell said,

'Please don't say Colin.'

'Well, somebody like somebody we know.' Joan shifted on her stool, the intensity of her good advice putting deep lines into her face. 'And don't you fret about it, there's plenty more fish in the sea.'

'Plenty of little fish.'

'What do you want?' demanded Joan. 'A barracuda?'

Nell laughed, 'That's not a bad description.' Joan's scowl melted and she laughed too, pleased with herself and with Nell's reaction. She bit into her salad roll.

'How about the cinema tonight?'

'I don't think so tonight,' said Nell. 'There's something on television.'

Joan had the sense not to ask what. She was relieved to see Nell taking things so calmly. Stephen Harmon overawed Joan out of her mind, but she could understand any girl being flattered if he looked her way, and after Stephen Harmon Colin – or even Bernard – might be an awful anti-climax.

She wondered what it would be like to have an affair with a man like that, and if she would ever find the nerve to ask Nell.

Nell knew how Joan, and most of her other friends, had interpreted the relationship. No one would believe it had been companionship and no more. But it should have been more, and it would have been. They had come so close to the word or the touch that would change every second of the years Nell had to live that a small stubborn corner of her mind still believed that moment was inevitable.

But the office staff at least had decided Nell and Stephen Harmon were through. After lunch, as Joan walked back into her office, Mrs. Storey spied Nell through the open door into the corridor, and nodded and smiled, her smile proclaiming eloquently that it was all for the best. Nell smiled brightly back. She was getting practice in smiles that meant nothing at all.

The afternoon passed. Stephen saw four clients. Nell took notes, and typed, and the procedure for each was routine and undemanding. At six o'clock she put the cover on her typewriter and asked, 'All right if I go now?'

'Good night,' said Stephen. 'See you in the morning.'

She cycled home and went in through the kitchen door. Pedro bounded as usual. His rope-burns from Sunday had been superficial and most of the time he forgot them altogether. Flo was laying the table, Ocky was sitting at it, and Elizabeth Attlesey was emptying a teapot into the sink tidy.

They had all heard about Celia. They looked at Nell and she knew that she must deal with this right now. If her grandmother started worrying about her being 'jilted' that could trigger another heart attack. So she smiled and asked, 'What are you all gaping at me for? Now don't tell me, let me guess.'

'Who's gaping?' said Flo.

Nell said, 'I know. Mrs. Greer's been on the phone to say that Stephen's ex-girl-friend's in town.'

'She's created quite a stir,' said Flo.

'I'll bet,' said Nell gaily. 'We don't see many like her around here. *And* she's buying a week-end cottage.'

Elizabeth Attlesey asked, 'Did he never mention her before?'

'No.'

'Is he still fond of her?'

'I don't know. Could be, I suppose. Laburnum Cottage, Marrow's Reach — that's over your way, isn't it, Ocky? What's it like?'

Ocky scratched his head. 'It'd be the Reids' old place. That's up for sale. What are they asking?'

Nell told him. 'And she doesn't need a mortgage. Colin says she's related to half Debrett.'

'Colin says?' Elizabeth Attlesey seized on that. 'Have you been talking to Colin about her? What does he think about it? I must say I'm very surprised at Mr. Harmon.'

'Well, you shouldn't be,' said Nell. 'He had a life before he came to Cheslyn Slade, and why should he tell us all about it?'

'He should have told *you*,' insisted her grandmother.

Nell shook her head. 'Not really. We work well together, we're friends, but that's as far as it goes.' She laughed. 'Anyhow, Miss Conway says she isn't going to let him walk over the moors any more since he nearly fell in on Sunday, so I'd better start looking around for someone who can call his soul his own.'

The phone rang in the hall and Flo went to answer it, calling quickly, 'Nell! For you!' She held the receiver, covering the mouthpiece with one hand, and as Nell neared her she said, 'It's a man. It doesn't sound like Mr. Harmon.'

Nell reached for the phone, but Flo held it back and said gently, 'You're laying it on a bit thick.'

'Am I?' Flo knew her so well. 'I do, don't I?'

'Not often,' said Flo. 'Is he still fond of her?'

'I honestly don't know,' said Nell, and tears welled so that Flo had to place the receiver in her hands. Flo stood there until Nell said, 'Well, hello, Ed, and how's life treating you?' Then she went back into the kitchen, where Elizabeth Attlesey was waiting to hear who was phoning Nell.

The surveyor's report on Laburnum Cottage was on Stephen Harmon's desk next morning, stating that the property was sound and the price was fair. Nell had already read it when Stephen came in at nine. He frowned as he did and then said, 'What the hell can one do about that?'

It wasn't a question, but hope stirred and she asked, 'Don't you want her here?'

'She can be a very distracting influence.'

Which was plainly her objective. She came into the office at midday. A client had just left who was suing for divorce, a sad-faced woman, prematurely faded, and then Celia came in, glowing and vital. She was certainly distracting. She made Nell feel like the young-old woman she had gone down the stairs holding the handrail.

'Do I buy the cottage?' asked Celia.

Stephen handed her the report, and she held it without looking at it. 'This says go ahead?'

'That says it's a sound business proposition, but I don't think you'll get your money's worth.'

She laughed her husky little laugh. 'Now I think I could get to like it here.'

'For how long?'

'How long are you staying?' She was wearing a black patent shoulder bag. She opened it and dropped in the report, going by touch, without taking her eyes off Stephen. Then she went round the desk to where he was sitting, stooped and kissed him, and said, 'See you, darling,' the catch in her voice making the caress as emotive as though they were lovers again.

Nell was convinced that this time she was blotted out.

Celia must have a blind spot, she must imagine she was alone in this room with Stephen. But Celia said, 'Come on, little Nell, show me out,' so Nell got up and went through the door and heard Celia following her down the corridor.

As Nell opened the glass-panelled door at the top of the stairs Celia turned huge amber eyes on her, seeing her very clearly. There was no catch in Celia's voice now. It was low, but incisive. 'Forget it. I want him back.'

'Why?' said Nell bluntly.

Celia's eyes widened even more. 'I'm sure you can think of reasons.'

'I can,' said Nell, 'but I shouldn't have thought we'd have made the same list. I hear you put cash at the head of yours.' She shouldn't have said that. She shouldn't have said a word.

Celia laughed, showing the prettiest teeth. 'Why, little Nell has spirit! And she looks such a meek little thing.'

'I am not meek,' said Nell raggedly, 'and if you call me little Nell again I'll prove it by shoving you down the stairs.' She didn't wait for any effect that might have. She went back.

Stephen was looking at the notes he'd made for the woman who wanted a divorce. Nell wondered if he was really looking at them and she said, 'Would you care for my resignation? I've just had words with Miss Conway.'

'About anything in particular?'

'For one thing, about what could happen if she calls me little Nell again.'

He smiled, 'I've been expecting that.'

No one should be so contained. Rattled herself, she resented the low-key note and said abruptly, 'She says she wants you back.'

'What does she expect you to do about it?'

'Tell you, perhaps?' She'd told him, but then so had Celia, by word and the deeds of Laburnum Cottage. 'Would you like to dictate a memo?'

'Yes, but not on that subject.' He picked up his notes. 'Although perhaps it is. I'm not a divorce lawyer. At least I wasn't until I came here and became Jack of all trades. But I've seen enough divorces to recognize the signs for a doomed marriage.'

He meant that marriage between himself and Celia would be doomed. Nell thought so too, although Nell could not have been more prejudiced. Celia had refused to marry him when he had little material to offer. She wanted him back in his old world of power and money. She knew he was going back some time and so she wanted him.

And he ...? Nell had no real insight into Stephen Harmon. But against her will she remembered the icon, and all the beautiful things he had collected, and how Celia Conway had seemed the rarest of them all.

'Too pricey for me here,' he had said, but not if he went back. He could afford her then, and another thing he had said the first time Nell went into the flat, that he wasted no time in bargain-hunting, he preferred to pay the price for what he wanted.

The collection was incomplete without Celia. And Celia, who should know, had no doubts at all that he was unable to resist her.

For the rest of that week, even without her physical presence, Celia Conway loomed large. Everyone who knew Nell heard about Celia. Her looks, her glamorous background, the fact that Stephen Harmon had so nearly married her, made delightful gossip, especially as Laburnum Cottage seemed proof that Celia Conway was in earnest.

But between Nell and Stephen all went exactly as before. They continued as an efficient working team and, as a bonus, good companions. Tuesday lunch time Nell had half decided to cycle home, but Stephen asked, 'What about lunch? You haven't fixed anything?'

She said, 'No,' and he said, 'Good, we can get this hammered out,' and she found herself over in the flat, taking notes, drinking soup and eating garlic sausage on cracker biscuits.

She spent Wednesday and Thursday evenings with Stephen, work on Wednesday, the theatre on Thursday. Celia wasn't mentioned, except that Nell typed out the house contract papers and put them in the mail.

She couldn't ask, 'What are you going to do about her?' Any more than she could have asked earlier, 'Are you staying in Cheslyn Slade?' Perhaps in her heart she didn't want to know, a coward preferring uncertainty.

Pedro's photograph appeared in the centre page spread of the *Clarion* on Friday, together with a picture of the subsidence as discovered, and one of it as the switch was thrown and great clouds of dust rose out of the earth. Nell's photograph, sitting at her typewriter, had a pained expression, and recalling the set-up she wasn't surprised.

The headline was 'Dog Gives Warning of Danger on the Moors,' and the caption under the picture said 'Pedro, the Hero of the Hour!'

Nell put the newspaper open on Stephen's desk, so that he saw it as soon as he came in. He read 'Danger on the Moors,' and laughed. 'It sounds like an old horror film. At the very least he should have rounded up a monster.'

'I like "gives warning",' said Nell. 'He didn't even see it until he fell in. The first warning we got from him was when he howled for help. Pedro, hero of the hour! I shall frame that.'

She would not frame it but keep it, remembering. As Stephen folded the newspaper and handed it across to her and they both smiled she prayed — you remember it too, beyond the laughter. Remember when you held me in your arms and didn't smile.

They didn't go over the hills that Sunday. Stephen went away for the weekend, staying with Sir Charles Fenby and his wife. Nell presumed the talk would touch on his rejoining the firm. She didn't know, he didn't tell her. Neither did she nor anyone else know if he would be seeing Celia.

But they all thought he would, they all knew he had been away. During the next fortnight the property transfer for Laburnum Cottage went through without a hitch and the decorators moved in. Celia came down, trailing stardust, dazzling the office staff and everyone else who set eyes on her.

Nell wasn't around when she came into the office, but she heard all about it and that Celia had been late at the flat that evening. They watched like hawks around here, Nell could have told Stephen.

Joan cornered Nell in the cloakroom next morning for an impassioned appeal. 'Can't you *see* he's making a fool of you? As soon as she moves down here he'll have no more time for you.'

'I don't think she can type,' smiled Nell, to whom no-more-time would have been a death sentence. 'That's my trump card, I'm the only secretary he's got.'

Joan lost her temper. 'You must think *I'm* a fool. If it was office work you'd be in the office, not gadding about or over at the flat.'

'There's no answer to that,' said Nell, and thought how strange it was that it should be friends who wished you well who said the things that hurt you most.

At least at home no one hectored her 'for her own good'. Her father and Flo and Ocky had too much sensitivity and Nell managed to reassure her grandmother that she was happy and enjoying life.

She did try a casual date to get her through one evening after Celia had phoned the office. 'Hello, little Nell,' Celia's throaty voice came clear as life through the receiver, 'is our man there?'

He was, and Nell left him talking to Celia, and walked down the corridor to where Mrs. Storey was sitting at the little switchboard, looking as though she would have loved to listen in but daren't.

That makes two of us, thought Nell. She went to the filing cabinet and collected some papers she was needing, and quite soon the small lights glowed that said the line was cleared and she could go back to her own office.

Stephen said nothing at all about the call, but Nell, faced with an evening wondering if he was meeting Celia, said, 'Oh, all right,' when Edwin Martin phoned again. Ed had persistence if nothing else.

And persistence, she decided after saying good night, was about all he did have. Her father was working still and she went into the workroom to announce, 'I don't care if Ed Martin is in line for a sweet factory, he's off my list. I think he's got candyfloss where his brain ought to be.'

John Attlesey grinned, 'Good. He was never on my list.' Tonight he had a small block of wood on the workbench before him and Nell asked,

'What's it going to be?'

Not a panel, this would be a three-dimensional carving. 'A rose,' said her father. 'I feel like making a rose.'

She stroked the wood. It would not be a faithful copy of a

flower, but when it was done the impression of softness and beauty would be so strong that you would hardly dare to brush it with a fingertip. And you would smell the perfume. 'Yes,' she said.

'For you.'

When she was a child she had had wonderful toys, a turreted castle marvellously furnished, little people, little animals, once a whole Wild West village. As she grew older anything her father carved that she wanted she could have, but she suspected that this gift would be fashioned with all his skill. It was a gift to comfort. She said, 'I'd like a rose.'

He said brusquely, 'I haven't been able to give you much. I'm not much use.'

'How can you say that – a man who can make a rose?' He had given her so much, not least the courage and the pride she needed now. She said, 'You've worked long enough for one day.'

'It isn't that late.'

She pulled a face. 'Well, it seems late. Any evening with Ed Martin is a long night. Have you had your supper?'

Flo had brought in some sandwiches, but he hadn't touched them. Nell opened one. 'Cheese and chutney. Shall we toast them?'

'That's a sound suggestion.' They went into the kitchen and toasted the sandwiches and raided the fridge, and talked and joked, each trying to cheer the other.

There were the remains of a roast chicken in the fridge and Nell held up the wishbone. 'Come on,' she invited, 'try our luck.'

This time when it snapped she had the 'lucky' half. 'There you are,' she said. 'I've got the knack back.'

Celia was more photogenic than Nell. Harry Irving surpassed himself the week Celia was featured in the *Clarion*, on the front page, at the door of the cottage, supervising the final touches of paint.

This was model-girl Celia Conway, the reader was informed, daughter of the late Colonel James Conway, and niece of Sir Edward Conway, fine art dealer . . . Not exactly 'half Debrett' but quite impressive name-dropping for Cheslyn Slade . . .

One month after seeing Laburnum Cottage and falling in love with it Miss Conway was moving in. She was enchanted with this 'beautiful little town' and she thought she was so lucky to have found her dream cottage that had such old-world character.

'Three up, three down,' said Ocky, 'and built fifty years ago. What's she on about — old-world character?'

Elizabeth Attlesey had produced the newspaper at teatime on Friday and Nell said yes, of course she'd seen it. It was a super photograph, and so it should be, she was a model, wasn't she? Probably Stephen had seen it too, Nell didn't know, did it matter?

Ocky sneered at Celia's gushings over the cottage. 'There's no roses round that door, and there's no laburnums either, for all it's called Laburnum Cottage. No garden at all worth the name.' Somehow the talk moved on to gardens, Ocky's favourite subject, and off Celia Conway, and John Attlesey folded the newspaper and slipped it down the side of his wheelchair.

They were still at tea when there was a knock on the kitchen door. Nell went and Colin stood there. He must have left his car at the front of the house and walked round. Beside Nell Pedro wagged a tail, forgiving and forgetting, it seemed, so long as nobody shouted.

This was the first direct dealing Nell had had with Colin since she told him that Celia had given up easily and gone, and that she was unlikely to be back.

He said quickly, 'I want to talk to you.'

She said, 'No, thanks,' and knew that her grandmother was going to call, 'Hello, Colin, how nice to see you. Do come in.'

He went in, passing Nell, and said hello all round the table, getting a smile from Elizabeth Attlesey and less welcoming acknowledgments from the rest.

Then he said, 'Nell, just five minutes. There's something I think you ought to know.'

If her grandmother had not been there, with that ailing heart, Nell would have told Colin what he could do with his bits of information. She was very near the end of her tether. The smiling face was a brittle mask that could easily shatter. But there must be no scenes in which Elizabeth Attlesey could involve herself, so she said, 'Aren't you the one for mysteries?' She picked up her cup and saucer. 'Come on.'

'Pedro, stay!' John Attlesey ordered, smiling at Nell and getting a grip on Pedro's collar. Nell smiled back; that smile was real if rueful.

'It might be as well,' she said.

Chagrin darkened Colin's face for a moment, but no longer. He had been made to look a fool last time he was here, and Nell's father knew it, but this time he was calm and in control. He was not getting his own back, nothing was further from his mind. He was here entirely in Nell's interests. It was giving him no joy, he was the last man to gloat.

In the drawing-room Nell put her cup of tea on the mantelshelf and said sweetly, 'Now, what do you know that you're determined I should know?'

'You saw the story?'

'Yes.'

'I did the interview.' Of course he had. He wouldn't let another reporter do it. Celia Conway was his scoop, as well as being such glowing and growing proof that he was right about Stephen Harmon and Nell was wrong.

'She talked to me.' He sounded as though someone had spilled state secrets. 'A lot of stuff not for publication yet. You can't start linking names at this stage.'

'Not in the *Clarion* you can't,' Nell agreed. Mr. Greer was a cautious editor, unlikely to publish anything that might come back at him.

Colin's voice dropped to a hoarse whisper. 'But in strictest confidence I can tell you there's going to be an engagement announcement before long.'

Nell said lightly, 'If Celia Conway does the announcing better check with Stephen before you publish.' Colin followed with his second momentous snippet,

'And Stephen Harmon is going back to London.'

'That could be more wishful thinking on her part,' said Nell.

Colin had expected vehement denial from Nell. He had been ready to be accused of jealousy or lying. His conscience was clear and his motives were high. Of course he hadn't wanted the shock to hit her too hard, but she had to know, and perhaps it was kinder in this case to be cruel. He had thought tears almost certain, perhaps even hysterics, and had planned ahead that if she became too distraight he would fetch Flo at once. There might be an embarrassing few minutes with the family, especially with Mr. Attlesey, but as soon as they were given the facts they must agree that the blame for Nell's distress lay squarely on Stephen Harmon's shoulders.

Colin was prepared for every emotion, except polite boredom. Nell was acting as though he had told her the colour of Celia Conway's kitchen curtains. His bombshells had gone off like damp squibs and, thrown off balance, it was spite rather than solicitude that bubbled to the surface.

He kept his voice down although he felt that someone ought to be shouting, getting it into Nell's thick skull that Stephen Harmon was leaving Elsgood and Elsey, and that Laburnum Cottage would be a week-end cottage for his wife and his friends and himself, and how would Nell feel about that? Did she know what a laughing stock she was making of herself? Did she seriously consider she stood a chance against Celia Conway?

He had the *Courier* in his pocket and he took it out and waved it under her nose. Celia's blazing beauty transcended the smudgy black and white. 'Look at her,' Colin spat, 'look at yourself.' There was a mirror and he was about to spin Nell round and hold her in front of it, apparently under the impression that it must be some time since she had seen herself.

She held him off with an outflung hand, her words short and sharp because she wouldn't prolong this a split second more than she must. 'Listen to me. If Stephen leaves here I leave here. I am a super secretary. Believe me. Accept that. I go along with him, with my little notebook and my pencil.'

Colin gasped. Her staccato delivery was giving fervent emphasis to what she was saying.

She said, 'I go barefoot over sharp rocks if I have to. I go anywhere, any time, anyhow. But if he asks me, and he will ask me, I go.' She paused, he went on gasping. She asked, 'Do I make myself clear?'

'You *are* crazy,' said Colin.

'No,' said Nell. 'Sorry if I'm confusing you. It's simple enough. I'm just saying mind your own business, will you?'

Colin was back to pity. He sighed and shook his head. 'I've done all I can.'

'Thank you,' said Nell. 'Perhaps you'd better take the front door. Pedro might remember where he left off last time.'

She saw him out, and then went back into the drawing-room to give herself a few minutes to cool off before re-joining the others. By the time she heard the faint squeak of her father's wheelchair coming down the hall she was feeling calmer, and almost regretting her outburst. Colin had been insufferable, but she could have kept her temper if she'd tried a little harder.

She opened the door and her father said, 'I did hear the car go, didn't I?'

'Poor old Colin,' said Nell. 'Last time Pedro went for him, this time I did. Now he's decided we're all crazy.' She laughed on a wobbling note. 'And I honestly don't believe he had a clue what I was talking about.'

It was county courts on Monday. Nell was out of the office with Stephen and Mr. Baker all day, getting back just before six o'clock.

As Stephen opened the door into the first office Joan jumped up. 'Oh, Mr. Harmon,' she gulped as if she had been eating dry biscuits she couldn't swallow, 'Miss Conway's waiting to see you in your office.'

'Thank you,' Stephen turned. Nell asked,

'Shall I wait?'

'Wait for what?' he said, so she followed as he went off down the corridor with long strides. Nell heard Joan call faintly,

'Oh – er – Mr. Harmon . . .' but either Stephen didn't hear or didn't bother, and whatever Joan wanted to say went unsaid.

Celia was sitting in the client's seat, and Colin nervously puffing at a cigarette was sitting in Nell's place. Obviously Joan had wanted to add that Mr. Greer was here too.

'Hello, darlings,' Celia smiled her wide smile. 'Have a

lovely day?'

Colin got up and Nell sat down, and Stephen went round the desk to his own chair, observing drily, 'I wouldn't go so far as to describe it as lovely.'

It had been quite successful, but it had been a very full schedule. Celia turned to face Nell. 'You would, though, wouldn't you?'

'Would I?'

'Oh, come now,' she made such play with her fabulous eyelashes that Nell could have sworn she felt the draught, 'a day with Stephen? Of course you would.'

'All right,' Stephen sounded weary, 'it's agreed we've all had a lovely day. Now, what can we do for you?' He looked at Colin. 'Mr. Greer?'

Colin stubbed out his cigarette and cleared his throat. 'Well, it's like this.' He sounded desperately ill at ease. He might be a reporter, but he didn't have his facts very well tabulated. He looked as if he was still trying to get them into order and Celia said smoothly, 'Colin has been asking my advice and I've suggested he should talk to you. It seems that little Nell told him that when you leave here she will be packing too.'

From the moment she saw Colin here Nell had had an ominous foreboding, but she hadn't expected quite such a bulldozer. She choked on indignation, 'It *wasn't* like that. I didn't . . .'

Celia's voice overrode Nell's, speaking to Stephen as though Nell was not in the room. 'Colin thinks she's mistaken, and so do I, but I do feel you should tell her you won't be requiring her services any more, because she's getting some very odd ideas.'

Nell was on her feet now, facing Colin whom she would never forgive as long as she lived. Celia was loving this hurting, she was bathed in a sensuous glow of pleasure, and Colin had given her the weapon. Nell said, 'Colin came to see me on Friday. He came to tell me that Celia said there would be an engagement announcement soon and that you were leaving Cheslyn Slade. I said if you did I thought you'd ask me to go too.'

Colin found his voice in a shrill and vindictive outburst. 'You said you'd go barefoot over sharp rocks to follow him.

Any time, anywhere, you said. You're making a clown of yourself. Everybody's sorry for you because you can't see that an affair like this has got no future.'

'And how is that your problem, Mr. Greer?' Stephen spoke with a deadly courtesy that chilled the overheated atmosphere like an east wind.

Colin stopped blustering. He said suddenly, 'I've known Nell all her life. In her own interests I want her made to see sense.'

'In your own interests,' said Stephen gently, 'I should advise you to be quiet. Any further scandal against Miss Attlesey or myself and I give you my professional promise that I will break you.'

There was a long silence. Even Celia was silent. Colin looked at the man sitting behind the desk and thought he had never seen eyes so hard or faced such implacable purpose. He had not wanted to come here. He had known he could do no good, but he had thought that Celia Conway would be able to persuade Harmon to sack Nell, that was why he had told her what Nell had said.

Maybe she could still. Harmon was angry now, but of course he had no loyalty towards Nell, and of course he wasn't serious about her. What man would be who could have Celia Conway?

Colin went without saying another word. Nell would learn before long, he reflected as he came out of the offices into the street. The prospect of being proved right in the end should have warmed him, but he felt distinctly chilly. He had never faced a really dangerous enemy before, and he had no doubt that Stephen Harmon never made a professional promise he could not fulfil to the letter.

As the door closed behind Colin Celia began to laugh. She threw back her head and her red hair rippled. 'You frightened him to death!'

'I'm glad to hear it,' said Stephen grimly. 'Who told you I might be leaving here?'

She smiled slowly. 'All sorts of folk, one way or another. Some time. When you're ready.' The smile dissolved into laughter again. 'I didn't think you'd be quite so hard on the poor lamb. He was only saying that little Nell doesn't know the score.' She turned in her chair to face Nell. 'And isn't that the truth? So wouldn't it be less trouble in the long run to tell her that she may be your girl-Friday but she is not your woman. Nor ever likely to be.'

Malice glowed green in her amber eyes. Stephen looked at her steadily, and was silent.

Nell couldn't speak. What could she say, except 'Speak for me, Stephen, fight for me,' and that couldn't be said aloud.

Celia said, 'Stephen, you must see.' She turned back to him. 'You're angry. I've never known you angry before.'

'We live in a changing world,' he said.

She looked uncertain for a moment, then she pulled her gorgeous grimace. 'All right, I'm sorry, I shouldn't have stagemanaged this little scene. You don't enjoy scenes, do you?'

'So you're sorry,' he said. 'Now run along, I've work to do.'

'Oh, darling,' she was soft and sweet as a kitten, 'don't be pompous, don't be a bore.'

He said in the same deadly voice he had used with Colin, 'Have you any idea how much you bore me? Go home, will you? Whether it's Laburnum Cottage or Richmond Hill. Get out of here.'

She said, 'No,' and then, 'It's Laburnum Cottage.' She picked up her handbag. 'Please don't be angry.' She went to the door, and hesitated, looking quite ravishing as she always did. She said in her lovely husky voice, 'I know I bore you. I bore myself.'

He was angry. Nell had often seen him impatient and aggressive, but she had never before sensed this white anger.

For a moment she almost felt sorry for Celia, but Stephen never even acknowledged what was after all a pretty pathetic admission. 'See you,' said Celia.

'No doubt,' he said.

Why was he so angry? Nell wondered. Because they had tried to force him into dismissing her, or because Colin had suggested Stephen and Nell were having an affair that was the talk of this small town?

It wasn't true. There was no affair, he knew that, but there wasn't that much scandalmongering either. She said, 'Colin

184

made the gossip sound far worse than it is. It's only nattering. It doesn't bother me.'

'It bothers me.' He got up and went to the window, looking out. 'You should have told me.'

He would be looking for Celia. Her car might be parked down there. Nell said, 'I'm sorry.'

'For God's sake don't you start apologizing!'

She nearly said 'Sorry' again. Instead she asked, 'Does she bore you?'

'She'd bore anyone who wasn't looking at her. She has a shallow little mind.'

That seemed too harsh a judgment. She asked, 'Why did you want to marry her if she bored you?'

'Because I usually did look at her when she was talking to me, and as you observed, she matched the icon.'

'*What*?'

He went to the cupboard in the corner. 'Do you want a drink?'

'No.'

He poured whisky. Celia had had the last glass out of that bottle and raised it to Nell and said, 'Good luck'. He went back to his chair behind the desk. Nell was sitting at her table, the typewriter in front of her. He could have been about to dictate a letter. They had sat here like this so many working days. And he spoke as though he was discussing a client's affairs, not his own.

'I was marrying Celia because she would have been an ornament to any home. She was marrying me for good and sufficient reason, so it was irrational that it should come as a shock when I had it spelled out.

'I overheard her talking to another man. He'd asked why me and she was telling him why.'

There was a light tap on the door and Stephen called, 'Come in.'

Mr. Baker stepped in, wearing his overcoat, carrying his briefcase. 'I'm off now, sir. There isn't anything else, is there? I have locked up the other offices.' He jangled keys like a jailor and Stephen smiled,

'Thank you. Good night.'

'Good night, Mr. Harmon. Good night, Miss Attlesey.'

Stephen went on with what he was saying. There were

often interruptions like this in an office. You picked up the subject again where you'd left it off. Nell felt she should have her notebook open and a pen in her hand. Except that they weren't talking about a client. This had happened to Stephen.

He said, 'Summarized, it was because if she travelled with me she could count on going first class by jet. She has money, but not quite enough. Her tastes are expensive.'

A ticket to ride . . . it could have been a figure of speech. Nell began, 'Perhaps she meant—' and he cut across in flat rebuttal.

'She meant literally what she said. I knew it, but until I heard her I hadn't let myself admit it. I cleared off for a day or two afterwards and did some thinking. My doctor's an old friend, he announced that it was overwork, a slight coronary.'

He said wryly, 'Celia was very concerned, very worried that she might be selling herself short, but I could still have been fool enough to marry her if she'd been prepared to marry me. I thought I was in love with her. I wasn't seeing too clearly and she could be as blinding as looking into the sun. All I had to do to keep her was stay around and carry on with the work I was doing.

'So I got out. My doctor knew why. No one else. And if there had been any doubts that resolved them.' The proof must have been bitter, but he almost smiled. 'She couldn't unload my ring fast enough when she learned that my prospects were a small-town lawyer's. Although I must say she did her best to sound as though she was doing me a favour.'

Nell said quietly, 'But you're not a small-town lawyer.'

'No.' He looked around and smiled. 'I couldn't stand the pace. As you know.'

'They're expecting you back?'

'They've been expecting me back ever since I left.'

She put her hands on the typewriter, pressing keys randomly and too lightly to strike, for something to do, something to hold. 'Back into "Celia's orbit"? That's what you called it, and she's still blinding as looking into the sun.'

'No,' he said. 'Five minutes ago she was ugly. She never looked ugly to me before, but then I've never been angry before. I never wanted to half kill a man until your Mr. Greer just now.'

She took the simplest point, the least important. 'Not my Mr. Greer.'

He said, 'I'm glad to hear that. Anger it seems I can control, but I'm not so sure about jealousy.'

'Jealousy?'

'As Celia pointed out, you may not be my woman, but it's now been forcibly impressed on me that I'm your man. I appear to have something in common with that mad dog of yours, anyone who's against you is my enemy.'

'What's safe?' she had once asked her father. He had said 'Love. Nothing else.' And she was safe from this day on.

'The things Greer said you said,' asked Stephen. 'Did you?'

Like Celia she had made a literal statement. She would follow him barefoot over razors if he asked her. She asked, 'Why?'

'It would make things easier if you did.' He held the whisky glass, but he wasn't drinking. Like the brandy the night Celia came it seemed to be going to waste. He said very slowly, 'I know that for me you are everything, but how do I prove to you that you're going to need me for the rest of your life?'

The hunger for him to come to her and take her in his arms was an ache. She said, 'You're a good lawyer. You could make out a good case.'

He got up. 'Have you ever considered that your grandmother may know what she's talking about?'

'Only recently.' Her voice was a breath through parted lips. He reached for her and lifted her to her feet and she whispered, 'You call this an ethical argument?'

Her head fell back, supported by his arm. He said, 'Objection overruled, my love.' He held her gently at first, his eyes dark and searching. Then as she swayed towards him he bowed his head to kiss her mouth, and this was the touch that was inevitable and irrevocable. And for both of them their whole world was here.

Mills & Boon's Paperbacks

JANUARY

WINDY NIGHT, RAINY MORROW by Ivy Ferrari

When Tina Rutherford's brother Bruno was tragically killed, she decided to go to Northumberland, where he had been working, to clear up his affairs and to meet his fiancée, Helen Copeland. But Tina found a far from warm welcome awaiting her from Helen's dour brother Adam . . .

THE VALLEY OF THE EAGLES by Eleanor Farnes

Juliet went to Spain and got involved with two men: Harry who was nice and calm and kind, and who loved her; Miguel who was like his mountain home – wild and dark and stormy. Yet might not the ease she felt with Harry be all too much like the situation between brother and sister? And the difficulties she experienced with Miguel be a guard against deeper feelings?

THE FAIR ISLAND by Anne Hampson

It was Estelle Marsland who had treated Cimon Duris's nephew so badly, but her twin sister Alaine who took her place on a cruise to Greece – and got abducted by Cimon for her pains as an act of revenge. Fortunately at the last moment he believed her story, but that was by no means the end of it all.

MAN OUT OF REACH by Lilian Peake

Dr. Adrian Crayford plainly regarded women as an interference in his life. 'They're an incredible nuisance,' he told Rosalie, 'and an irritating distraction from things that really matter. And the more attractive they are, the greater distraction they are. So I keep them out. Full stop.' And Rosalie was attractive – and attracted to him!

20p net each

Mills & Boon's Paperbacks

THE LITTLE NOBODY by Violet Winspear

Gard St. Clair was dark and wild and mysterious, like his house on the Cornish cliffs. And Ynis was going to marry him – or so he told her when she recovered from the accident in which she had lost her memory. Ynis had to believe him – yet what could a man like Gard possibly want of her, a little nobody straight from a convent, when a far more suitable woman was his for the asking?

PAINTED WINGS by Lucy Gillen

Llanwellon Cottage, in a peaceful Welsh valley, was just the ideal place for Deryn to get on with her work as an illustrator of bird life. Ideal? Well, it was until an unwanted visitor arrived, in the person of Dominic Gregory, and proceeded to turn her life – and her heart! – upside down.

MAN IN A MASK by Beryl Palmer

Penny's courtship with Mark Kenway had been by letter and the first time she met him was on the night of his return to England, the night of the fancy dress ball given by his aunt to announce their engagement. Penny's world would have been torn to tatters when she overheard his remark, 'I would marry Methuselah if it meant keeping the house in the family,' if at the same party she had not also met that certain bearded masked man who was so sympathethic . . .

SOUTH TO THE SUN by Betty Beaty

Of all the professions open to women, the one with the highest marriage rate is surely that of air stewardess. Here is the story of one of them, Susan Shelton, and the officers – fickle or faithful, gay or serious – with whom she flew on the sunshine route to South America.

THE FLOWER ON THE ROCK by Jane Arbor

In any other circumstances Honor would have been thrilled to be going to the lovely Pacific island of Grand'terre. But it was the family home of Piers Sabre, who had just cruelly jilted her and whom she only wanted to forget. How ironic that the first man she met on Grand'terre, Piers' cousin Arnot Lord, had got entirely the wrong idea about her and was determined *not* to let her forget!

20p net each

Mills & Boon's Paperbacks

FEBRUARY

THE TIME OF THE JACARANDA by Margaret Way

Adrienne saw Saranga station as a means of escape – but how could she escape its owner, Grant Manning?

THE NIGHT OF THE BULLS by Anne Mather

Dionne had returned in desperation to the Camargue, and to Manoel who hadn't wanted her before and certainly didn't want her now . . .

NO FRIEND OF MINE by Lilian Peake

Elise had never liked Lester Kings when she was a child, and now he had come back into her life she still didn't like him!

OLIVE ISLAND by Kay Thorpe

Nicky loved her job as travel representative in Corfu, but Nikos Alexandros thought it was unfeminine. What business was it of his?

A THOUSAND STARS by Anne Hampson

Lisette thought she had found love again with Sula Condylis – but then he didn't know how she was deceiving him . . .

MEANS TO AN END by Lucy Gillen

Alison couldn't marry Danny unless she had some of her money – and it was all in the hands of her trustee, Stefano Illari, who wouldn't part with it!

BUTTERFLY MONTANE by Dorothy Cork

Parma had come to New Guinea to marry Alec Rivers – but Pierce Adams had got entirely the wrong idea about her.

MANDOLINS OF MONTORI by Iris Danbury

Craig had given Grentha a china donkey – a sign of love. But how many other girls had he given china donkeys to?

NILE DUSK by Pamela Kent

Romilly couldn't stop herself thinking about Crighton Bey. But was he interested in her – or only in her inheritance?

20p net each

FREE! YOUR COPY OF OUR CATALOGUE OF MILLS & BOON ROMANCES NOW AVAILABLE

If you enjoyed reading this MILLS & BOON romance and would like a list of other MILLS & BOON romances available, you can receive a free Catalogue by completing the coupon below and posting it off today. This opportunity to read more MILLS & BOON romances should not be missed. Your free Catalogue will be posted off to you immediately.

Over the page are listed 50 selections from our current catalogue. This list may include titles you missed and have had difficulty in getting from your usual stockist. Tick your selection and post the coupon to us with your remittance. We'll do the rest. Happy reading!

CUT ALONG THIS LINE

HAVE YOU MISSED ANY OF THESE MILLS & BOON ROMANCES?

**ALL PRICED AT 20p. SEE OVER FOR HANDY ORDER FORM
PLEASE TICK YOUR REQUIREMENTS**